PENGUIN BOOKS

LACHLAN'S WAR

'An excellent book . . . Cannon, in just a few words, can give a familiar image an arresting vitality' *Literary Review*

'Brilliantly conveys a sense of displacement and despair which is deepened by the background war . . . A book that remains with the reader' *Time Out*

'Cannon is not only an appealing writer but an extremely good one' *Sunday Herald*

'Brilliantly written characters and pace-gathering plot make this, quite simply, unputdownable' *Eve*

'A fine tapestry of plot and character . . . page-turning, entertaining and comic. An incredibly moving, wondrous piece of writing' *The List*

'Bold, fascinating, moving . . . It runs along at a cracking pace. Cannon is a natural storyteller' *Tablet*

MAY ⋯Y. 7.

D1147183

ABOUT THE AUTHOR

Born in Glasgow in 1958, Michael Cannon left school at the age of seventeen to become variously employed, among other things, as an engineer, civil servant and worker at the construction of the Sullum Oil Terminal in the Shetlands. He is the author of two previous novels, *The Borough* and *A Conspiracy of Hope*, and currently works at the University of Strathclyde. He lives near Glasgow with his wife and daughter.

Lachlan's War

MICHAEL CANNON

ABERDEENSHIRE
LIBRARIES

WITHDRAWN
FROM LIBRARY

PENGUIN BOOKS

PENGUIN BOOKS

Published by the Penguin Group
Penguin Books Ltd, 80 Strand, London WC2R ORL, England
Penguin Group (USA) Inc., 375 Hudson Street, New York, New York 10014, USA
Penguin Group (Canada), 90 Eglinton Avenue East, Suite 700, Toronto, Ontario, Canada M4P 2Y3
(a division of Pearson Penguin Canada Inc.)
Penguin Ireland, 25 St Stephen's Green, Dublin 2, Ireland
(a division of Penguin Books Ltd)
Penguin Group (Australia), 250 Camberwell Road, Camberwell, Victoria 3124, Australia
(a division of Pearson Australia Group Pty Ltd)
Penguin Books India Pvt Ltd, 11 Community Centre, Panchsheel Park, New Delhi – 110 017, India
Penguin Group (NZ), 67 Apollo Drive, Rosedale, North Shore 0632, New Zealand
(a division of Pearson New Zealand Ltd)
Penguin Books (South Africa) (Pty) Ltd, 24 Sturdee Avenue, Rosebank, Johannesburg 2196, South Africa

Penguin Books Ltd, Registered Offices: 80 Strand, London WC2R ORL, England

www.penguin.com

First published by Viking 2006
Published in Penguin Books 2007
1

Copyright © Michael Cannon, 2006
All rights reserved

The moral right of the author has been asserted

Typeset by Rowland Phototypesetting Ltd, Bury St Edmunds, Suffolk
Printed in England by Clays Ltd, St Ives plc

Except in the United States of America, this book is sold subject
to the condition that it shall not, by way of trade or otherwise, be lent,
re-sold, hired out, or otherwise circulated without the publisher's
prior consent in any form of binding or cover other than that in
which it is published and without a similar condition including this
condition being imposed on the subsequent purchaser

ISBN: 978-0-141-02620-6

ABERDEENSHIRE LIBRARY AND	
INFORMATION SERVICES	
2640824	
HJ	720149
FT PBK	£7.99
AD	RDN

For Denise

I

During a freezing November sunset in 1941 Dr Lachlan McCready stands near the cliff edge contemplating his final house call of the day. In his gloved right hand he holds a cigar whose tip alternately glows and dulls with the gusts and lulls of wind coming up from the bluffs. Anyone looking out from the croft would see an ember in the growing gloom that seems to pulse in time with the soft concussions of the surf below. But the curtains are drawn against the elements and the occupants wait without curiosity.

To the informed observer Dr Lachlan McCready, sporting his cigar, beard, glasses and soft felt hat, bears more than a passing resemblance to a more illustrious colleague: the father of psychoanalysis. It is not a comparison the doctor would like to think he invites, for Lachlan has as little truck with the teachings of 'the Viennese witch doctor', as he refers to him, as he does with astrology or the theory of humours. Lachlan's dismissal of Freud is one of the many robust opinions that jostle for ascendancy in the fertile mind of the old man. By the age of ten Lachlan had formed views on many things, from the Aardvark to the Zygote, and, despite an eventful and sometimes traumatic life, found little cause for revision.

'Trust a Scot to build a house in a lightless gulley,' he says, throwing his cigar in the direction of the ruminating sheep and beginning his careful descent. Talking to himself is another of Lachlan's more obvious idiosyncrasies. For the past twenty-seven years most of Lachlan's meaningful conversations have been with himself, a habit broken by an event that the evening's proceedings are destined to unfold.

The afternoon snow has hardened in the Atlantic gusts to a hard crust. The fields appear crimson, colour leached from the sky as the submerging sun draws light towards the point of its disappearance.

He knocks. The door is opened almost instantaneously. The brightness of the interior belies the outside. Perhaps they are one of the few families paying attention to regulations. There is no hall. The door lets on to the parlour. The accumulated heat from the peat fire arrests Lachlan on the threshold. The younger Mrs Dougan is waiting. 'Isabel,' he says in recognition. She greets this with a wry downward smile and an easy movement that slides the coat from his arms. All her gestures are self-deprecating. He has remarked to himself before that she seems one of life's bit players, a character whose passing would not interrupt the momentum. The older Mrs Dougan calls him from the hearth. She is a large, handsome woman with masculine features and hands once more powerful than Lachlan's. Her son bears her imprint. The difference between the two women is striking.

'I cannot believe, Morag, that I have been summoned to visit you. You will outlive us all, if we outlive this war. I would more readily believe I have been asked to prescribe a hearty meal for that daughter of yours.' This is pitched at a volume the younger woman is intended to hear. It elicits a soft laugh from the next room. And there is an implied compliment of kinship. Isabel is not Morag's daughter but her daughter-in-law.

'I know, Doctor McCready. She is a good girl. I would not have called you. Nor would she, for herself.'

Lachlan makes a pretence of examining the older woman. Both know her only illness is age, the inevitable wear of heavy work over a long life in severe conditions. Her hip is porous. The large hands are deformed by arthritis. In good weather the croft glistens with sea-blown spray. He can only guess at the pain this woman endures without complaint.

'My bones are old,' he says. Both know he is talking about her. Both know there is nothing he can do and that the pretence of a consultation has been conducted for the benefit of Isabel. The misshapen hand takes one of his.

'See what you can do for her . . .' She is not a woman accustomed to talking sotto voce and has to stop as Isabel enters from the bedroom.

'Asleep,' she confirms of her children and, embarrassed by this single utterance, takes up position behind her mother-in-law's chair.

'And the other boy, the evacuee?'

'Frank.'

'And Frank?'

'No . . .' She hesitates. He is used to patients' perception of a social gulf between himself and them. But she is an extreme case. 'I was going to ask you to look at him too . . .'

'Can you fetch him then?' And when she goes, to Morag, 'Is Murdo not here then?'

'Is he ever here, doctor.'

'Fishing?'

'At night? He is . . . wherever he is . . .'

He senses a worried exasperation with her son and will not press. He neither expected nor wanted to see Murdo, but asked for the sake of form. Isabel has returned with the boy.

'This is Frank. He came with some papers . . . I seem to have lost them . . .'

'You will make the poor boy sound like something that came with instructions. And what does Frank have to say for himself?' While saying this Lachlan makes a further pretence of examining the boy, looking at his nails and palms. Running his hands down the back of the legs, he feels the hollows behind the knees. His case is obvious. He is pitifully underweight. The eyes loom unnaturally large. Shadows smudge the sockets. Lachlan notices the rhythmic facial twitches the boy seems to be attempting to suppress. He assumes they are caused by their voices in the confined space until he realizes the spasms coincide with the bangs of the breaking surf below, barely audible to him. He has seen men in France subjected to days of bombardment react like this.

'That's just it, doctor.' Isabel is animated. 'He won't talk and he won't eat. I've tried everything. I'm worried. I'm more than worried . . .'

'We both are,' Morag adds.

Lachlan takes in the obvious profile of the boy.

'Show me what you have been giving him to eat.'

He is shown to the stove where a soup practically the consistency of stew stands on the heat. Stirring with the relinquished spoon, he dredges up the lurking bone. Standing back, he makes three instantaneous diagnoses. It is his great strength, or weakness, never to be undecided and to act with complete conviction upon his judgement. He returns to the hearth and the audience of three.

'Isabel, I want you to give Morag two and a half teaspoons of whisky in warm water each evening half an hour before she goes to bed. No more than half a cup of water, warm not boiling.' When dispensing placebos he has always found that the more elaborate and precise the directions, the greater the advantage the patient, in this case Isabel, derives. 'For you, Isabel, I prescribe at least two bowls of that hearty soup next door every day and at least two meals beside. There is more than one patient in this house. With two children and Morag the last thing we need is you coming down with something. And for the boy – get his things together. I'm taking him home with me.'

The speed with which Isabel complies with his last request suggests to Lachlan more than simply the obedience he is accustomed to. He knows that her circumstances, worse than they appear, are too much for her. One less responsibility can only be a relief. She stands in front of the boy and ridiculously mimes his impending departure, pointing alternately to him and to Lachlan, clasps her hands to illustrate their new compact and walks towards the door. Without acknowledgement to her that he understands the boy disappears and returns clutching a Gladstone bag he could practically sleep in.

'Won't go anywhere without it,' Isabel nervously explains.

At the door she touches Lachlan's arm. Before he can remonstrate she has forced two cabbages on him in lieu of the fee they both know he will not accept. The boy, waiting outside, is already stamping in the cold, blowing a plume of breath through the tunnelled fingers of an ungloved hand. Awkwardly Lachlan tucks a cabbage between each elbow and his ribcage, the bag now suspended a foot from his hip. Still standing inside, Isabel points to the boy, her gesture concealed from him by the half-closed door. 'We thought . . .' she has lowered her voice, obliging Lachlan to lean indoors to hear, '. . . perhaps he is . . .' With an extended forefinger she points horizontally to her temple and rotates her wrist, as if screwing, or unscrewing, something into her skull. He infers 'touched' from the aspiration too faint for him to hear.

'We'll see.' He disagrees. Embarrassed by the presumption of her own diagnosis, she closes the door without another word. The doctor labours uphill with the boy following.

He stops feet from the car. The immobile sheep are where

he left them, now pewter against the snow. He extends both arms to let the cabbages drop and places his bag on the ground. The boy does likewise.

'One thing I cannot abide is a cabbage. A strawberry, yes. A cabbage, no. We'll keep them if you want them. Do you?' He allows sufficient time for response. 'Thought not.' He picks up the first and throws it in the direction of the sheep. It hits the snow with a dull noise and rolls a few feet down the soft declivity with a protracted crunch, leaving a compressed furrow in its wake. 'Your turn,' Lachlan mimes, with, he fancies, more inspiration than Isabel. The boy grasps what is expected of him. His first attempt does not clear the fence. Parallel ropes of snow shudder from the wires. The second is better, matching Lachlan's own with the same pleasing noise. The sheep remain petrified.

'Come here.' He guides the boy to the front of the car. Leaving him, he reaches inside, starts the engine and turns on the headlights. Overlapping cones illuminate the boy starkly, the light dissipating over the dark Atlantic. Lachlan returns to the boy. 'Don't be afraid.' Cradling the nape, he tilts the boy's face to his own, rotating the head from side to side to study the depression of the temples, the lateral planes, the occipital curve which he traces with his hand, cupping the depth. He is not making any attempt to identify the boy's ethnic group; that was done infallibly on first sight. Lachlan has his own taxonomy that has nothing to do with racial prejudice. As he casts a last dispassionate look over the face his eyes meet the boy's. He sees a weary patience in the cast of features that has come with endurance of continued scrutiny, and worse. Because there has been no complaint, or resistance, Lachlan realizes the indignity of this ad hoc examination and drops his hands apologetically. But the eyes do not disengage, and in that brief moment there is a charged intensity in the exchange of something understood and reciprocated, that startles the older man enough to make him take a step backwards. He exhales two tusks of freezing air from his nostrils. The boy is shivering. The ill-fitting trousers come half-way down his calves and his legs are so thin that the ankles hang like clappers, suspended from loose cuffs.

'Get in.' Lachlan turns on the heater to revive the boy and reverses over the crest of the hill. Headlights receded, the sheep make their slow way to the cabbages.

'Isabel's husband,' Lachlan says in the warm cab. 'You probably know enough to make up your own mind. Swine of a man. Every possibility he beats the poor woman. Rumours have it he has women up and down the coast. Even although it's common knowledge he doesn't seem to have any shortage of takers. Pulls them in like line mackerel it's said. There must be something about him that makes women suspend whatever judgement they might have while he's around. Can't say I understand it. He hasn't any scruples I've ever encountered to prevent him. When he can't have women it's said he anchors at random and lands to sodomize animals. I don't know about that. Too much of a womanizer I'd say. I'm not saying he wouldn't rob a bank. Women, larceny, embezzlement – if he wasn't so stupid, smuggling – yes. But animals – I doubt it.'

He continues in this vein till the headlights sweep in a crescent to illuminate the ashlar frontage of Lachlan's house. Lights are burning within. Agnes MacLeod, the housekeeper, awaits them in the hall.

'Dinner was served twenty minutes ago.'

Lachlan knows this is nonsense. There are only two of them in the house. She wastes nothing and would not serve to an empty chair.

'Dinner is somewhere simmering and will be the better for it. Agnes, this is Frank. He is going to stay with us.'

The old lady has taken in every detail of the boy's neglected appearance within a second of him crossing the threshold. She is accustomed to Lachlan's generous caprices and accepts the new arrangement without question. In her mind she has already run the child a hot bath and is making an inventory of clothes, discarded or altered, that could be used for him till they buy more. She shakes his hand formally. When she reaches for his bag he deflects her hand with a shy shoulder.

'Run him a bath.'

'I'm glad you thought of that for me, doctor. That medical training has not gone in vain.'

'Find him some clothes.'

'And where would clothes for a poor child be found at this time of night in a house like this?'

'Buy him some clothes. Until then you can . . . improvise.'

'I dare say I can.'

'But first we feed him.'

'We?'

'No bacon, pork, or anything to do with a pig. He's starved himself rather than eat the Dougans' ham broth. God only knows what else he has endured there. No shellfish either.' He indicates to Frank that he should put the bag down and takes both the boy's hands in his. 'You are welcome here as long as you wish. No one in this house is going to make you eat anything you do not want, but you must eat.' The intensity of this exchange surprises Agnes. This arrangement is not something Lachlan would customarily get involved in. He values his privacy too much. 'Go upstairs with this lady. She will make up a bed for you. Then we will find something you will eat.'

Lachlan passes one of the boy's hands to Agnes who takes it and begins to lead him to the stairs. She is alarmed when her fingers encompass his wrist. With an inarticulate grunt he strains backwards for the Gladstone bag he can barely lift.

'You are certainly fond of your bag,' she says, brushing the fringe out of his eyes with her free hand.

'If I'm right it's all he has. What's for dinner?'

'Mussel soup, then pork escalopes.'

2

Three months before Lachlan made his clifftop house call Gail Kemble sat in a farmhouse kitchen turning her ankle this way and that to admire the clumsy silhouette of her wellington boot. With an amused detachment she notices that moist earth and what she assumes to be cow dung have cleaved to the sole. She realizes that she should have left the boots outside and with an effort slides an ankle from each and carries the parallel boots to the door. She returns to the bench and sits down heavily. A month of voluntary labour has not accustomed her to the rigours of this life. Mrs Campbell puts a cup of tea in front of her. A cigarette is already burning in the upturned hubcap they use as an improvised ashtray. Gail watches parallel columns of rising steam and smoke, framed in the daylight. Her eyes are drifting in and out of focus with a sense of warm languor she knows she cannot allow to possess her at this stage in the day.

It is mid-morning. In her previous existence this meant she would have been teaching for just over an hour. She has been up since first light and now no longer needs the dawn inventory spoken aloud. Mr Campbell concluded she was a good worker from within an hour of her arrival, in clothes entirely unsuited to the tasks she had undertaken to perform. Like Lachlan, Hamish Campbell is a man of instantaneous judgements. He keeps his own counsel. His business acumen is suspect but his psychological marksmanship is unerring. Within three days of being told the same thing each dawn, Gail interrupted Hamish on the fourth repetition to recite the list and instructions verbatim.

'You're a quick learner.'

'It's not the instructions that are taxing. I got them the first day. The only reason I didn't interrupt before now was because I thought they would vary.'

'They will.'

'To save us both time, why don't I go ahead on the understanding that I'm doing the same thing until you tell me differently?'

'I'll teach you the tractor tomorrow, if you're game.'

'I'm game.'

He had anticipated some squeamish debutante being foisted on him and his wife, a girl who would stand high-heel-deep in slurry wincing at everything. His wife has passed on the rumours about other land girls on adjacent farms. Mrs Campbell does not keep her own counsel. Rumours have it that other girls sleep till noon, awaking only to paint themselves and fornicate. He has reminded Mrs Campbell that these rumours originate from a religious quarter so extreme that prudence must be exercised. Mrs Campbell does not believe these tales any more than her husband does. She has met the young ladies in question who seem to her nothing more than high-spirited girls unfortunate enough to be billeted on puritanical fanatics. Away from home for the first time, they are intent on extracting what fun they can from their new circumstances. But rumours are the currency of the village and she can no more help herself passing them on than can the source of the rumours themselves.

She turns round from the stove at the sound of an engine entering the yard. It is not erratic enough to belong to the farm. The only engine she has heard that runs that smoothly is Dr McCready's, and no one has called him. She hears a muted exchange, tantalizingly too far out of range for her to distinguish the actual words.

'Did you hear?'

Gail, abstracted by the smoke, looks round. She had not noticed anything. Before she can answer Hamish comes in.

'There's a man from the Ministry here.'

'Tell him that if they dropped as much paperwork on the Germans they'd have surrendered by now.' The man, in a trenchcoat and shoes as unsuitable for a farmyard as those Gail first turned up in, stands behind Hamish. Eileen Campbell's comment was intended to be heard.

'He's here to talk to Gail.'

'What does she know about livestock?'

And stepping aside to allow the man access: 'I don't think he's from agriculture.'

This does indeed turn out to be the case as David Anderson introduces himself to everyone. Standing up to shake his hand, the first thing Gail notices is the perfect clarity of his accent, Inverness, she believes, eschewing the singsong cadences of the locals here. The second thing she notices is slurry on his shoes, and the third the toe protruding from the hole in her sock. He also contemplates both their feet. In mutual embarrassment they sit down and tuck their feet underneath their respective chairs. Once the obligatory tea has been offered and delivered, Hamish invites his wife to join him outside to allow the others privacy. She loiters in the hall, out of sight and within earshot. At his peremptory cough she joins him.

The man from the Ministry seems discomfited by the sudden privacy. Gail decides to help him.

'Agriculture?'

'Education.' And in a rush, to pre-empt the objection, he anticipates, 'I know you may have come here to get away from all that, get your hands dirty, make a difference . . .' He falters after his good start.

'Actually, I came here for a change.' She notices her nails are filthy and wonders if this is what he was alluding to. Dirty nails would apoplex her mother. Somehow this thought comforts her. She thinks of the forms she filled in to come here and wonders where he has unearthed the information to locate her.

'Have you carried out some kind of skills audit to find local people with experience?'

'As a matter of fact I'd never heard of you till last night in the pub. The thing is, we have a bit of a situation here.'

3

In most parts of the British Isles the prospect of conflict has involved subordinating prejudices for the common weal. The interchangeable men from the Ministry concern themselves more with quotas and national defences than the basic education of children marooned on a wind-blown promontory on the West Coast of Scotland. More urgent matters are afoot. Make do and mend is the order of the day. Here in the village of Rassaig, however, things are different.

Since anyone can remember there has been a primary school in Rassaig and another some ten miles up the coast run by Catholics. The Catholic school roll is made up from all the villages in the district that arrange transportation for the children. The segregation ends at the onset of secondary. Everyone is obliged to send their children to the same secondary school.

Mobilization stopped these arrangements. There was not the transportation or the teachers. In the cities, retired teachers were brought out of mothballs. In Glasgow and Newcastle and London old men, gaping like fish, were tormented by children they no longer had either the inclination or stamina to discipline. Myopic elderly lesbians had obscenities chalked on the back of their tweed jackets as they peered at textbooks whose font had inexplicably shrunk. In Rassaig a compromise arrangement was organized by yet another man from the Ministry. All primary pupils were lumped together in the local school. In the commandeered village hall three 'teachers' turned up every day at the ad hoc secondary school. It had a catchment area of five miles, encompassing Rassaig and two satellite villages.

The youngest of these unfortunate instructors was a fifty-five-year-old woman. The two others were men, one five years her senior, the other indescribably older than that. Each had an eclectic portfolio: the old man taught mathematics, science and all technical ramifications thereof, including woodwork; the woman taught domestic science, to perpetuate the same bondage to sink and cooker which had held her in thrall; the ancient man taught everything else, including humanities, geography, 'rhetoric' (his advertised specialty) and Scottish country dancing.

The affair was a sorry catalogue. These good people's good intentions were misconstrued, deliberately or otherwise. Word percolated back to Gavin Bone, Elder of the Free Presbyterian congregation in Rassaig, that dancing was to be taught. A strongly worded letter arrived at the 'school' suggesting that the 'unregenerate' might like to practise this 'impiety' in the privacy of their own homes. The ancient man, a God-fearing Methodist, penned a response explaining that the joyousness of dance was a celebration of God, not a denial. He went on to explain that private Scottish country dancing was in fact a contradiction in terms as a minimum of eight was normally required for a reel. His rhetorical subtleties served no purpose. Mr Bone threatened a boycott at the first sound of an accordion.

Round two consisted of the younger of the old men attempting to teach the mechanics of pollination. This was a rural community. The working population comprised mainly fishermen with a plot or farmers with a boat. No one could legitimately object. Gavin Bone loitered after hours peering suspiciously through the windows. There was something indecent in the lovingly chalked depictions of pistil and stamen.

When the old man guilelessly drew the practical analogy between the fertilization of plants and that of livestock, the Free Presbyterian community took note. The next logical progression was from the coupling of beasts to that of humans. They interrogated their children, gathering evidence. The last straw came one Friday afternoon when the ancient man, intoxicated by the prospect of two days without the drudgery of this ghastly and thankless work, gave way to his artistic bent in an attempt to raise their minds above the quotidian and intoned a 'filthy' poem by John Donne, 'combining', as was subsequently reported by a parent following interrogation of a hapless schoolboy, 'sex and geography'. A third of the class fell off the roll instantaneously. The school closed. The three teachers returned to wherever they came from. Old arrangements were restored for secondary pupils. The bus ran fifteen miles inland. The reinstated curriculum did not include rhetoric.

Against her better judgement Gail allowed herself to be persuaded into returning to the primary school classroom. She knew nothing of its new ecumenical constitution, or the tensions this entailed. Her assurances as to her shortcomings had been airily waved away. Mr Anderson seemed equally cavalier when she broached the subject of checking her credentials. Her references were never taken up. In retrospect she would realize that this should have given her a clue as to how desperate the authorities were. She reasoned to herself that there was little danger of anyone in Rassaig emerging as a prodigy. If she could shed some light on these children before war closed in still further, then so much the better. At her insistence this was to be a probationary arrangement. Mr Anderson said he would talk to the Campbells who, he was sure, would be happy to allow her to stay here. The stipend that came with the job would more than cover accommodation. There was enough space if they wanted to get more help. He was no expert, but he imagined that with the approach of winter work around the farm was probably tailing off. The Campbells would understand her services were more urgently required elsewhere. Without explaining the context, or what her duties fully entailed, he left the house telling Gail he had no doubt she would 'go down a storm'.

4

Lachlan and Frank have had a jolly day. Frank, Gladstone bag at his side, sat in the car or was invited to sit in the parlour while Lachlan attended to the prosaic round of flu, bunions and one case of particularly bad piles. Refusing to subscribe to the public assumption of Frank's imbecility, Lachlan has proceeded on the theory that treated normally, with nothing demanded of him until he shows the inclination to volunteer it, the boy will come out the end of the tunnel. He has explained his theory to Agnes, who is quick to point out that children do not *normally* accompany doctors on house calls. Nor are they privy to the kind of uncensored opinions she has overheard him pass on to the boy. For a reason he will not and cannot explain, Lachlan believes his candour is part of his compact with Frank, silently sealed during their clifftop exchange.

When Frank has gone to bed, Lachlan and Agnes have speculated as to his age. They think he is around twelve years old. He is tall enough but still underweight, although making progress. Lachlan believes the boy to be naturally slim and tells Agnes not to expect to plump him up too much. At lunchtime Lachlan took Frank to the Drovers for a pub lunch, introduced him to the locals, who expected no more from the boy than the shy stares they received, and sat with him sharing bread, Orcadian cheese and local chutney. After warming himself with a single malt Lachlan strolled back to the surgery, the warm spirit and the presence of the silent boy suffusing him with a quiet, rare happiness. He was particularly charming to his afternoon patients, especially the ladies, many of whom left thinking the old man a card and wasn't it strange he never married?

Washing his hands for the final time, Lachlan leaves the surgery and goes to find Frank in the lounge.

'Get your coat on.'

Being modest, Lachlan's domestic needs demand no more than a tidy house, clean clothes and a good dinner. Consequently Agnes has no one on whom to lavish the attention brimming in her surfeit heart. Her husband is long dead. She has two adult children. Her son has been in the merchant navy since the close of the last war. In her mind he is floating somewhere in a dark expanse that, in sleep, she cannot disassociate from purgatory. Restrictions being what they are, letters carrying exotic postmarks arrive erratically, like wind-blown spores. Her daughter 'emigrated' to Leeds fifteen years ago and is engrossed, the way Agnes was at her age, holding a family together. So Agnes has been prodigal in her attentions to Frank. When Lachlan tells him to get his coat on the boy, for the first time in a long while, is presented with the dilemma of choice. Within a week of his arrival at Lachlan's he is fully equipped. All his clothes are comfortable and expensive. Missing nothing, Lachlan notices the ease with which he wears these, seemingly accustomed to the best.

Taking his stick, Lachlan strides out the front door and points up the hill. They walk together in the gathering dark, Frank lumbering with the inevitable Gladstone bag, the lights of the village winking on around them. It takes half an hour to reach the summit, a wind-blown ridge that gives a prospect of the crescent bay they have just left. To the right there is a small harbour, illuminated at this distance by a dim necklace of lights. To the extreme left a barely visible jetty is being absorbed into the dark sea.

'People here don't pay much attention to the restrictions.

I've yet to see a warden around these parts. Rationing doesn't bite either. Not so as you'd notice.' Holding his stick horizontally, he bisects their view of the village. 'If you were to take a line from the point of this stick to the sea you'd notice there is a little corridor of darkness. It's not that there are no houses that have put on their lights, it's that there are no houses. That's because what we call one village has been two settlements that have grown towards each other but can't consummate the marriage.' Lachlan laughs at his own little joke. Frank stares at the scene before him.

'Moses must have felt like this separating the waves. From here to the harbour lives everyone not of the same persuasion as those from here to the jetty. It's not an absolute division but it's a good enough generalization. The harbour lot comprise a large proportion of Catholics who, as far as I can see, seem to think they have a monopoly on guilt. From here to the jetty are our Free Presbyterians. They sit in their buttoned-up Sundays frowning across the abyss. They live with the abiding fear that somebody, somewhere, is having a good time. As far as I can tell their only consolation is in the fact that those who are not the elect get their eternal comeuppance. They can sit upstairs and see everyone else cook. It's a bit like watching the Sunday roast, except it goes on for ever. It's a grim theology. I've never yet managed to find whether all of them think themselves the elect. If you're not, why bother?' By this time Lachlan is thinking aloud. Taking stock, he turns to the boy. 'The rest of the world is on fire and this lot from the jetty sit stoking a dislike for their neighbours just because they commit the cardinal sin of trying to enjoy themselves. The other mob has people just as bad. People are dying all over Europe to defend the freedom most locals here take for granted, and look what they do with their liberty. Honest to God . . .'

5

Lucy Vernon and Harriet Pearsall are getting ready for a night out. They are the other two land girls in Rassaig. The Campbells, who accommodate Gail, are people of firm convictions, the strongest of which is tolerance. Gail has never fully appreciated how fortunate she is, having never seen the adopted domestic circumstances of the other two. Lucy and Harriet are not permitted visitors.

Lucy and Harriet have had the misfortune to be billeted on the McHargs, Ewan and his wife Elsbeth. It is from the McHargs that Gavin Bone receives much of his intelligence, generating the rumours of slovenly 'foreign' girls of easy virtue.

Lucy's behaviour does little to scotch these rumours. It is Saturday and she is adamant she is going out. Harriet, weary, would be happy with a good book and an early night. She has been persuaded by her friend to make the effort. Ewan McHarg is standing just outside the gloomy room the girls have been given. Lucy is confronting him, arms akimbo.

'You want a bath *again*?' He succeeds in sounding both incredulous and aggrieved.

'Again.'

'Both?'

'We're not livestock. We need more than a bath a week.'

'There are restrictions, you know.'

'I'm from London, dearie. You don't have to talk to me about restrictions. I haven't noticed you and the missus practise them.'

Somehow he feels there is something indecent in her mentioning anything to do with him and Mrs McHarg as a couple, although, as God and the long, long nights are his witness, there is nothing indecent in Mrs McHarg.

'It is right to be frugal.'

'Cleanliness is next to godliness. Isn't that what your mob say?'

He dislikes mention of God from her mouth even more than mention of himself and his wife.

'You'll have to share then,' and quickly, as an afterthought, 'one at a time!' He does not want rumours of impropriety although he has often furtively wondered what two naked young women would look like together. Even if they stood immobile with no part of one touching any part of the other, Ewan believes that two naked women would be more than twice as alluring, and therefore pernicious, as a single naked woman. There is an erotic synergy here that can only be the work of the Devil.

'Fair enough,' Lucy concedes, and turning to Harriet without closing the door, 'first or second?'

'First, if you don't mind.'

'All the same to me.'

Ten minutes later, lying back in the shallow bath, Harriet coils her hair and secures it above her head, thinking how it could never be all the same to her. She cannot imagine consenting to use someone else's bath water. From her brief acquaintance she has come to like Lucy but recognizes something blowsy in her.

Five minutes after that, the evening feed distributed, Ewan McHarg sits in his room adjacent to the bathroom, clenched fists trembling. From the soft lapping he can imagine the larger, darker of the two girls, not the mock blonde tart from London, soaping herself in the next room. She has legs as long as a horse's. He has washed a horse's legs before. And applied a poultice. The little blonde is blonder than she was two days ago. Before that a dark crevice outlined her centre parting. Does this mean she would have a dark cleft? No doubting the colour of the taller girl. That brunette delta is probably being soaped at this very minute. It is true; the Devil is in the detail. 'Begone!' he pants and forces himself to think of Mrs McHarg.

An hour later the girls have left, lily of the valley wafting from their room. He can hear their voices recede as they walk towards the Drovers. Locking the bathroom door behind him, his minute examination of the soap can only disclose one pubic hair, a corrugated grey follicle whose provenance, by elimination, can only be traced to Mrs McHarg.

Lucy has arranged for them to meet Gail in the Drovers. It is this that has prompted Harriet to go. She feels an affinity with the quieter girl. With Lucy it is the demand of their daily rota, of having always a task to hand, that keeps them companionable. She thinks three unchaperoned hours of Lucy would be too much. Feeling guilty at entertaining such a thought, she slips her arm through the younger woman's and they walk on, Lucy singing softly in the dark. They reach a junction in the main street. The Drovers is a hundred yards up the hill.

'I'll catch you up.'

Thinking Lucy has to pull her stocking up or somehow put herself to rights to make an entrance, Harriet says she will wait.

'No. Honestly. I'll catch you up.'

'What? You expect me to go into the pub on my own?'

'You won't be on your own. Gail will be there.'

'How do you know?'

'I asked her to be there half an hour ago.'

'So she's on her own?'

23

'I don't see what the problem is, being on your own in a pub.'

'Because we're comparative strangers here. Some women don't like sitting on their own in a bar. I don't. It invites comment.'

'Who gives a fuck about comment? If you're that worried you'd better not leave Gail alone.' Harriet is too angry to answer. Failing to notice, Lucy stretches up and kisses her, leaving a smudge. Laughing, she licks her hanky and wipes off the offending mark. She turns and disappears in the direction of the harbour, heels clicking into the dark. Harriet turns and walks up the hill.

Gail is smoking a cigarette and talking animatedly to Lachlan, who stands to admit the other girl to their company and goes to the bar to fetch them all a drink.

'Lucy left me at the junction.'

'I wonder why?' Both girls laugh.

Lucy clicks her way down the hill to the harbour. Douglas Leckie is waiting for her near the stairs. Laughing, she touches him.

'Not here.'

'Where then?'

He guides her down the steps. The oars plash softly towards his fishing boat.

'I wish they'd observe the restrictions and keep these lights down.'

'Worried about a U-boat, or your wife?'

He rows determinedly on. She laughs at his silence. He clambers aboard the small fishing boat and helps her on deck. He gestures her down the stairs. She expected an overpowering smell of fish but the cramped space smells of tobacco and engine oil. In one corner is a rumpled bunk. She is aroused at the lack of anything remotely feminine. Having been silently purposeful in bringing her here he looks hesitatingly around, as if thinking of a suitable preamble. She pre-empts him by lifting her dress over her head and stepping out of her pants.

As Gail returns the favour by overriding Lachlan and standing the next round, Lucy lies, eyes closed, cupped palms beneath her crooked knees, pulling her thighs progressively wider. Soft eddies radiate from the gently heaving craft and she too is carried out in accumulating spasms. Experience having taught her to keep quiet, she exhales a whistling climax, eyes suddenly opening to her vicarious partner. Douglas, transfixed in mid-thrust, feels she is surprised to find him at the other end of his member.

'Go on, lover,' she encourages. But the damage is done. He withdraws. She smokes a cigarette to give him time to collect himself. She lets him know she is prepared to go again, but by this time he is already climbing the three steps to the deck. As they row back he tries to keep the urgency from his voice.

'When can I see you again?'

'Anytime. Pop over. Those miserable bastards won't have you in the house but you can find me knee-deep in shit any day of the week.' They both know it is not what he meant but she is already preoccupied, thinking ahead to the next thing as she always is: the bar, the faces, her friends.

6

Lachlan's first emergency call out at Rassaig, twenty years previously, exemplified the philosophy he had formulated on life and death and the professional manner in which he would conduct himself thereafter. It was a breezy September afternoon. He saw the two vehicles clearly on the metalled road that bisected an expanse of gorse receding on either side into the autumnal distance. The police car sat squarely on the road, the other vehicle at a tangent, half askew in the ditch. One policeman, the more senior of the two, was leaning into the vehicle through the passenger window, talking to the prostrate figure behind the wheel. His younger colleague stood in the middle of the road looking completely redundant. As Lachlan approached he saw the younger man vomit. Lachlan drove round the hunched policeman and sticky pool and came to a halt beside the damaged vehicle. As he reached across for his bag he noticed the truncated telegraph pole, like a large exclamation mark, tilting from the impact, push up and out from the number plate of the other car.

He took two careful minutes before coming to a decision. From the smashed window on the driver's side he could see across the seat to the policeman, stroking the driver's shoulder, speaking soft, reassuring nonsense. The snapped portion of the telegraph pole radiated out from the smashed pelvis like some grotesque erection, through the mutilated steering wheel and out the space where the windscreen had been. The pulse was weak and erratic but unmistakably there. Infinitesimal noddings of the drooping head suggested a man who had

26

fallen asleep over his newspaper. With a sure movement Lachlan took out a large syringe and a bottle of morphine.

'What are you doing?'

'Killing him. For some reason, God in His boundless mercy, having seen fit to allow this man to become impaled, has decided to revive him long enough to let him appreciate that the rest of his short life will be spent in excruciating pain.'

The policeman looked as if he was about to remonstrate and thought better of it. He watched as Lachlan administered as much fluid as he had only seen injected into a cow before. The nodding stopped. Lachlan continued to feel the pulse till it failed. Reaching deftly into the inside breast pocket Lachlan retrieved a wallet. He flicked it open on the dented bonnet, inspecting the card that first disclosed itself. The man is some kind of agricultural salesman, animal feed and fertilizers Lachlan expects. That would explain the samples strewn on the back seat. Rifling further, he discovered cash and what he suspected would be there and hoped not to find: a photograph. The salesman is standing with his hands on the shoulders of the woman seated before him, presumably his wife. His hair looks as if it has been painted on and reflects light. His suit is formal, the collar restrictive. They both wear unnatural smiles, poised erectly like a Victorian couple in contrived arrangement, held by unseen struts for the long exposure. On the woman's lap is an infant, the head outlined by a ghostly second image, recording the child's movement before the closing shutter froze them.

Lachlan McCready was born in Morningside, Edinburgh, on 14 December 1877. A late and only child of conscientious and loving parents, he was given every advantage their reasonable means could provide. His father, an insurance loss adjuster who rose through the ranks by means of diligence and a reputation for integrity, wanted to ensure that his son enjoyed the professional standing he felt his own indeterminate status lacked. Lachlan was christened, both parents being regular if not devout worshippers. He was educated at one of the private merchants' schools, the fees requiring of his parents sacrifices both were happy to make. Happy, confident and precocious, Lachlan found little to tax him academically. His father wanted him to read law but didn't demur at his son's preferred option. Lachlan matriculated at Edinburgh University Medical School in 1895, graduating some seven years later. During his studies he lived in rented accommodation, the darling of a species of genteel elderly Edinburgh landladies who rented to 'proper' young people. Unbeknown to him his parents, on a dwindling income, retained the house they could no longer afford in anticipation of his possible return. They entertained expectations of him as a young intern, with a younger wife and child who would stay with them while their son worked every hour God sent, as young interns do. They would help with the grandchildren till Lachlan achieved the status when he could delegate and take over the responsibility they had gladly adopted.

His easygoing manner concealed a naturally introspective side to Lachlan's nature. His ready wit ensured he made friends easily and he had a reputation for gregariousness he neither deserved nor sought.

A few of his University friends with artistic leanings tore from themselves angst-ridden poetry of the worst sort. He observed everything and said little about what mattered most. While members of the gregarious circle he moved in discussed politics, female emancipation, sex, religion, Madame Blavatsky and anything else that exercised their young minds, he wondered why it was that they failed completely to discuss something that occupied his.

It took some time for Lachlan to realize that not everyone

saw things in the same way he did. He had been born with the visual equivalent of perfect pitch, a facility to recognize beauty in the most obscure configurations. Clutter could be exquisite. He experienced the same sensation observing recesses disclosed by the scalpel on the dissecting table as he did watching the mist clear from the Forth. Where others saw in terms of function he viewed from an additional perspective. The striae of separated muscle fibres, his landlady's blue jug glimpsed through the half-open door on his way out, the skittish intelligence in the horse's liquid eye as it strained in the traces all afforded him the same joy. He became accustomed to but not complacent about this faculty, and once he realized it existed in many others only to a diluted extent, or not at all, he never spoke about it.

His father fell ill. The prognosis did not require a medical degree. Lachlan was grateful his father remained alive long enough to see him graduate. His mother died within a year. He never knew the fantasy he failed to fulfil. Settling his parents' affairs, he did come to appreciate the financial sacrifices they had made. The day he buried his mother he came to appreciate emotionally what he had apprehended, if at all, only as a fact: that in the natural order of things we are born to be orphaned. He thought himself stupid to have arrived at such an obvious conclusion so late.

His sense of calm was infectious, his tranquil manner pacifying those he came in contact with. He thrived on the constant duress of instantaneous decision-making that agitated others to the point of stupefaction. He preferred the succession of often mortal dilemmas to plotting the prognosis of slow recuperation or gradual decline. His exposure to women had been limited to chaperoned visits in their genteel lodgings, or faculty parties he attended to humour friends. He had few female acquaintances. He spent two years doing relief work in Africa and the next eight years working in the hospitals of Edinburgh and its environs, steadily scaling the ladder. He was not ambitious; this seemed a logical progression given his expertise and a natural gravitas he had acquired. Contemporaries married off and consigned him to the category of confirmed bachelor. He drank in moderation most evenings, read voraciously and socialized when the mood took him.

During an early autumn evening in 1912 Lachlan walked the length of the New Town terrace, flowers in one hand, a bottle of Chablis in the other. The flowers are for the two hostesses, the Misses Crawford. The wine is for him, to make the evening more palatable. He is fulfilling his duty as a past tenant, an obligation he is called upon to dispatch once every few years. The Misses Crawford have a new quota of 'guests'. In order to break the ice, and set the tone, they invite selected past tenants to an evening buffet to meet the latest intake. Turning round at the door, he takes in the concertinaed perspective of the terrace, a succession of oriel windows giving back the light in receding increments, the short walk eliciting a catalogue of memories.

He is roused from his thoughts by the door being opened. He has not even rung the bell. The Misses Crawford beam from the threshold. They have been awaiting his arrival. At thirty-five he realizes he is the elder statesman. The demands of children have excused the contemporaries he used to meet here. He remembers a previous incumbent who occupied this role, an awkward bachelor who obviously couldn't say no, who failed to hide chronic shyness behind the paraphernalia of his pipe, who sucked and puffed and spluttered and was terrified by the twenty-year abyss that separated him from the ranks of the young. Lachlan walked into the lounge prepared to outdo this uninspiring prototype, to be pleasant and bored. Among the petrified bric-a-brac he has unconsciously committed to memory he sees younger incarnations of himself and, to his astonishment, women.

He teases the Misses Crawford about their moral erosion. 'Women guests! If only in my time.' They exchange a look with each other and laugh in unison, 'That Doctor McCready!' They enjoy being scandalized. He knows they will police the sleeping arrangements with Prussian ruthlessness. He is introduced to some of the young ladies. He hadn't expected suffragettes and he wasn't disappointed. Most of them struck him as female equivalents of all the male guests the Misses Crawford had ever entertained. They are young and clean and wholesome women destined, in five years, to partner the same kind of young and clean and wholesome men they are currently rubbing shoulders with. One woman stands slightly apart. She is the only woman smoking. She looks only slightly less young than the others but this, and her air of rueful tolerance towards the young man at her side, stammering through a long anecdote, marks her out.

'Our Kate,' says Miss Crawford, seeing him observe her. This is said at a volume intended to introduce the two. The woman looks up. Lachlan smiles and, obliged by the introduction, crosses the gap. The young man is now caught in a dilemma: should he limply abandon the anecdote or go for the quick conclusion? He knows no better than to try and finish. The presence of the composed-looking older man at his side aggravates the stammer. Lachlan finds himself contemplating the carpet, knowing from experience that the more attention is focused on the poor boy, the worse things will become. He casts around looking for a diversion but the room has grown quiet. The boy, now aware that he has become the centre of attention, is paralysed. A succession of consonants escapes him. There is an elaborate little stand at Lachlan's side supporting a grotesque vase. Calculating that it can withstand the concussion on the carpet, Lachlan decides to put the boy out of his misery and kick the stand. His foot collides with hers as she beats him to it. The ensuing confusion releases the boy. The stand is put to rights, her apologies waved away, general conversation restored.

'You left the vase intact,' Lachlan says to her.

'I'll get it next time. Are you a relative?' He cannot place her accent.

'Why would you assume that?'

'You're younger than Jean and Doris and older than everyone else.'

'Kate smokes,' says one of the Misses Crawford, interrupting with the tiered sandwich plate. 'That's London for you.'

'Kate thought I was related to you. I could be your son, or Doris's.'

Doris, circulating with an identical plate, is waved across by Jean to share the joke. 'That Doctor McCready!' they say, and separate.

'Previous lodger. I've been asked back for tonight to keep the tone. You seem to have your feet under the table: it took me two years to be on first-name terms.'

'If you were here for two years why didn't you get rid of the vase?'

'You should have seen the place when I arrived.' He feels her cigarette is a prop. She seems to advertise a confidence he is sure she does not feel. But then, he reflects, he cannot know how composed he appeared at her age. 'Do you have a second name, Kate?'

'Roddick. Do you have a first name, doctor?'

'Lachlan.' The preliminaries dispensed with, an uneasy silence falls. He fails to understand why this happens and is irritated. He is a socially adroit man in his mid-thirties who delivers traumatic news daily. She looks like a composed young woman. Then he realizes what bothers him. He likes her; more, he is attracted to her, and her face is beginning to adopt the same expression of rueful tolerance she directed at the stuttering boy. On point of principle he determines to stay until he breaks the ice, but immediately he is called away.

'Duty calls . . .' Even saying it he is aware it sounds limp.

'Don't let me detain you.' Her smile seems genuine. He wonders if she is being ironic.

He is shuffled by the Misses Crawford to meet a series of young people and finds himself saying the kind of thing he might have ascribed to the pipe-smoking predecessor. It was never this difficult before. He is aware she is watching him from the other side of the room and puts his woeful performance down to this. When she leaves the room he is relieved. When she fails to return within half an hour he is piqued. He eats a desultory sandwich and when he turns back for another finds the students have devoured everything.

Within another hour the soirée is breaking up. The food is gone, the night is young, the students are hungry. The Misses Crawford hand him back his unopened wine at the door. They brook no denial. 'House rules. No alcohol. Surely you remember, Doctor McCready?'

'There were no women here either at one time. Perhaps you're introducing vices gradually.'

'That Doctor McCready!'

Kate is standing on the raised step on the other side of the front door, unlit cigarette in hand. He is hesitant to hope she is waiting for him.

'Can you stand here for a minute?'

'Of course.' He is perplexed by a sense of pleasant apprehension.

'If you stand there they can't see me smoke from the hall.'

'They don't mind you smoking in the house.'

'They think smoking in the street is common. I must say,' she lights the cigarette and extinguishes the match in one of the potted plants, 'I agree.'

He laughs and finds he has nothing to say to this vital, smiling young woman.

'I was told you were a catch,' she says.

'I think of a catch as something that breathes its last on the ground.'

She exhales the next question with the smoke while studying the half-buried match. 'Are you still hungry?' He can see from her false preoccupation that she is nervous and is heartened by this.

'I didn't think about it. Yes, I suppose I am.'

'Would you like to take me to dinner?'

'Yes.'

'I'll get my shawl.'

'No, allow me.' There is no need. The door opens and a disembodied arm belonging to one of the Misses Crawford hands the shawl out. He turns to Kate, suspecting collusion, but there is no mistaking the surprise on her face. As the door gently closes they both laugh. He offers his arm.

She is a nurse, working in Edinburgh to avoid the pitfall of growing up and dying in the same postal district. He walks her back home after dinner. The door is locked. She has not been given a key and is obliged to ring. Both Misses Crawford beam from the other side of the open door at the fruition of their scheme. He is obliged to say goodbye more quickly and formally than he intended, his airy 'Good evening' incorporating all three. Only later, walking away, does he realize he has made no arrangements for their next meeting.

He equivocates for two days and finally telephones. He is surprised when she answers and is caught flat-footed by her response.

34

'Why did you wait so long?'

'I . . . I wasn't entirely sure you wanted to hear from me.'

'I asked you out last time.'

'Strictly speaking, that's not true. You asked me if I wanted to take you out.'

'You should be a solicitor, or a Jesuit.'

She is armed with a key when he next walks her home. They have the luxury of the hall to themselves for two minutes before one of the Misses Crawford walks the diagonal length from lounge to back stairs and nods gentle encouragement to the doctor as she disappears. He would not presume to test the security. If they wanted complete privacy they have his flat. He knows from Kate's behaviour that she will not be constrained by social rules she considers absurd, but, despite her sometimes flip manner, there is a seriousness to her that touches a similar chord in him and precludes him from making any suggestion that they sleep together.

She stops smoking. Unoccupied, her hands flutter. Something of this nervousness communicates itself to him. Walking in the Botanic Gardens, he kisses her on impulse and only succeeds in restraining himself from telling her he loves her. That night, alone, he analyses his feelings. He is of the opinion that 'love' must be the most abused word in the language, debased by common coinage. He will never use it inappropriately. The following afternoon he tells her he loves her.

They marry that winter. She is ten years his junior but looks younger. Both are virgins, brought together, as he puts it, by the well-intentioned connivance of older virgins still. It was a kind calculation. The first time he saw her naked was their wedding night. She stood, her clothes on the floor around her, inviting assessment. He took in the flare of her pelvis and, kneeling, pressed his face to her stomach.

They conceived quickly. It was part of their plan to start a family as soon as they could. Coming home, late and tired, he would nightly run his hands over the protuberance of her belly, inventing features of their baby he claimed his clairvoyant examination revealed. He marvelled at her green-veined breasts, the beauty of her gravid movements.

As her time approached her desire to be near her mother outlived her fear of parochialism. They moved to London. He met her family, visiting as often as his punishing hours would allow. They held a doctor of his seniority in some awe.

He is urgently summoned home. She has had a discharge. She sits in the lounge looking stricken. He draws the curtains. When his clairvoyant hands fail to detect any movement he adopts a professional manner. She had anticipated a consolatory smile and hopeful news. She starts to cry. She is vomiting before the ambulance arrives, her pulse shallow, her respiration quick. Their baby died before it saw the light of day. She developed septicaemia before the dead foetus would abort. From being the provider of a family he overnight became a widower of considerable means. It was 1914. The looming conflict seemed somehow pertinent to the context of his life. His sense of beauty abandoned him.

In 1916 Lachlan stands at the tent entrance watching the stretchered ranks being laid out. 'You're only allowed to die in straight lines around here.' He is musing aloud to himself but within earshot of the orderly. The man makes no response. Looking across at him, Lachlan recognizes in the almost granular complexion a weariness that surpasses even his own. He hands the orderly his flask. Those of Lachlan's rank do not like this fraternizing. They see it as bad for morale. Whatever idea Lachlan has had of his place in any hierarchy disappeared with Kate's death. Noises have been made. He has been told that one of his seniority need not attend, personally, to all the wounded. The cover is so makeshift, the conditions so brutally inadequate that he has wondered if they are being ironic. What do they know? So he has shrugged at their hints. If they persist he is prepared to be bullish. 'What else would I do?' he has astonished his senior officer by saying, and, nodding towards the tents, 'I will stay here.'

He has a reputation for macabre humour. He has seen some terrible things, but nothing that he considered worse than the sight of his dead wife with their dead baby inside her. He will not explain his motives for refusing to leave, that he is not here to help forget but to honour her memory by occupying himself and not giving way to despair. What strikes him at the field hospitals is not the severity of the injuries, or the number of casualties, but the sheer arbitrariness of death. Fortune does not favour the brave. To be first is to be foolhardy. Reticence is no guarantee of safety either. And among the battalions of dead and mutilated he formulates the philosophy that is to inform his professional behaviour for the rest of his life: not the preservation of life but the annihilation of pain.

He had not inherited his parents' comfortable and modest leanings towards religion. Nor was he convinced to the contrary. In a thicket of otherwise fixed opinions Lachlan was prepared to be guided by a healthy scepticism and convinced by convincing arguments of either persuasion. It was not his personal tragedy, but the sheer aggregate of human suffering he witnessed that convinced him. Pain as a warning, a deterrent, he could understand. But motiveless pain that did not warn, did not aid recuperation and was presented to him daily in all its various guises, dispelled any thought he had had of a benevolent overseer. He lost patience with the chaplains.

'Are you a Catholic?'

'Anglican, sir.'

'Are there any other denominations here?'

'You mean among the men?'

'Of course I don't.'

'There are Baptist chaplains, but none that I know of assigned here.'

'So what happens if you're a dying Baptist?'

'We all worship the same God.'

'But not in the same way. It seems to me that although you say that, you all think the other has got it slightly wrong. If they haven't, then why are you different?'

'I don't quite see it that way, sir.'

'And the more extreme, the more exclusive.'

He waits for an answer that does not come and realizes he is being unfair. Even if the chaplain has an answer, he cannot give it. Lachlan has rank on his side.

His restraint didn't last. Three days later the inadequacies of the field hospital were made manifest when the dead and dying began to arrive in numbers he hadn't seen before and no one had planned for. The first arrived in ambulances and continued to come in vans, horse-drawn carts and any form of transportation commandeered for the purpose. Lachlan took charge. The logistics of the situation demanded a brutal assessment. The most severe and those certain to die stayed. The rest he ordered moved on, knowing many might not survive the juddering ride. The field hospital was now wildly beyond capacity. Further casualties would have to be diverted elsewhere. The dying were given as much relief as he could administer. The most severe cases were treated as best they could. At the sound of commotion he left the makeshift theatre to find chaos outside the tent. Trucks had continued to arrive. Either his orders had not been carried out or the drivers had refused to go on. The whole compound was littered with wounded. A junior doctor was shouting at a driver. Lachlan strode across. Both fell silent at his approach. The driver's eyes seemed unnaturally bright against the grime of his face.

Looking at him, Lachlan recognized the symptoms. The man seemed capable of shooting anyone.

'Are there any more wounded coming?'

'How the fuck should I know? Ask the Kaiser.'

The other doctor interrupted. 'We're told this is all we are going to get.'

'We were told that after the first arrivals. Get on the telephone. Find out what you can,' Lachlan said, and, turning to the driver, 'sit down somewhere. Have a drink.'

'No time.' The man swung himself back into the seat and drove out of the compound.

More casualties continued to arrive until drivers, seeing the hopeless confusion, took the initiative and drove on. Medical supplies ran out. They were reduced to carrying round water and applying primitive first aid to those lying on the ground. They worked through the night, carrying lights. Dawn disclosed figures, like Lachlan, moving between the injured with the same sense of numbing fatigue. In this half-light everybody seemed to be shading into death.

Among the medical staff he noticed a Catholic chaplain, administering extreme unction. The soldier the chaplain now kneels over is no more than ten feet away. He is obviously dead, his young face contorted in a rictus of pain. Laying his bag on the ground, the priest removes a small bottle, sketches a cross over the dead soldier's forehead and anoints the eyes, ears, lips, nostrils and hands.

'I thought you only did that when they were dying, not dead.'

The chaplain looks across. He looks scarcely older than the soldier. Lachlan is perplexed. He had expected someone older to assume such responsibility.

'Don't you realize that five miles that way German priests are doing the same thing over their dead?'

'I certainly hope so, sir.'

For the first time in his adult life Lachlan shouts, pointing at the corpse.

'Dear God! What kind of an expression is that to face annihilation with?'

'Sir, if you'd like we can step inside the tent.'

'Don't patronize me! Not only do you say the same words when they're dying, you invoke the same God as those others over there to justify them killing one another.'

The chaplain's expression infuriates him. He realizes he is being treated with the same circumspection as the insubordinate driver, on the verge of snapping. He turns away. The chaplain kneels over the soldier again and resumes his prayer.

The war ended. He returned to London. He still had accommodation with all his effects there. But there were no ties to renew. Kate's relatives treated him with renewed respect. He was now also a veteran. He and they only succeeded in reminding one another of the woman who wasn't there. He packed up on a whim, left instructions to the estate agent to sell up, and took the overnight train to Edinburgh. He realized his mistake as he walked out the grimy cavern of Waverley. His friends had changed, but not as much as him. He looked for a bolt hole and found the vacancy in Rassaig for which he was ludicrously overqualified. He told the few taken into his limited confidence that this was a temporary arrangement till he decided what to do. He bought a car and left a forwarding address.

He drove north-west, from one coastline towards another. Consulting the map, he found no distinguishable landmarks. This was reflected in the view of nothing beyond the circumference of moorland that moved with him through the mist. As late-morning sun began to penetrate, the air seemed to grow luminous. For no reason he could explain he stopped. Beside the cooling engine the silence was complete, the space within visible radius charged. He waited, not knowing why. The mist quickly lifted. Overnight pools had gathered. The earth was tawny and purple with gorse and heather. With no reason for deviation the road disappeared into vanishing point. As the last wreath drew up to evaporation Lachlan found himself standing on a metalled strip like a placed ribbon across a mosaic of flashing groundwater. His sense of beauty returned in a cascade of sensations and he was lacerated with the thought that she was not there to share it with him.

The temporary arrangement, that had lasted for twenty years when Lachlan made his clifftop house call, was a period that only established its full continuity in retrospect. For the first few years he still contemplated moving, but the alternatives that presented themselves paled beside Rassaig. He became addicted to its austere beauty. The work was not difficult. Most of the locals were appreciative and accepting. He was assimilated before he knew it. Without making any attempt to socialize he had a vacant place held for him most nights in the Drovers, that he came willingly to occupy more often than not. His friends were mostly fishermen and farm labourers, the local postman and, after a wary probation, Brendan Keenan, the Catholic priest.

His first half-dozen meetings with Brendan consisted of tersely polite exchanges in the Drovers. The ice was broken by their first professional exchange. Nagged to make an appointment, he sat across from Lachlan in the surgery watching the doctor contemplate his blood pressure.

'I could tell you to drink less.'

'You could. And I could tell you to make a novena. And which of us is more likely to follow the advice? We only ever meet in the Drovers. If I do what you say we're never likely to see one another again. Do you ever take your own blood pressure?'

'I'm not the one who made an appointment.'

'Do you know the one about pots and kettles, Lachlan?'

'If you don't pray for me, I won't nag you.'

'Done.'

He knew that most of his medical school contemporaries would have thought he had sold himself short, a man of his talents languishing in a village prey to the vagaries of the Atlantic, discussing mackerel quotas and the purity of breeding strains, but he did not care. In the quiet of this backwater he came to a slow and private reconciliation with himself.

Every evening he avidly read the newspaper, his reading accompanied by a running commentary Agnes learned quickly to ignore. He watched Nazi predations with a sense of dread, and regretfully acknowledged that on this topic he agreed with Churchill. His occasional sortie to the cinema served only to fuel his indignation. It was here, in the Pathé News reports, that he saw footage of Chamberlain waving his pathetic slip of paper. It was here that he listened to the strident propaganda of Dunkirk and wondered if he was the only one in the audience, or nation, to understand what the euphemisms presaged. The day he sat beside the radio and listened to Chamberlain announce a state of war he looked out of the window and wondered if any of the poor bastards around here had the faintest idea what this really meant.

Staring into the fire, he did some thinking. Coming back from France he had passed through some of those sad English shires. The devastation of a generation of young men coming to grief was bad enough in the cities; it had utterly destroyed some of the rural communities. Looking around, he took inventory and realized what conscription would entail for Rassaig. If he was correct, the conflagration that was about to burst over Europe could swallow a thousand times over the complement of men this village could provide and their sacrifice would not matter one iota in the general scheme of things. He knew that if everyone thought likewise the darkness would spread, unopposed. He decided that short of falsifying medical records and telling outright lies he would do what he could for the men of this village, especially the younger fathers. The country needed food, now more than ever. Many already worked in reserved occupations and he used what patronage he had to have others similarly employed. The more adamant refused his help. Some did not wait for conscription. He had seen this patriotic fervour before and saw them off with an outward smile, shaking their hands, wishing them well, advising caution, taking silent inventory of their health and strength, the proportion of their intact limbs, and all the while remembering the stretchered ranks, skin bags of excrement and viscera, slipping away before he or the chaplains could get to them.

Nightly he read. Kristallnacht. Czechoslovakia falls. Poland is carved up. Hints of euthanasia in Germany. News of rationing introduced. Scapa Flow bombed. Denmark, Norway, France, Belgium, Luxembourg and the Netherlands all capitulate or fall. Something filthy has been spilled that darkly blots the map as it spreads. U-boats sink merchant shipping. Families atomized by blitzkrieg while men flail in freezing water.

And nightly he would go to his eyrie, the vantage point he had taken Frank to, and he would look at the scene before him and wonder how long this fragile tranquillity would last.

7

'And this is Miss Kemble. She has come a long way to help. Can we show our appreciation as we practised?'

'Good morning, Miss Kemble.' It is a ragged salvo. She thinks they cannot have practised much. Having dispensed with the introductions, the man from the Ministry rubs his hands redundantly and departs on the pretext of leaving her to it.

'Leaving me to it,' she repeats to herself. To what? She has been taken aback by this denuded, makeshift classroom. She cannot remember what she expected but she knows it wasn't this. She also knows this is not the time to equivocate: this vital first hour is crucial to obtain their confidence and respect.

'We won't start with the register. We'll start with each of you introducing yourself, since I've already been introduced to you.'

'Miss, why do you talk funny?'

'I don't find it funny. My accent is different because I come from another part of the country. Another country in fact.'

'Miss, are you a filthy Hun?'

'Miss, he talks funny and he's from here.'

'You can talk.'

'Yes, I can.'

'Your big sister's the town bike.'

It is a little boy and girl who are arguing. It is the girl's sister who has been insulted. She thinks they are both too young to understand what they are saying.

'Quiet, both of you.' But the dialogue continues and threatens to bring in those on the periphery. She claps her hands, the sound louder than she had anticipated, reverberating in this empty space. All the children immediately fall silent, some alarmed, the gesture more potent than she expected.

'We won't use the word "Hun" in here. We'll use "German" and we won't call them filthy. Not all Germans can be held responsible for what some of them are doing.' And to the boy, 'Your behaviour was ungentlemanly.' They giggle at her choice of words. 'Apologize for what you said.'

'Your sister's not the town bike. She was but my dad says it's that English girl now.'

Gail turns away, frowning. They do not understand what they are saying and order has been restored. How upset would Lucy be knowing her reputation is common currency? She spends the rest of the morning getting them to talk about themselves. From this brief assessment she believes that she has here the same mixture of abilities she has encountered in half a dozen classes. Some of the children are very poorly dressed. She guesses their means are as various as their abilities. Many are very reticent. It is almost as if they believe this invitation is a trap.

At lunchtime most of the children disperse to their homes. The majority live within walking distance. Three stay behind. One has a packed lunch in greaseproof paper. The other two, brother and sister, have some woeful-looking sandwich between them. Gail thinks that even if rationing bit here, and it doesn't, there would be no excuse for this. Eileen Campbell has been lavish packing Gail's lunch. She shares this with her reluctant pupils, thinking how much more enjoyable it would be to go to the Drovers. During the remainder of the lunch break she looks at the supplies. The textbooks are tattered and too few in number. In the course of the afternoon reading lesson pupils have to double up, and in some cases share three to a book. Coaxing answers from them, she gets the inescapable impression that they are paying more attention to the cupboard behind her.

She disbands the class early, remaining behind with the intention of writing out for David Anderson a list of what she needs. This shortage of textbooks means that it is impossible to stream the children into groups. Unless they are segregated she knows the inevitable result: learning progresses at the pace of the lowest common denominator, leaving the more gifted bored. And the bored become insubordinate. David Anderson did not make clear the conditions she would be expected to work under. She feels she has been conned. If she had known she might not have accepted. But she is here now and it is not in her nature to do anything half-heartedly, especially when children are at stake.

She does not stint in her list. If he expects her to make sacrifices he can strain every official sinew to get what it needs to make a go of this. The austerity of this classroom is terrible. How can children be encouraged in such a severe place? Thinking this, her eyes turn curiously towards the cupboard behind her that seemed to be the object of so much nervous attention.

8

An extract from Gavin Bone's journal, November 1940.

We are all dead in trespass and in sin. We are all spiritual corpses. The best that we can do is to tremble at the threatenings, embrace the promises and yield obedience to Him through whom we are saved.

Gavin usually prefaces his writings with formulaic paragraphs discussing man's unworthiness and inclination to evil, culled from printed sermons he has pored over. It is when he wanders from dogma or memorized phrases that his prose begins to degenerate.

He pauses, pen above paper, hesitant how to continue till he remembers the previous night's conversation. He had returned surprised to find Ewan McHarg alone in his parlour, Mrs Bone nowhere to be seen. On seeing him, Ewan immediately launched into a tirade against the lodgers, growing increasingly vociferous till Mrs Bone entered, presumably from the bathroom, still putting herself to rights.

Exercising their duty, the McHargs have told me yet again of the doings of those foreign women. All women are skittish creatures. This one has the morals of a hot bitch, as do others who don't do something about it and by that I mean stopping themselves. This latest piece of intelligence I have of the blonde one exceeds even my worst expectations.

And she was seen rowing out to a boat with that papish oaf no doubt for her carnal pleasurings to wallow in sin lying on the nets or if that was a bit wet his bunk. And after that going into that hellish den for drink and an alleged game of dominoes. Ewan has been diligent. I see the fervour of righteous excitement when he tells me about her.

He recalls the tirade stopping and the additional details, delivered in private, as Mrs Bone retired to the kitchen.

But I don't understand the thing he is saying about the soap.

9

The same week Gail receives her visit from the man from the Ministry, Frank sits perched in a high-backed chair in the corner of the Dougans' parlour on a blustery Tuesday afternoon. He is practising remaining absolutely still. This has become his strategy. His unforeseen reprieve at Lachlan's hands is three months hence. Most children are at school. The grandmother is resting. Even from his brief sojourn here he has noticed that she sleeps more and more frequently, as if rehearsing for the perpetual sleep that will soon engulf her. Evaluated by Murdo and considered unfit for learning, Frank sits, ignored. His hearing has become attuned to something the other inhabitants of the house fail to notice. Soft as it is, the noise of incessant battering from the waves below causes him to twitch at each collision. Maintaining a semblance of composure, even when alone, has become a sustained act of concentration.

Gradually he becomes aware of a second rhythm superimposing itself on the first. It began quietly but is getting louder and more frequent. It sounds like a soft impact followed by the noise of escaping air, as if a punctured football is being repeatedly stamped on. Intrigued, the boy climbs softly from the chair and leans from one side to another in an attempt to find the source.

It is coming from the direction of the couple's room. He does not know if they are in, having returned with the grandmother to what both assumed was an empty house. The periods she can spend with him are shortening as the demands of her illness punctuate her day with sleep.

There is a sudden violent increase in the noise, like a spasm, and a sound he can only think of as a drowning man coming up for air. Astonished, he crosses to the bedroom door and pushes it noiselessly ajar.

Isabel Dougan is kneeling across the bed, her head towards the doorway he stands in. The upper half of her body that he can see is fully clothed. He cannot see her face as it has been pushed into the mattress. In the tangle of her hair he can see Murdo's sinewy hand. The grip suggests relentless leverage. From the shudders as she pushes against it, straining for air, he can see the force used. Murdo stands behind her. From the height of the bed and his perspective Frank can see the man's corduroy trousers, rumpled like an accordion around his ankles. Braces trail on the planking. There is a puddle of dripped seawater beneath one scarcely visible boot. From the trousers to the underside of the bed Frank can glimpse the upper part of calves, knees and lower thighs, contoured cylinders of wiry black hair. The enormous latent power terrifies the boy. The legs flex rhythmically in time with the concussions as he pushes against her. Isabel's skirt has been bundled up in corrugated folds on the small of her back. Murdo's other hand loops round her waist, pulling the lower half of her body upwards as he pushes her head down.

Murdo's visible torso is also fully dressed. He does not see Frank. He does not see anything. His head is straining back and upwards as his pelvis pushes in, his eyelids fluttering. Frank can see the workings of his huge neck, the fleshy throat swallowing. This is an organism totally preoccupied with its own sensations.

With another spasm Isabel wrenches her head to one side. The sound is almost like a scream, as she draws in air, followed by a sob. The sight of the boy standing in front of her registers. She looks as if she is about to cry out again when the hand rotates her head, face downwards, and pushes it again into the mattress. This has been achieved by him without looking down. She wrenches in either direction. This seems to afford him more pleasure as he arcs into her with a hoarse grunt. At his climax she kicks backwards and squirms. He looks down to find a hank of hair in his hand and the terrified boy standing opposite.

She is sobbing between draughts of gulped air, now lying the length of the bed, trying desperately to pull down her skirt. He is slowly hoisting up his trousers. The boy notices with growing fear the attenuating thread of glistening sperm from the still tumid glans. The man tucks the strange thing away with more care than the boy has seen him exhibit with anything. He is aware he has witnessed some adult collision he should not have. Instinct tells him to run but he is too frightened to move.

Murdo adjusts his braces and walks round the bed towards the door, paying no attention to his huddled wife. His next action is almost as an afterthought, as he draws abreast of the boy.

'Did no one in idiot land ever teach you to knock?' He slaps the boy in a sharp chopping motion, the hand encompassing the area from ear to jawline. The boy falls, his head ricocheting off the doorjamb, causing him to slump against the bed. Without further comment the man walks slowly out, the bedroom door left ajar behind him, the house resounding to the habitual bang as he slams the front door.

The boy gets unsteadily to his feet. He does not look at Isabel, knowing somehow that she does not want to be seen. In the corner of the room one of the floorboards has been disturbed and for no reason he can divine he walks over and looks into the space. Startled at what he sees, he turns back to Isabel. She is now sitting on the bed dabbing the gap between her legs, the handkerchief disappearing up the bell of her skirt. Again he looks into the space, taking note. He turns away, keeping his eyes to the wall furthest from Isabel, and walks out of the room, closing the door softly behind him. He returns to his chair, ear and cheek still throbbing from the slap, and sits as still as he can, twitching at the incessant surf.

10

Impervious to the winter sunburst that sank into the Atlantic in arresting splendour, Gavin Bone is making his way back from the jetty. It is early Saturday evening. He is muttering disgust at the sallies of noise from the distant village hall.

As the light fades the noise increases. He can see the winking doorway as an interrupted beam as people come and go from rehearsal. An accordion wheezes and he can hear the stutter of a drum.

There is a ceilidh on tonight. Locals from neighbouring villages will shortly be pouring in. Gavin knows that in the fullness of time these transgressors will be brought to book, but occasionally he wishes that He would make His dictates more palpable, indulge in some Old Testament severity, perhaps launch a discriminating tidal wave on the stroke of midnight publicly to chastise those who profane the sanctity of the Sabbath. Walking on, he contemplates this evening's entry in his journal.

Within an hour all light has faded. Various vehicles have arrived and the proceedings are well underway. Drink is flowing under the harsh lights. Drawn by curiosity, Harriet and Gail arrive together, trying to make as unobtrusive an entrance as possible. Short of wearing their land girl uniforms, both are conservatively dressed. This is strange to them. Gail expected something like the Drovers, scaled up. She is pleased by the sight of children. Despite the drink it is more of a family affair than the girls anticipated. She is also glad to see the fair proportion of other young women present. For her and Harriet there is always an initial awkwardness walking into the Drovers, comprising as they do most of the young female contingent.

Their arrival has passed off as uneventfully as they hoped. Both look round for Lachlan. He is not here. This is altogether too noisy for Lachlan's tastes.

Lucy is running late. Working up for an effect, she grew as impatient with Harriet as Harriet was with her, urging her to hurry. She told her to go on. Harriet needed no second bidding, catching Gail at the village cross. Neither has mentioned it to the other but neither wants Lucy's notoriety to rub off.

She arrives colourful and smiling. She brings with her the unmistakable feel of an infusion of oxygen into the place. Both the other girls have been persuaded to take part in a reel, laughing at their own ineptitude and allowing themselves to be good-naturedly nudged into position. The proceedings do not stop when Lucy arrives but everyone in the place knows simultaneously that she is there.

At the end of the dance Gail is happy to bow out. She stands apart, changes the monstrous measure of gin she has been presented with for a beer, and studies the faces. Lucy has thrown herself into the proceedings with predictable verve, enjoying being manhandled. As the main door continues to open and close Gail sees a figure standing outside, arrested in a series of tableaux each time he is framed in the light. Puzzled, she dismisses this until she realizes she has seen him somewhere before, in the same context, hovering on the periphery of the schoolroom gazing in. He is too old for primary, too old for secondary. She assumed he was there as some kind of janitor. His face is illuminated again, framed by the light in an aspect of childish longing. She feels suddenly compelled, puts down her drink, refuses the offer of making up a set and walks outside. After the warmth of the interior

54

and without a coat the cold is bracing. When she speaks her breath hangs momentarily suspended before dispersing into the dark.

'Alan, isn't it?'

He swallows, nervously summoning a reply. 'Angus.'

'Of course. Angus. Sorry.' A mutually uncomfortable pause falls. 'Isn't it cold just standing here? Why don't you come in?'

'Not allowed.'

'Not to drink.' She is puzzled by his age. Does he come under the legal age? Even if he did, would it be enforced here? 'There are . . . young people in there too.'

'Not allowed.' He looks acutely embarrassed but dogged. She sees from the intermittent glimpses they get of the interior that he is fascinated by Lucy. She recalls now something she had heard about him, mentioned in passing, that he was 'slow'.

'I'm too cold to stay here. Are you sure you won't join us?'

'I'll stay.' For the first time he directs his attention at her. She estimates he must be in his late teens or very early twenties, but he looks like a beautiful child. 'Thank you, miss.' His face breaks into an artless smile and she feels suddenly saddened at such gratitude for such scant attention.

The door opens. Lucy comes out. The light behind her disappears with the closing door. Her face is suddenly illuminated, an oval sheen of sweat, as she strikes a match.

'I'm not interrupting anything?' Gail introduces them. After staring unaffectedly at her for the past twenty minutes Angus is now unable to make eye contact and stares fixedly at the ground. 'Cat got your tongue, handsome?' Lucy spends the remainder of her cigarette being kind to the boy, despite his inability to reply. Finishing with a long exhalation of blue smoke, she throws the butt on the ground, makes a half-hearted attempt to tread on it, smiles goodbye and has gone as suddenly as she arrived.

'Are you all right?'

'I'm happy here.' With Lucy gone he can speak again. He cannot expect the night's quota of happiness to be any more fulfilled. When the door closes on Gail he looks at the cigarette end till the smouldering tip extinguishes.

She returns feeling somehow that the night has been thrown out of kilter by her meeting with Angus. She dances again, then takes her beer over to a table where she settles with Harriet and a few others. She is irritated by the scrutiny of a big man across the room who has been staring unashamedly at their table for ten minutes. She steels herself to return his look until he smiles, then she looks away.

'Don't let him get to you.'

'Is it me, or us?'

'I didn't notice him staring till you arrived.'

'Arrogant bastard.'

'Yes,' Harriet concedes, laughing. 'But he is rather splendid.'

'He certainly thinks so.'

'He's the first person I've seen who's managed to make you swear.'

'It's this beer.' They both laugh. The night wears on. As they collect their coats Lucy says she has arranged a lift for all three of them. Make that five, no, twenty minutes' grace and meet her out back. After twenty minutes they are left with dispersing cigarette smoke in a jaded hall.

There is a single vehicle at the back, a dilapidated Vauxhall rocking on protesting springs. The windows are partially obscured with condensation. The girls look at each other and back towards the door they have just come out of. Before they can go back in, the large man who has been staring insolently comes out. He seems amused at the spectacle of the car and the girls' embarrassment at their friend's behaviour. Douglas Leckie, searching for Lucy among the departing throng, comes round from the outside of the building. He is transfixed by the rocking car.

'She's keeping up the war effort,' Murdo says, to anyone. There is a sudden strangeness to the lines around Douglas's mouth. He leaves through the hall without speaking or looking at any of them.

'Would you ladies like a lift?' He purposely looks at each of them in turn. There is nothing sardonic in this scrutiny and Gail wonders if Harriet feels the same sensation she experiences, a kind of pleasing discomfort she knows she could not adequately explain to her friend. They arrived in Rassaig to confront many preconceptions, few of which were flattering. And Lucy's behaviour hasn't helped. She is frequently looked at by the local men, a flicked glance that takes inventory of her breasts and thighs and ricochets off when confronted by her own gaze. Aside from Lachlan few look directly into her face, and she is flattered by the directness of this man's manner.

'No thanks,' Gail responds for them both.

'No charge, of any kind.' His stress is on the second last word.

'No thanks.'

'Tell me, does your friend accept coupons?' And, as they turn away without answering, 'Does she hand them out?'

They begin walking, linking arms and matching each other, stride for stride, slowing as the lights recede behind them.

'That man . . .' says Harriet. The pause hangs.

'Yes?'

'I can't explain.'

'I can't explain it exactly the same way.'

'And Lucy . . .'

'I know.'

'Maybe he wasn't so far off the mark saying those things about coupons. Maybe he's got a sense of humour to go with that look.'

'That'll be the look you can't explain.'

'And us standing there as if we're at a bus stop and Lucy in that car for anyone to pass by . . .'

'I know.'

'Some day I'll see the humour in this,' Harriet says, and for no reason they both begin laughing, leaning against each other, snorting condensation, covering their mouths with their gloved hands. They are young and healthy. The night is cold and beautiful.

II

Frank's arrival in Lachlan's household has prompted something of a dilemma. Lachlan has long since given up asking Agnes to use his first name, despite the fact that he uses hers. The desire to maintain the distinction of employer and employee is entirely hers. Both speak to Frank with equal unaffected concern, which begs the question of what terminology he will adopt for the doctor if he emerges from his silence.

And then there is the additional problem of dinner. Each night Agnes serves dinner to the doctor before disappearing back to her own modest parlour. She knows everything about his domestic arrangements, given she supervises them. He knows almost nothing of hers. She lives in apartments whose furnishings and dimensions he can only guess at. He showed her round ten years ago when she applied for the position and left her to 'cheer them up' at her discretion and his expense. Short of being deprived of a salary and accommodation, she would manage if he left, which is not to say her self-sufficiency is any reflection of her feelings for him. If anything were to happen to her then, in the domestic sphere, he would be utterly lost. Both know this and both know the other knows.

Her ability to cook is matched by the discrimination of his palate. Every evening she delivers a simple, impeccable dinner to him in his front room and disappears for the remainder of the evening. They may bump into each other in the top hall as she turns down his bed or offers supper on colder evenings, but generally their last exchange is a 'goodnight' spoken loudly by the first to go up the stairs to bed. His meal is eaten the way he prefers, in silence. When eating he gives himself over entirely to concentration on the activity, because her food and his wine deserve no less. There is a dining room he uses half a dozen times a year for the more formal occasions he is sometimes called upon to host. But his parlour table, scarcely larger than two tea trays, suffices for his solo meals.

It is unthinkable to Lachlan to relegate Frank to the kitchen, or Agnes's parlour, for his meals. He is not an employee. But to eat with him alone somehow seems to Lachlan insulting to Agnes. Despite the distance she has sought to maintain, and which he suspects does not feel, he is unwilling to reinforce domestic apartheid by having her act as Frank's servant too. So the good doctor ruminated for ten minutes and came up with a decision.

'Agnes, I'll have dinner from now on in the dining room, with Frank.'

'Very good, doctor.'

'And you too.'

She raises fewer objections than he anticipated, perhaps guessing at his dilemma, perhaps looking forward to spending more time with the boy.

'Call someone in to check the hearth and flu.'

'That will be the sweep, doctor.'

'We'll burn a fire. Get rid of the mustiness. There's no need to pull a face like that, I'm not calling your competence into question. Body parts atrophy if not used. Must be the same with a house.'

'You'll want to amputate the attic then, doctor.'

'A through draught for a couple of days should do it. Do something with the furniture, will you? Let's make it less like a morgue. Those curtains, who chose them?'

'You did, doctor.'

'Are you sure? Well, anyway, make them more like . . . your curtains.'

'And what are my curtains like, doctor?'

'How on earth would I know? Cheerful, I expect. And by the way, just because his beliefs might restrict his diet, there's no need for them to restrict mine.' She raises her eyebrow sufficiently to make him realize he may have overstepped the mark. With a gruff apology of sorts he dons coat and scarf for last orders at the Drovers.

They settle into a routine. He comes home of an evening to the room she has somehow cheered up. A fire burns from late afternoon every day. She has imported his favourite chair. He sits reading the paper as she busies herself in the kitchen. Frank usually sits on the hearthrug, endlessly reassembling a child's jigsaw he has been given. A hatch links the two rooms and they can hear her cheerful clatter as she cooks. If feeling gregarious Lachlan will talk about his day, making the kind of disclosures that brings a tut of disapproval from the other side of the wall. At Agnes's instructions, Frank sets the table. Within a week he is entrusted with carrying the hot dishes. The trio sit down, the boy eating silently, missing nothing of the exchanges. It is not lost on Lachlan that this is the nearest he, and perhaps the boy, have come to a family meal. He avoids the introspection this thought gives rise to by talking. He has taken it upon himself to educate Agnes's palate.

'It defeats me, Agnes, how a woman who can cook the way you do can drink tea with everything.'

'I drink tea after a meal, doctor. I think the food stands for itself. I do not understand how you, being, I have heard, an educated man, need to drown the flavour in grape juice.'

'Wine does not drown. Caffeine drowns. Wine enhances. And you do not even have the excuse of your religion.' Agnes is a devout Catholic. 'One thing that can be said about your mob compared to some of the others is that they aren't abstemious when it comes to the bottle.'

'I believe you will find that more people here drink tea than wine.'

'There are more people here read comics than serious newspapers.'

'We are fortunate to have you to enlighten us from our quaint ways.' She clears away the dishes. He lights a cigar. Frank, after a nod from Lachlan, retires to the hearthrug to stir puerile jigsaw pieces in an attitude of boredom. Agnes returns with a deliberate cup of tea. Pleasantly tired, Lachlan pours himself another drink. He is willing to let the matter rest. It is she who reopens the conversation.

'I'm sorry you find it regrettable I drink tea.'

'Think nothing of it.' But it is obvious that she does. 'I apologize if I've offended you, Agnes.'

'You haven't offended me, doctor. We can't all share all your enthusiasms.'

'Any time you want a drink, feel free.'

'I'll bear it in mind.'

Her asperity hasn't escaped the boy, who looks up from the hearth at one then the other, as if following a rally.

Lachlan gestures in the direction of the lounge. 'And if you want to read . . .'

'I only dust your books and files, I don't open them.' She takes a thoughtful sip. Her next comment is made with the cup still raised, half concealing the lower half of her face. 'Although I've never dusted that book in your surgery.'

The steady stream of smoke he is placidly blowing terminates with an abrupt puff as he coughs.

She has identified Lachlan's major idiosyncrasy. The close examination of Frank's skull by the car headlights, on the night of the boy's reprieve, is not an isolated incident. Lachlan makes

'Surprise me, doctor.' Her tone is flat, tolerant.

They are both distracted by a preparatory cough from the hearthrug.

'Phrenology,' says Franz.

12

Shortly after her pupils dispersed on her first day of school Gail sought out Lachlan to ask advice. She found him in the surgery waiting room, the paper hoist in front of him. 'Everyone is healthy – or dead,' he explains. It is obvious from her manner that she would like some privacy. To avoid interruption he takes her to his surgery and sits her opposite him.

'I'm not here about my health, so there is no need to make notes.' He has inexplicably retrieved a large hardback notebook from a bottom drawer and seems to be squinting at something behind her. 'I'm here about the school, or, more accurately, the children.'

'What about the children?' From the seriousness of her tone he has abandoned whatever he was doing.

'Their manner. It was . . . subdued. I don't think there's any point in asking Mr Anderson anything.'

'Who's he?'

'The man from the Ministry.'

'He's a functionary. He might do better under Comrade Stalin. There's a shallowness to his cranial arch I associate with blind obedience. It's common enough around here.'

'Can't say I've noticed.'

'Stand outside either of the churches as they empty and look closely. Anyway, about the children.'

'What was my predecessor like?'

'A mindless sadist who would have made an even better apparatchik than the other one. I thought he had a crew cut. Turns out his head was completely flat. Beat learning into the children. Terrorized them into remembering facts and probably put a fair proportion off ever learning anything again. I'm sure he'll do well in the army. I'd be surprised if he hasn't made sergeant by now. That poor boy, Angus, isn't the cleverest boy in the village, but he deserves to be better educated than he is. He preferred to be considered a moron than go back to the class and face the teacher.'

The following morning, while the children were still in the playground, she had searched the cupboard, an airless alcove the size of a small room, racked on one wall with dilapidated shelves. Among the stubs of chalk and stacked slates of past pupils she found a large leather belt. She was intimidated by its density as she weighed it in her hands. She could surmise its purpose. The sheen of the receiving end testified to exuberant use. The dark stain where it had been held suggested enthusiastic handling. She could sense something of his relish. She was revolted.

The belt was on display on her desk as the pupils filed in. A frightened silence descended. Realizing they had mistaken her motives, she marched them in a ragged crocodile to the jetty. On the way they came across Angus, who, as ever, had been hanging around on the periphery. She asked him to come with them. Although bitterly cold it was a beautiful day. They remained cowed. At the end of the jetty she handed the belt to Angus and told him to throw it as far out as he could. It convulsed in its arched trajectory. She expected laughter or some cathartic outburst at the splash but turned only towards a row of questioning faces.

'You will never again be beaten as long as I am here. Not understanding something is nothing to be ashamed of.'

This produced a cheer and they walked back in a nebulous group. Her hat blew off with a boisterous gust. Angus set off in pursuit and shyly presented it to her. The children laughed at the spectacle of her trying to tuck away the flying abundance of her hair in a high wind. She laughed and spontaneously threw her hat in the air, which Angus, spontaneously, set off in pursuit of again.

By the time they returned to the schoolroom Angus had allowed his pace to drop and lagged behind. She made a point of speaking to him. His employment seemed to consist of whatever odd jobs he could find. 'Folk always need something doing,' he explained. There seemed to be no supervision. Judging from his appearance his income was as irregular as his hours.

'I don't want you to stay outside the schoolroom. I want you to come in. You don't have to join in if you don't want to. You can just listen.'

And that's how she came to recruit her new pupil. He felt hulking among the children and scaled-down furniture, and wanted to leave at the first amused titters he elicited. She sent him to the village hall to find one of the old adult's desks used during the aborted teaching experiment. He sat at the back, making himself as unobtrusive as possible, and the children, as children do, came to accept him as part of the furnishings.

13

Miklos Cherny moves to the drawing-room window to look out on the street below. Behind him he can hear his wife, Ida, give final instructions to the caterers. The window he looks from is on the first floor of their terraced house. The narrow street slopes down towards the river. A frost has descended with the night. The air looks brittle. A passing dray horse snorts a vivid plume and he sees a momentary spark in the darkness struck from its shoe against the frozen cobbles.

The room is not yet lit. Passersby in the street looking up would see a silhouetted figure, dark in his evening suit, his shadow projected by streetlight against the coffered ceiling.

'Come away from the window,' his wife instructs, lighting the room. He enjoys staring down into the street. He has always enjoyed the spectacle of passing life, but not the prospect of being observed. Nothing acts normal knowing it is under scrutiny. And now that the room is lit that is what he would be, a watched observer. Ida thinks staring out of a window is common but he has never had her preoccupation with social norms. He was born into this house, this money. His father had the same attenuated sense of social discrimination his wife possesses. He thinks it must be to do with poverty. His father made enough money to get out of Josefov and move his family to the grandeur of this Mala Strana house. And then he died and went back to the Jewish cemetery of his birthplace. All that striving to cross the river and climb the hill, only to go back again, like the Grand Old Duke of York in the nursery rhyme the English governess taught them.

Now in his late fifties, he has grown plump, not with the protuberance of a gross stomach but with a gradual spreading that has widened him, splayed his pelvis and ribcage, inflated his hands and chin and cushioned his eyes. He feels his centre of gravity is lowering. Perhaps eventually, he will be like one of those toys it is almost impossible to knock over. He has no personal vanity about his appearance. It is the penalty he gladly pays for his sedentary life and the relish of food. His lack of concern is obvious: he carries his weight majestically.

Ida is also thickening. Unlike him, she has a regimen that fails to combat the inevitable. They are both aware that they are becoming more alike. He is pleased. The children are grown, and gone. They are becoming old together. Beneath her social aspirations and failing attempts to keep her figure she shares almost all his opinions.

It is a cold December night in Prague, 1923. Miklos cheerfully awaits the arrival of his guests, having left the arrangements to Ida. As long as the food is good he is happy to take care of the rest. His amiable manner usually predominates most gatherings. He is a man who would make the best of whatever he has, with the wit to see that what he has been given is more than could reasonably be expected.

Natasha has told him he has 'a genius for happiness'. The expression pleased him so much he spent the remainder of the week repeating it to anyone who was vaguely interested. He repeats it to himself again as he awaits her arrival. It is not only the appositeness of the words that pleases him but the fact that it implies he possesses a quality he knows he has no right to claim. He has spent his life among competent men and women and even kept company with the exceptionally intelligent, such as Natasha. But he has never rubbed shoulders with genius, and even if he had, suspected it would not rub off.

He likes to think of Natasha as his protégée. Ida has told

him, without rancour, that the influence travels in the other direction, that his mind is pedestrian in comparison to the younger woman's. Ida is as fond of Natasha as he is. Intellectually the two women are poles apart. Ida staked her claim in the domestic sphere.

'She's here,' she says.

'Come away from the window,' he replies, 'it's common.'

He can hear the door being opened below, her coat taken in the hall. She comes up the stairs looking around curiously. She has dressed in her usual subdued manner, simple and elegant. She is what he would describe as a handsome woman, her jaw too determined to be pretty, her features mobile, her expression alert. Her looks will only improve. She exchanges a kiss with Ida and turning to him asks, without preamble, 'Who's coming?'

'Friends. Do me this courtesy, Natasha – be nice.'

'I'm always nice.'

He groans. A large part of his social repertoire is histrionic, pretending to be upset, astonished, hurt, drowsy. He enjoys being an overgrown child. Natasha has chided him for it. Life is not a trivial matter. Given her history, he can see why she thinks so.

'If people say something wrong, please don't point it out.'

'I'll try not to.'

'People don't change, you know. They don't alter their point of view just because you point out a flaw in their thinking.'

'They might.'

'It might surprise you to know that most people don't have arguments to back up what they think. They have opinions because they just do.'

'If that's a description of the friends you have coming I can see it's going to be a long night.'

He turns to Ida for corroboration. 'See, she's doing it again.' But his wife has gone to irritate the caterers by reviewing the arrangements she has reviewed twice already this evening.

Among his many concerns Miklos runs a small publishing house. Knowing little about the industry, he had an image of modest print runs of exquisitely produced books for distribution among the Prague literati. He even attempted to design the colophon himself, eventually handing over his attempts to a professional for completion. In envisioning the enterprise it was more appearance than content he thought about.

His finances did not depend upon the business, but it began to be such a drain on his other resources that he seriously considered abandoning the whole enterprise. At this point Natasha arrived as a part-time proofreader and incrementally assumed complete editorial control without resistance when she realized no one else was up to the task. With Miklos's blessing she also took on the job of translation.

She hailed originally from the Ukraine, one of three daughters. Her far-sighted father had had all three educated as well as his considerable means allowed. This was done in a small-town community that viewed an educated woman as an anomaly. The family was forced to uproot, during yet another of the habitual anti-Semitic pogroms, leaving with what they could carry. Natasha could argue cogently in several European languages. Their impoverishment bothered her less than it did her sisters. She was happy to forfeit past luxuries for the opportunity of being part of the intellectual life of this capital. Provincial indolence would have killed her.

The guests begin to arrive, individually and in couples. Miklos greets each new arrival from the head of the stair, his broad face creasing into an easy smile, introducing them to the guests already present with easy aplomb. They begin to arrive thick and fast and he is obliged simply to wave the latest additions into the company with an expansive gesture.

Natasha is having difficulty making small talk. There is an intensity to her that deters. The caterers are circulating with cocktails. She drinks two martinis in quick succession. She does not normally need the stimulus of alcohol to talk, but Miklos's remark about opinions generally being groundless has given her pause.

Miklos makes an exception for the next guest and brings him across.

'Natasha, you are abandoned.' His face adopts an expression of bottomless woe.

'I've been standing alone for a minute enjoying watching the proceedings.'

Miklos raises his eyebrows. 'Well, if that's all . . . I too enjoy watching proceedings, usually out the window. Ida says it's common. What do you think, Gregor?'

'I'm sorry. I don't understand.'

'Looking out the window. Is it common? Is it normal?' He turns to Natasha. 'Gregor is a doctor. He'll know. Gregor, are common and normal the same thing?'

Gregor is unable to judge if the older man is being serious. 'Pushed at short notice for a distinction I'd say "common" has social connotations that "normal" doesn't.'

'No wonder they pay you so much, or if they don't, they should do. I think "normal" is an abstraction. Personally I don't know anyone who is normal and don't aspire to either. But tell me, what about the common cold? It doesn't confine its attentions to people with no taste. But I see you're looking perplexed. I'm only joking. Natasha disapproves of triviality.'

'You have too much money, Miklos,' she says.

'And you will help me earn more, in the worthy cause of

educating us further.' He turns to Gregor. 'Natasha is the translator I told you about.'

Having set the tone that neither of the others will maintain in his absence, he excuses himself with the obligation to circulate. Gregor has as little time for triviality as Natasha does.

'What did Miklos tell you?' She knows that on a one-to-one basis Miklos is far more serious than his public persona would have people believe. She is certain he would not trivialize the circumstances that brought her here.

'He told me about your family's unfortunate deportation.' She raises her eyebrows at the euphemism. He fails to notice. She begins to ask him a series of questions, her manner almost forensic. She draws him on the question of religion. He is as cynical as Lachlan.

'I think it's institutionalized superstition. I think it's responsible for a great number of evils by perpetuating ignorance. Dependence on myths keeps people from thinking for themselves. What we call "evil" is a result of moral ignorance. Enlighten people and they will stop behaving badly. Take your deportation, that was the result of a collision of spurious theologies. I think that if only—'

But she has listened enough.

'Do you know what I think, I think it might do you the world of good to run away from a burning house in the middle of the night with only the clothes on your back. I think it's astonishing that an intellectual fop, who has never faced a crisis greater than a broken collar stud, feels he has the right to pontificate on others' actions.'

Seeing the telltale signs, Miklos has begun to make his way across the room towards them. She catches sight of him from the corner of her eye and holds up her hand in the universal gesture, causing him to halt. He turns to his guests, wiping mock perspiration from his forehead.

'Miklos might have told you about our "unfortunate deportation". He told me something about you too. I know you were brought up as a Jew the way I was. I know you have chosen to give up your faith. That is your right. Perhaps if you had been unfortunately deported for your religion you might not have shrugged it off so easily as an intellectual exercise. I don't know, your motives are your own, but a consequence of your decision is that you have no idea of the worth of what you abandoned. I've seen you at many of the concerts and Miklos tells me you read everything that we produce and more. He also tells me you're eminent in your field, so you're obviously a cultivated man. I don't decry your learning, but that's not what elevates us. What does is our contemplation of the divine. I feel sorry for you that you feel compelled to deny that portion of yourself that participates in eternity.'

They are by now the centre of a small, circumspect vacuum.

'Dinner is served,' shouts Miklos. He is premature. Seeing the heat of the exchange, Ida is in the process of changing the seating arrangements when the door is opened by her husband and she is caught in the act. Natasha and Gregor are compelled to sit opposite each other.

The noise of the cutlery seems very loud to Natasha during the meal and she can hear her own chewing. Gregor confines his conversation to those at his side. Afterwards she seeks him out.

'Perhaps I shouldn't have been so forthright. But really, it had to be said.'

'I take it that's the nearest thing I will get to an apology.' This is so far from the truth she is nonplussed. He offers his hand. It would be churlish not to accept.

As she shakes it she says, 'I don't think that if we tried for three hours we could find a single thing we agree on.'

They share a departing taxi.

Miklos says, 'It's a match made in heaven.'

Ida says, 'I give them a month.'

General opinion agreed with Ida. Neither Gregor nor Natasha altered their opinions one iota. The only concession she would make to herself, in secret, was that she had done him a disservice. But really, what could he have expected, introducing himself like that?

Unlike Lachlan, Gregor Brod did not cavalierly dismiss the teachings of 'the Viennese witch doctor'. He kept an open mind to advancements of any kind, believing development to be another incremental progression in human improvement. He was a meliorist, and although he did not believe in human perfectibility, he did believe that if we all tried a little harder to be nicer to one another the world would improve by orders of magnitude.

He was a neurophysiologist. In politics he was, predictably, a liberal. He reminded Natasha of one of those tireless men, prominent in the Victorian era, who combined large families with boundless zeal for espousing good causes. It took her the month that Ida had allocated to find these things out, because he was an unassuming man.

They adored each other. When it became obvious to them both that neither would change they saw little point in deferring things further. They married the following autumn.

Within ten months of marrying they had their first child, a boy. Two more boys followed at eighteen-month intervals, Franz the youngest. Gregor, ever the rationalist, had said that their children should be born in a manageable cluster. This would both make best use of the nursery resources and would mean that they were both sufficiently young to enjoy a shared and active retirement when the children were grown.

Seven years after Franz a girl, Nina, arrived. The active retirement would have to be deferred. Their daughter compounded the happiness both parents already thought complete. Natasha spoke only Russian to the children at home. Gregor would return from work feeling he lodged at a club he was not a member of.

The only argument they ever had, and it was ferocious on her side, was over the issue of the children's faith. She refused to have the rigours of existentialism foisted on them.

'You believe in nothing. Nothing isn't something that can be taught. It's an absence. You arrived at a point of scepticism. You chose to give something up. If they choose to do the same then that's their decision, but they have to have something to abandon first. They should at least be afforded the same opportunity you were. I shouldn't have to tell you this.'

He conceded, not just because of her vehemence but because he believed the weight of argument favoured her. His habits of decency had been formed before doubt assailed him. Even if she had not prevailed she would have brought them up in the faith clandestinely. Their mother was a Jew. They were Jews. It was that simple.

The concession Gregor won, by giving in to her on this issue, was his supervision of the children's secular education. The children showed as much promise as any child brought up in a polyglot household with the run of an extensive library and two keenly intelligent parents would. Even so, Franz exceeded expectations.

Money was not an issue. The boys were educated at home until the age of eight. Gregor devised the curriculum. An ardent advocate of the League of Nations, he took upon himself the task of teaching history. Scientific objectivity was left in the hall. His selection of events chosen to illustrate a preconceived view was worthy of Gavin Bone. According to Gregor, the past was littered with dictators who temporarily assumed control before history prevailed. Despots were becoming fewer in number as monarchies fell. Governance of nations on rational principles and in harmony with one another was simply a matter of time. And we were to take example from the larger sphere in our everyday conduct: 'The first man to throw a punch is the first man to run out of ideas.'

By the age of eight, and half a dozen playground encounters later, Franz realized how utopian his father's views were. His mother predicted it all. She had contemplated getting the boys secret boxing lessons but resisted the temptation. She had won the more important battle. She reasoned that a few weeks among their contemporaries, a few skinned knees and they would acclimatize. And she was right.

But the stain was spreading. As Lachlan watched from a distance, with a growing sense of dread, Gregor, from a more immediate perspective, was incredulous. This could not be happening. News of the treatment meted out to German Jews arrived by hearsay, then via more formal channels. He abandoned his medical duties to pitch himself with almost frenzied desperation into political activities. And like Benes, his President, and the other Czechoslovakian diplomats, he listened in stunned disbelief to the news that Chamberlain and Daladier had gone to Munich to surrender a portion of his country to the Germans at a conference to which they had not even been invited.

The scientific endeavour that Gregor so fervently believed in as a means of curing the world's ills had gone into the production of weapons. Fragmentation of order was dragging Europe into another dark age of warring fiefdoms and carnage that would pass unnoticed in the scheme of larger atrocities. Gregor thought his disillusion complete. He had no idea how far he had to go.

Natasha had. She had seen this before. She began making arrangements before German troops marched into the

Sudetenland. The diaspora that had deposited her family in Prague had spread others across Europe. She had relatives she could call upon. When Gregor returned dumbfounded with news of their country's betrayal he found half the furniture gone and most of the family's belongings in three trunks. The boys stood in the hall, each holding a Gladstone bag which seemed to grow larger as their heights diminished.

Although well travelled, Gregor had never lived anywhere else. To leave now seemed another betrayal. He climbed the stairs and found his wife dressing Nina for the journey. From the curve of her back he could only guess at her exhaustion and realized immediately that she had been right, about this and practically everything else.

Farewell letters were stacked on the mantelpiece, stamped and addressed. He asked for two hours' grace to put his affairs in order. She gave him one and called him down to the eldest boy's bedroom. The sore throat the boy had been complaining of since waking, and to which Gregor had paid cursory attention that morning on his way out of the house, had worsened. Fearing the worst, Natasha had been praying since early afternoon, hesitating to bring this to her husband's attention because she knew the conclusion he would draw: that the health of the state had monopolized his concern at the expense of the health of his family. When she told him what she had been doing he pushed back the bedclothes silently to conclude that her prayers had been as effective as his political activities. The confluent rash ran down his cheeks, neck and shoulders to dissipate across the chest. The diagnosis corroborated what she already knew: it was scarlet fever.

Suspecting the damage was already done, he ordered no one to leave the house and for the boy to be kept separate until they could establish whether or not the others had been infected. The other two boys presented early symptoms by the following morning. Nina seemed immune. Natasha paced the downstairs rooms. She had no doubt about her husband's skill. It was delay, not disease, that could prove fatal.

By the time the illness had abated Gregor knew it was too late. He emerged from their self-imposed quarantine to get food when the first vehicles rolled in. He stood in the recess of a shop doorway, his scarf round his mouth, listening to the rumble of half tracks and troop carriers. He could feel tremors through the soles of his shoes. The citizens looked on, silent, resentful.

Within two days there were machine guns posted at every bridgehead. The number of armed men seemed disproportion-ate to the population they had come to subdue. The first evidence that reached them was anecdotal. A Jewish cemetery had been desecrated and a restaurant they frequented burned; what was presumed to be the Jewish owner found in the smouldering ruins.

Miklos visited. Natasha answered the door.

'If I let you in you risk infection.'

'The atmosphere's better in there than out here. I'll take my chances.'

She was surprised at his appearance. He had lost weight and dropped his histrionic repertoire. Nothing was trivial any more. He sat down warily.

'What times we live in, Natasha. My genius for happiness is being put to the test.' She watched him work up to something. 'They smashed the press.' She absorbed this in silence. Like him and Gregor she knew they had left it too late. News of suicides spread before official pronouncements.

There was a sense of contained panic. Funds were seized. The Prague Bar Council, members of which had been guests in their house, ordered all non-Aryan members to stop practising. More ominous still, the organization for Jewish emigration was closed. People clustered outside the British Consulate shouting that they wanted to get away. Gregor thought it a bitter irony to appeal to the nation that had sanctioned his country's dismemberment.

While they could still be had he took the English newspapers. When these became scarce he became one of those to whom week-old copies were clandestinely circulated. The German Foreign Office in Berlin was prepared to admit to the British press that 'some people opened their mouths too wide. Some neglected to get out in time.' Prague was condemned as 'a breeding place of opposition to National Socialism'. The head of the Gestapo in Prague was happy to be more definite to foreign journalists: 'We have ten thousand arrests to carry out.'

They had been living out of half-disgorged trunks in the desperate hope of a quick exit. When the children were in bed the couple sat leaning towards each other across the kitchen table, preparing themselves for the unthinkable conversation they had deferred as long as possible and knew they must now have. For the first time they acknowledged to each other what both of them knew the other had already apprehended. He was the one who said it.

'We won't be able to leave as a family.' She nods, staring at her knuckles. His hand covers hers. 'We will send the boys ahead.'

She had a series of destinations westward already plotted out. The persecution that had driven her from the Ukraine had spread extended family members across the continent. They had all been diligent in communicating, keeping the heritage of their extended family alive. She shows him the list, pointing.

'They can go there first.'

'No, Natasha. They cannot all go there.'

'What do you mean?'

'No one honestly believes it will stop here. Not us and not the British and French who allowed this to happen to us so it wouldn't happen to them. The Germans will move west. The boys look . . . the way they do. To look the way we do is a liability. The people you want to send our sons to will soon have to look to their own future. We can't, in all conscience, ask one family to look after three children who look like us.'

'But to separate them . . . They have never been apart . . .'

'We are going to have to smuggle them. They stand a better chance of getting out if we smuggle them individually. We can pass one of them off as a family member of whoever we get to take them, but not three. Whatever else the Germans are they're not stupid.'

There was one final argument for the boys' separation that logic dictated but that he could not bring himself to enunciate: if scattered, the chance of at least one of them surviving was greater.

'Each of the boys should carry money and a letter of introduction. In all probability these relatives will be risking their lives on behalf of children who aren't theirs.' His hand still covers hers. She cannot bring herself to reply. She fetches writing materials and leaves him to the task.

An effortlessly verbal man, Gregor normally found the translation from thought to word instantaneous. But he stared at this paper and found himself unequal to the task. He was writing to his wife's relatives, people he had never met, his appeal based on ties of blood and a common faith he did not share. But that was not his problem. He had already accepted his wife's arguments: the children were Jews because their mother was a Jew. He was unequal to the task because he was entrusting half his heart to the unknown.

By the early hours he had produced a terse communication that he laboriously copied out two more times. Coming upon this the following morning, his wife again copied it in English, Russian and French, adding a postscript of her own in each of these languages. Each document was sealed in a vellum envelope that was then placed inside a larger one.

Franz does not remember either of his brothers' departures. All he recalls is the lack of playmates in an increasingly empty house and parents who had stopped speaking. He remembers being roused in the middle of the night and being taken in complete darkness to the lane at the back of the house. The local baker's van idled. He was handed his Gladstone bag, a thick envelope and a bound cylinder of banknotes to conceal in the waistband of his trousers. He remembers the exchange among spluttering exhaust fumes. Till the day he died the smell of carbon monoxide evoked for him this leave-taking. Both parents kissed him in a silence broken only by the coughing engine.

Nina was too young to send away. Even if she hadn't been, neither parent could send her. The plan, although neither of them could bring themselves to call it a plan, was for mother and daughter to leave at the first opportunity, with Gregor following when he could. Three addresses in encrypted form were sewn into the lining of their luggage. The boys would be collected on the way. The family would unite in Paris before seeking passage to New York. The thought that sustained Natasha was a nurtured image, improbably cinematic although she knew it to be, of Liberty's torch being disclosed through the mist to her family, huddled but intact on the forward deck.

Franz remembers leaving with the smell of fresh bread. The journey from then on is a confused memory, a series of tableaux that blurred and ran into one another with the light-headedness of recuperation. He remembers transferring to a number of different vehicles, usually at night. In one he hid under a tarpaulin. No one ever asked him for money. After the border he travelled unaccompanied on a train, bemusedly watching fields pass by, his ticket stamped by a puzzled-looking official. By then his sense of dislocation was such that he would not have been surprised had the train come to the end of the world and plummeted off. At a rural station outside Paris he heard his name being called and a shouted general enquiry in Russian. He knocked on the window. A friendly-looking man boarded the train and took him off. Had he not been so traumatized he might have recognized a family likeness. The man took the envelope and slid it into his breast pocket. His offer to carry the bag was politely refused.

They drove in the direction of the disappearing train. Franz spent the remainder of the year in a tidy Parisian suburb. The family was kindly. In the spring he sensed something of the same unease he had felt at home towards the end of his illness. Almost on the anniversary of his departure from Prague he was sent to a small village in Brittany. The new people did not have the same family resemblance and spoke only French. They dressed him in different clothes and sent him to the local school. He felt the same way he had hiding under the tarpaulin.

Every evening the father listened ever more anxiously to the radio, a habit he had seen his own father adopt. Talk at school was all of the Germans. He sensed a feeling of growing circumspection towards him. The people he stayed with tried to disguise it but he knew they felt the same. What Gregor had feared most was happening. Franz, so obviously Jewish, was a liability. The more tenuous the links became to the successive families that fostered him, the less the likelihood of him being concealed to put at risk the same families his presence endangered.

In May he was shipped across the Channel. Three days later the Germans rolled into France.

His cylinder of cash was still intact. His letter had been read by his successive hosts and handed back. He was told he would be met off the boat at Plymouth. He was given a telephone number and name if for some reason his contact did not arrive. He disembarked with the departing throng feeling everyone in the world had a destination except him.

The link was now indeed tenuous. He was met at the quayside by David Munroe, brother-in-law to Leon, the man who had seen him off from France. David had married Leon's sister. She died on her thirtieth birthday. Working as a buyer, David had met Irene Dougan, Isabel's sister, on a trip to Scotland to look at cottage textile industries. The loss of his French wife had left him more emotionally redundant than genuinely bereaved. His work involved travelling. By disposition he could not stay at home, but intermittently craved a home to return to. He was based in the south of England. Irene saw him as a ticket out of Rassaig. There was no pretence of great love on either side. She knew he would be an indifferent husband and a good provider.

They married in Rassaig and settled in Chelsea. He stayed at home for a week before resuming his itinerant life, leaving Irene lonely and pregnant. She suffered the nausea alone, suspecting a man of his vitality must have other women. She never asked. Over the next couple of years he seemed to be home only long enough on each occasion to impregnate her. They had three children. His reaction to her exhaustion was to employ a home help. It never occurred to him to stay longer.

A man of considerable acumen, he foresaw the coming war and realized the opportunity for someone in his line of business. War meant a demand for uniforms. He established a small clothing factory. It was a risky enterprise that survived at subsistence level until, calling in every favour his limited

85

patronage allowed, he won the company's first order. The workforce was comprised almost entirely of women. He demanded a great deal from them and paid extravagant bonuses. It was a winning strategy. A second order meant expansion of staff and premises. He established a track record of delivering on time. He regarded the growing threat as a licence to print money.

He moved his family to a bigger house. He employed more domestic help, a woman who turned up without forewarning looking for instruction from a mystified Irene. By this time Irene's children were her family. She neither knew nor cared about her husband's suspected affairs.

Communication between the brothers-in-law had been intermittent and finally stopped, not because of a growing coolness but because each recognized the other's commitments. David's first wife had returned to France to die. He had a keen sense of obligation to his brother-in-law. Both knew there was no chance of Leon's appeal being refused.

At each change in location Franz spoke less and less, like a slowing locomotive. He came to a standstill on the French side of the Channel. This cheerful, immaculately dressed man chatted amiably all the way to a large house in Chelsea. He handed the boy over to his wife who by now had ceased to be mystified by her husband's caprices. 'Refugee I said we'd keep. Doesn't say much,' was his only comment. Undaunted by the prospect of her sleeping back that night, he was up and out before the family stirred.

Somewhere in this inadequate transition Franz became Frank. Two days after his arrival he solemnly handed his envelope to Irene. Baffled by the Cyrillic script of the first two paragraphs, she folded the document and handed it back. 'You keep it safe for me, dear.' She never demanded anything of him. She could see premature marks of care in his young face. Had she had more information she might have been able to treat him more like one of her own, but like so many of David's surprises he had come unannounced, with no history and no indication of how long he was staying. David might reward her efforts by taking him away tomorrow. The boy never spoke. She thought him incapable of education, or at least the kind of rudimentary education on offer now there was a war on.

He hung around the house for a few months, eating with the family, surreptitiously reading the newspapers David left around following his infrequent visits. With the mother, children and domestic help he practised evacuation to the Anderson shelter. Nothing surprised him any more. These rehearsals did nothing to reinforce in Irene's simple mind the reality of the situation. But she panicked at the first genuine siren and moved everyone to hastily rented accommodation in Somerset. The first raid on London, late in August 1940, incinerated their factory.

David arrived at work to find a doused hole, bewildered relatives of the vaporized security man having been forced back from its smoking periphery by the firemen. Suddenly redundant, he returned to his childless house. Irene had no idea of the extent to which they lived beyond their means. The extravagance of their domestic arrangements was a fraction of their extravagance.

The first thing to go was the domestic help. He had the good grace to turn up in Somerset with news of the debacle for Irene and an envelope, with as generous a settlement as their drastic means allowed, for each of the helps. The indefinite upkeep of the country accommodation went next. They were released from the terms of their lease when David made it quite clear to their landlord that there was no point ruining an already ruined man. With a sense of foreboding they all returned to a darkened London. The house in Chelsea was beyond his means to maintain, and her energies to clean, but he could not unload it in the middle of a crisis. He was an energetic man. It was a matter of time and continued health till he revived their fortunes. In the meantime Irene closed up the rooms they did not need and went back to cooking with thrift learned of necessity in Rassaig.

They found a family camaraderie in retrenchment. Adversity drew them together. The forced economies he saw as a personal indictment cheered her. She had grown up in a place characterized by vegetation that clung and she found reserves even she did not know she possessed. He saw the value in her he had been too preoccupied or obtuse to notice. She was happier than she had ever been.

The national evacuation programme was in full swing. When the children were asleep he sat her down.

'If we are to send them away we have to decide now.'

'No. I can't. I won't send them away. It might be selfish but I've never been separated from them yet and I couldn't bear it now.'

He was prepared to defer to her. Up till now all he had invested was money.

'I can't imagine the thought of life without them any more than I can the thought of them being brought up by strangers and not knowing me.' And having said this she thought of Franz and for the first time realized the appalling sacrifice he represented.

'All right. We'll stay. We'll see it through . . . or not, as a family. I'm happy to go along with you on this but I don't think either of us can take the decision to expose Frank. He's not blood. It's not fair.'

'What do you think we should do?'

'Most of my contacts are in the south. Most are no safer than this. I'll telephone Isabel.'

'No. It should come from me. I'll telephone Isabel.'

The following afternoon a drinking companion of Murdo's turned up at the croft to say someone had called the local pub last night hoping to leave a message for Isabel. Her sister was looking for her. She was to call the number he had written down. She could reverse the charges. Leaving her mother-in-law in charge of the children, she went to the only public phone box, situated ludicrously on the exposed wharf. The concrete floor was intermittently swamped by higher tides. The noise of the sea made for halting exchanges. She had to wait her turn and shout into the concavity of the next approaching wave.

Franz found himself on yet another night-bound train. Perhaps it was his imagination but when he changed at Glasgow the rural darkness seemed to deepen the further north he travelled. He did not know what his parents had intended for him but he knew it was not this.

The station he found himself finally deposited on comprised two concrete platforms linked by an overhead walkway. The ticket booth was closed. The departing train wavered along parallel moonlit streaks until it, like them, disappeared into moorland. The man who emerged from the otherwise empty waiting room was not cheerful, immaculate or talkative. He made no effort to take the Gladstone bag. Later that night, when Franz was getting undressed in the Dougans' house, the same man entered unannounced in time to see the cylinder of notes fall from the waistband. Murdo picked it up, flicked through the unfamiliar currency and pocketed it. 'It's our secret,' he said.

Until then Franz had not considered his plight captivity, but he did so now. And one day, a month after his arrival, a large envelope arrived. It was from London, and contained within it a short note from David clipped to a smaller envelope.

The smaller envelope was for Franz, its frayed discoloration testifying to much handling and the delay of its transit. The lack of other official stamps suggested it had travelled by the same surreptitious route he had. He opened it in private and in silence, poring over the same Cyrillic script in the same handwriting that had dissuaded Irene from examining his credentials. And he knew, with precocious certainty, that this was the last chink of light that had escaped from a room whose door was now closed for ever. As his contemporaries in the village school, a walk distant and under Gail's tutelage, familiarized themselves with long multiplication and the dates of Magna Carta, he slowly absorbed the fact of his family's dissolution.

So Franz listened to the surf and waited. By now he saw himself as a harbinger, preceding annihilation. He had come a long way. Rassaig was remote. By entirely different reasoning he had come to the same conclusion as Lachlan: the tranquillity of this place was fragile. Whatever followed him might take longer to get here, but its progress was inevitable. Sooner or later it would come.

14

The day after Franz dropped his four-syllable bombshell, Lachlan went back to see Isabel Dougan. His pretext was a follow-up visit to the mother-in-law. His real intention was to find out if Franz's silence had been total during his stay with the Dougans. He was looking for any kind of clue to the boy's antecedents and intended asking for the papers Isabel referred to so absently, that might be the only link to his past. But his intention and the pretext for his call escaped his memory when Isabel opened the door. If she had ever worn makeup he had not noticed, but even heavy cosmetics wouldn't disguise the mark on her face. The previous night she had interrupted Murdo in the bedroom raking his hand into the space created by floorboards he had just pulled up. Standing, he had shouted, 'Where the fuck is it?' She didn't know if he addressed the question to her or discovered her behind him as he spun round shouting. She credited the next second to instinct. She explained to his mother that it was not his fault: he had been taken unawares. The arc of his hand followed the line of sight as she hove into his peripheral vision. His hand was only half closed as it made contact with the side of her face, otherwise it would have dislocated her jaw. She slammed into the bed. The look she cast him was more accusatory than her subsequent accounts. The look he cast at her was bewildered, not apologetic. He kicked the boards back into position and left the room.

She tries to refuse Lachlan's examination. There is no structural damage and the swelling will subside. He orders a cold compress and leaves her something for the pain. The mother is asleep and he does not disturb her. Murdo is nowhere to be seen. Lachlan is glad. The only thing that would have forced him to hold his tongue is the knowledge that the victim of any public recrimination would be the same one who is suffering now. Against her objection he leaves with a promise to return.

Despite running late he makes a point of finding Michael Murray, the constable. The exchange occurs in the Drovers. The younger man seems preoccupied with the blemishes of the table as Lachlan speaks. They have spoken enough times for Lachlan to know he is listening. Michael, nodding, hears him out.

'I know. It's not the first time. You're not the first person to mention it either.'

'Nor the last, from what you say. How bad would it have to be before we can do anything about it?'

Michael is heartened by this 'we'. Lachlan is renowned for being opinionated and ploughing a lonely furrow. He has never been a member of a team. This is not empty rhetoric.

'Bad enough for her to press charges or someone who witnesses it to come forward.'

If Lachlan needed further proof of inequity this is it: as long as he continues to do so in private Murdo can beat his wife with impunity, and the fact that this constitutes nary an atom of the suffering being experienced elsewhere does not lessen the misery of a woman being punched behind closed doors. But Lachlan does not need further proof. The tragedy, from his perspective, is that Murdo has a legitimate excuse for not fighting. He suffered some kind of accident as a child, falling into a freezing sea and perforating an eardrum. He lives now with tinnitus in one ear. Bouts of disorientation are infrequent but unpredictable. When he feels them approach he can do no more than navigate home and lie in a darkened room till the nausea subsides. Tragically, it is at such times when he despises his own weakness that Isabel likes him best. She will minister to him tirelessly. He will ask for nothing and dislike her for witnessing his humiliation. When he recovers she is exhausted and he is colder.

He was avid to enlist, first in the queue when recruitment was announced. The prognosis of his condition was such that he could not be entrusted with any responsibility. His humiliation was compounded when he was referred for a second examination with the lame, the twisted, the flat-footed and the stutterers. He sat in a waiting room with these untouchables breathing deeply to quell his anger at being similarly classified. The regret of the recruiting officers at losing one of his build was nothing in comparison to the smouldering resentment with which he heard the news. He was, by disposition and physique, a natural warrior. And from experience Lachlán knew that such men were not good survivors. The temperament that would have propelled him into the fray would have earned him an early bullet. Murdo's tragedy, from Lachlan's perspective, was that he remained intact when decent men were being blown to fragments.

Thanking God for his intervention, Isabel tried to console Murdo as best she could: people need to be fed even when there's a war on, especially if there's a war on; it requires more courage to face a gale than an enemy. These attempts simply stoked Murdo's simmering anger. At such moments he despised her. Irrespective of the consequence to his family he would have been glad if an advance invasion force had landed on the coast. He knew nothing about Nazis, but he would happily have hunted down and killed as many Germans as he could until they killed him.

He temporarily assuaged his anger by pitting himself against ludicrously superior forces. He would listen to the shipping forecast in anticipation of putting to sea in the teeth of a weather front that sent everyone else scuttling to harbour. On a pretext of business he went to Glasgow and haunted the bars, looking for someone sufficiently sinister to challenge him about his civilian clothes. He had nothing but contempt for conscientious objectors, and when someone referred to him as one he spun round in anticipation. But the man was drunk and too small. On the way out, and almost as an afterthought, he slapped him off his barstool.

Two hours and six pints later he found what he wanted in a bar off the Trongate: three uniformed soldiers, the biggest as big as him, kit bags at the ready. He made a point of unceremoniously kicking their luggage out the way as he bawled above the throng for his drink. The smallest of the three was the most sinister and his reaction was instantaneous. There was no verbal escalation that resulted in a punch being thrown. The soldier snatched up a cane from an old man at his side and brought it down with enough force partially to detach Murdo's ear. Galvanized by pain, Murdo ducked down and ran the soldier into a pillar, breaking his jaw from an upward butt delivered by the back of his head. The competition was so unequal there was no pretence of one-on-one. They had not come this far together to lose their comrade to a bar-room psychopath. The fight spilled into the street. They left him there twenty-five minutes later. Murdo had kicked one of them so hard in the side of the head that the eyeball burst. With one eye, he was confined to logistical tasks while his comrades went to Burma. Neither came back. The man who had unwittingly done him a favour lay in the street spitting. The fight had concluded with Murdo face down while the only soldier still capable jumped up and down on the back of his head. The soldier staggered off with his comrades, strands of hair attached to his hobnailed soles. Murdo's skull was perforated. His nose, jaw and ribs were broken. An outstretched hand, fingers curled underneath, had been repeatedly stamped on.

They went to the Royal Infirmary. He lay in the Victoria for three weeks. He returned to Rassaig more taciturn than ever. Rumours of his association with the Glasgow criminal fraternity spread. He continued to go out in calamitous weather, pull the larger dogfish from the net and beat the still palpitating ones to death against the bulwarks.

Lachlan reflected that if he could have somehow falsified Murdo's medical record to qualify him for active service, he would have done so.

15

The schoolroom has undergone a transformation. With an ultimatum to the man from the Ministry to requisition the list of goods handed across, or find himself another supply teacher, Gail has managed to prettify the place. She has even written to her parents to have some things salvaged from past teaching positions sent on. Charts of various kinds now bedizen the walls. She has had Angus screw up in pride of place her favourite artefact, a shallow glass case containing several cruci-fied butterflies who, when unpacked, continued to coruscate through the dusty glass.

Within a short time she believes she has managed to create an atmosphere whereby most of the children are happy to come to school, and those who are not are not afraid to. She has separated the children into sections for reading and arithmetic. Everything else, as she predicted, goes at the pace of the slowest. She is a slender resource and has done as much as could be reasonably expected. During the last part of the day she reads to them a child's edition of *Huckleberry Finn*, simplified into manageable chunks. They are into the second week of instalments when Gavin Bone walks unannounced into the schoolroom.

'This is not work.'

Several of the children automatically stand at his entrance. Initially stunned by his rudeness, Gail takes stock. She has a vague notion that the parents of the standing children are members of the same congregation as this arrogant bastard. She is further incensed by the fact that they will not sit despite her gesture to do so, seemingly awaiting his permission.

'I have no idea who you are and what credentials you presume to possess that you think entitle you to criticize my methods, but do not ever walk uninvited into my classroom again and speak to me in this manner.'

It is his turn to be stunned. He physically steps back.

'I am not accustomed to be spoken to by women who—'

'The limitation of your experience is of as little interest to me as your opinion of my teaching. I am sure the sheer tonnage of what you are unaccustomed to would sink a liner.'

She is so angry her eyes are smarting. The silence is complete. The standing children are aghast, anticipating some Old Testament apocalypse. He is so astonished he turns away, as if temporarily dispelling the sight of her will confirm the fact that this is an hallucination. But when he turns back she is still there. A woman, a young woman, has not only spoken back to him but has seen fit to upbraid him in front of children, some of whom have parents in his congregation. His eyes wander over the classroom till they settle on Angus. Of all those at a desk he is the only one not observing the exchange. His eyes are fixed on the ground in his overwhelming desire to remain inconspicuous. Gavin addresses himself to the boy.

'Angus. A young man of your years in this . . . place. It is indecent. Step outside.'

'Angus, you are not officially a pupil of mine, so I can't order you to stay. You don't have to go if you don't want to, which is more than I can say for this man.'

Gavin turns to her. He has a public voice of sudden fortissimo, perfected in the barn on startled livestock in imitation of denunciatory sermons from pulpit belters it has been his privilege to hear. He is about to direct this like a lighthouse beam at Gail when she pre-empts him.

'Paul, please run and fetch your father. Say we have an intruder in the school.'

Eager to fulfil the commission, the boy scrapes back his chair. His father is the constable, and a Catholic. Gavin envisages the uniform, the boots, the Catholic relish as he is escorted off the premises, the official reprimand, the unofficial glee. He walks out with as little forewarning as he arrived, heading in the direction of his journal, there to give full expression to the denunciation he was prevented from voicing in the schoolroom.

News of the exchange spreads like wildfire through both sections of the community. For the first time in Agnes's experience she hears Lachlan cackle. Gail's stock has risen, certainly with the contingent who live nearer the harbour. To reassert his standing among his own, Gavin has been more publicly severe than ever in his observance of Church discipline.

Unaware of her notoriety, Gail continues to do her best. She persuades Angus not to let the prejudice of the older man dissuade him from trying to learn. His reading has progressed to the halting narrative of a precocious seven-year-old. He has confessed to her his longing to be able to sit in front of the *Oban Times* without dissembling. The paucity of this ambition saddens and shocks her. She has spent half an hour, three nights out of five, staying back to help him. He now haunts the schoolroom. She half suspects he has nowhere else to go. Anticipating that Gavin Bone will do what he can to discredit her, she feels these solitary lessons will provide ammunition. But she will be damned if she will abandon this boy because some warped old man doesn't like being talked back to by a woman.

Reading aloud to her after four o'clock, Angus was stopped short by a new arrival. Gail's back was to the door. From the consternation on Angus's face she expected to turn around and find Gavin. Instead she saw Lucy, who managed to get as much innuendo into 'Late lessons?' as she suspected Gavin would. It was clear from the effect of Lucy's arrival that they would get no more work done. Gail finished the lesson off. The three left the schoolroom together, walking to the junction that separated the girls.

'Going my way?' Lucy asked Angus. He fell in behind her without comment.

'You didn't say why you'd come,' Gail said to her, mildly anxious at the turn of events.

'Fancy going out later?'

'I can't tonight.'

'There you are then.'

And the exchange stopped at that. Gail could hear Lucy's voice and their footfalls till they disappeared in the direction of the McHargs' farm.

The following afternoon, having accustomed the children to expect something beyond the syllabus, Gail diversified.

'You all know what this is.' She handed it round, allowing each child in turn to examine the texture. When the piece of coal was returned to her she held it aloft. 'Did you also know this was part of a forest, long, long before anyone else was here?'

16

Having heard the first word Franz uttered in Scotland, Agnes expected a torrent of reminiscences, and asked him a number of questions till Lachlan told her to stop. His expectations were more realistic. 'Who knows how much that one cost him?' he said, once the boy had gone to bed. His instruction was that the order of the day should be the same as before: talk to him in the expectation of being listened but not replied to.

'There is at least one thing we can now be sure of, doctor. We know that he can understand.'

'I always knew he understood.'

'It must be a marvellous skill to have, doctor, the ability to predict things after they happen.'

But she knew that he was right; he had always known. And she went to bed piqued that on this occasion his insight had been keener than hers.

Lachlan has plans for Franz's education. But he will not force the issue till the boy is forthcoming. He continues to take him on house calls, to lunches at the Drovers and on evening walks. The dinner conversation is still confined to the table-top exchanges of the doctor and his housekeeper with Franz unashamedly listening to the proceedings, as if preparing to adjudicate. He no longer has the absurd jigsaw and childish toys Agnes provided him with. Against her advice Lachlan has given him the run of his library, and Agnes, who will casually decapitate a chicken, looks over Franz's shoulder as the boy pores over *Gray's Anatomy*, and considers it ghoulish.

Confirmation of the boy's understanding has not led to any

circumspection on Lachlan's part. Finding Franz reading about the lymphatic system, Lachlan is happy to hold forth on patients, past and present, whose ailments are pertinent to this field of study.

'Don't you at least think you should try and disguise certain names?' Agnes asks.

'Nonsense. Look how long it took him to say a word. He's not going to blurt it out. And even if he spoke as much as you do, he is obviously intelligent. I trust to his discretion.'

'I would not say, doctor, that intelligence is any guarantee of discretion. You must have passed exams and look at the way you talk to him.'

'And I would add,' he continues, ignoring her comment, 'that the shape of Franz's head corroborates my theory. It would be impossible for the boy not to be intelligent with a head shaped like that.'

She returns to her cooking, exasperated. He raises the newspaper, satisfied. Franz, taking up a pencil, makes a note in the margin of the anatomy textbook, unnoticed.

Having corroborated his theory in his own mind if not Agnes's, Lachlan is curious to know just what level of intelligence the boy has. Poring over *Gray's* is no guarantee of anything. He could be simply exhibiting the same macabre curiosity that would prompt a schoolboy to poke a dead cat with a stick. Lachlan is content to wait. He feels life has dealt him enough surprises. Unlike Agnes, he has an abundance of patience.

The following week he is sitting in the surgery making another of his haphazard notes on the record of the last patient, when there is a soft knock on the surgery door. He tuts with impatience. It has been a long day. He believed his last patient was his last patient. He is looking forward to asking Franz to play chess with him.

'Come in.'

The door opens. Franz stands on the threshold. The boy has never knocked before. He either enters a room or reads elsewhere until called upon. There ensues a charged pause. Lachlan is about to fill this.

'There is a woman here.'

The voice is soft. Lachlan cannot place the accent. He is anxious to hear more.

'Does she have an appointment?'

Franz disappears from the frame of the door. Lachlan hears a murmur. The boy returns.

'No, she does not.'

'What did she say?'

'She moved her head, like this.'

'What is her name?'

Again the boy disappears. This time Lachlan hears the reply. From her voice he knows the identity of the patient.

'Mrs . . . she told me but I cannot say it.'

'Urquhart.'

'Yes.'

'Tell her I will be with her in a moment.'

The boy gently closes the door. On this occasion Lachlan would have preferred if he had left it ajar. He hears the murmur of Franz's voice again and a response, followed by the boy's voice. This seems to be a muted dialogue. Of all the people to whom he should start talking, Rhoda Urquhart is the worst, or best. She will not demand anything of him by way of a response. She does not conduct conversations, she sustains a running monologue as a continuous commentary of her experiences and fictitious ailments. She is old. In the past few years Lachlan has watched her slip from idiosyncrasy to near lunacy. She is a single woman, as rare a specimen here as he is himself. What family she had she has outlived. She lives on a farm, too old to manage, the land leased on. She no longer has the distraction of a punishing regime to occupy her. Lachlan thinks her condition symptomatic of chronic loneliness. It is strange, he thinks, that some people are born into a remote landscape that ill befits them for town existence and still succeeds in unhinging them by the resonance of its solitude. She used to shop once a week but now makes daily forays into Rassaig and has become something of a diversion in the village. Previously abstemious, she will now command the hearth of the Drovers with a pint in her hand and pontificate at the ceiling. People are kind. She has become something of a sacred cow.

Lachlan wonders if he will hear better if he puts his stethoscope to the door. This fails. Risking observation, he opens it a crack. She is in mid-flow.

'You're not from around here.'

'No.'

'It's my hysterical lung, y'see, sonny. Lot of them won't believe. Doctor McCready believes. Good man. Most of the others are spies.'

'What are they spying on?'

'Hysteria of the lung runs in the family. Lots of my ancestors went to Canada after the clearances. Spread the condition through Saskatchewan. I'm thinking of going there.'

'Will that be possible? Will the war not mean that you have to stay here?'

'What war?'

Although he would love to hear the boy being drawn out, Lachlan thinks it advisable to intercede.

'Rhoda, please come in.' She precedes him into the surgery. 'I will join you in a moment.' Closing the door behind her, he turns to the boy. 'Would you be good enough to tell Agnes I will be ten minutes late. One other thing before you go – do you play chess?'

'Yes.'

'Perhaps we can play a game after dinner.'

'That would be good.'

Fifteen minutes later, having sent Rhoda off with a placebo for her hysterical lung, he finds the boy in the dining room reading the newspaper whose formal prose daunts Agnes. She is staring through the communicating hatch, waiting to catch his eye and nod meaningfully towards the small reading figure.

'Any news?' Lachlan asks casually.

'I think there are lots of things happening that this newspaper says nothing about.'

'Did you read a lot at home?'

'Always.'

'And is your name really Frank?'

'Franz. Franz Brod.'

17

The guilt of sin is imputed from our first parents. The corruption of their nature is ours, conveyed to all posterity. Sinfulness proceedeth from the sinner, not from Him. Being perfect He cannot be the approver of sin, which is a transgression of His righteous law and will bring upon its author His wrath, with all its attendant miseries. It is the privilege of His immutable will to leave His iniquitous creatures to pursue temptations, to wallow in corruption so that they be chastised and humbled and come to realize their dependence on Him.

That a teacher should be a woman and not appreciate her place is receiving instructions and not giving them is bad enough. That woman who usurps her betters place . . .

Here Gavin stopped, temporarily defeated by the positioning of the possessive apostrophe. Reflecting that punctuation should not impede the afflatus when it is upon him, he draws a large red mark through the previous sentence. 'That woman who occupies a place that any man would be better suited to hold . . .' Even the blinkers of Gavin's fanatically restricted vision could not prevent him from realizing that this was not true. Some of the farmers and fishermen of his acquaintance are semi-literate. Put them in a schoolroom and the sense of displacement would be as great as that of some primitive monster transported to the teacher's desk. This last inadvertent reflection is pertinent to his train of thought. Summoning himself, he cancels the last attempt and begins yet again:

To put a woman in a man's job is a perversion of the natural order and look what happens, I am spoken back to in public and threatened with the law. She will be made to learn that there are larger laws, His laws. And now I hear she is holding up pieces of coal. Coal was made by Him for us to burn to keep warm. And here she is talking about creatures stuck there since before our first parents arrived . . .

18

If Lachlan was expecting a prodigy whose tactical insight would confound him from the outset, then he was disappointed. The truth is that he did not expect a prodigy, and he was a little disappointed by the ease with which he beat Franz in their first game of chess. Reflecting later that night, he realized he had beaten the boy with the same ease with which he defeats the harbour master, who is a fifty-year-old man of solid but not scintillating intelligence.

The second game Lachlan won with equal ease, although he noticed that the boy seemed to pay more attention to Lachlan's moves than his own. The following evening, a Wednesday, was chess night in the Drovers. Chess night consisted of eight or ten sufficiently competent people playing at several boards while darts were conducted in the corner. Against Agnes's strictures about the effect that smoke and such company might have, Lachlan had Franz wrap himself against the cold and took him to the pub, ordering him half a Guinness for medicinal reasons. Amid general laughter Lachlan offered to write a prescription should the barman prove unwilling to pour it. The drink arrived and the boy took it, settling himself near Lachlan avidly to watch. Having proved his speaking credentials only to Lachlan, Agnes and Rhoda of the hysterical lung, Franz was treated with a certain good-natured condescension. One player being left redundant without an opponent, Lachlan was asked to perform what was considered locally as the prodigious feat of playing two simultaneous matches. He reluctantly complied. Lachlan played for his own stimulation, not public esteem. So he played his two opponents, defeated one and achieved a stalemate with a second he would have beaten had his attention been monopolized by the game. There followed several games of speed chess, the tactics growing sloppier as the evening progressed. Having dispatched several more opponents, Lachlan ordered Franz to drink up, downed his own whisky against the night and walked back to the house chatting to the boy who seemed to have stored what conversation the night's activities provoked until they were alone.

The following night the doctor was uncharacteristically dyspeptic. Agnes's dinner had not improved the world. Franz had set the chess pieces up in readiness. Rather than upset the boy, Lachlan sat opposite him, moving uncomfortably in his chair, contemplating a vindictive bubble of trapped wind. The doctor's attention is desultory and at one point he excuses himself to stand by the back door and raise his leg to break the seal on a blissful fart.

'That will be the Drovers' lunches, not my cooking.' Agnes has startled him in flagrante. The doctor is stoical, not embarrassed.

'It is age, Agnes. It comes to us all, women included. The days of definitive and predictable bowel movements have gone. I compare my intestines now to the bilges of some decrepit old scow, disgracing the flag of convenience.'

It is the exaggeration of poetic licence. Feeling considerably better, Lachlan returns to the game to find himself in trouble. It takes what concentration he can muster to summon a stalemate. The following night his undivided attention barely produces a win. Several harsh realizations simultaneously dawn upon him. He has been playing the same game for the past fifteen years. A winning strategy that needed no revisiting has left him strategically flat-footed when faced with someone capable of predicting his next move. Indulging all his idiosyncratic interests is all very well, but he has lost whatever mental flexibility he once possessed. Ever since he can remember, at University and beyond, nothing presented him with any great difficulty; he is accustomed to being cleverer than his contemporaries, and sequestering himself in Rassaig he has been the only fish in the smallest of pools – until now.

The boy proves more talkative over subsequent games. From the brief answers to deliberate questions Lachlan begins to build up an intelligible picture of Franz's background. The following nights produce three consecutive stalemates. On the next of these Lachlan knows Franz has conceded a stalemate in deference to himself.

'I think our games are finished.'

'I have not won.'

'I think we both know you could. You have watched my only game and beaten it. I will not get better. You will only improve and you are better than I am already. Tell me, did you play at home?'

'Always.'

'With your father?'

'Yes.'

Lachlan appreciates the need for caution. In their brief exchanges they have studiously avoided talk of the fate of Franz's family.

'And did you beat him?'

'Never.'

This is doubly humbling, coming as it does on the night of his first reversal in Rassaig.

'He was a doctor?'

'Yes. Like you. But he did not visit people in their houses. They visited him. In hospital. He looked at brains. He knew about phrenology also, although I do not think he gave it much . . . credit.'

It is the first time he has spoken about his family in the past tense. They both gaze for a few moments in silence at the dormant pieces till Franz begins carefully to replace them in their box.

The following afternoon Gail returns from school to a note from Lachlan asking her to come and see him at her convenience. Glad of the air and the chance for conversation other than Eileen Campbell's, she walks to the house. Lachlan is in the lounge. At his insistence she agrees to stay for dinner. His invitation accepted, Lachlan disappears into the hall. She hears him tap on one of the doors, presumably leading to the back of the house, and when it is opened say, 'One more for dinner.'

'And what evening will that be, doctor?'

'This evening.'

'Unlike Our Lord I cannot stretch a fish. Perhaps you could find out if the young lady is partial to mackerel portions.'

'I'm sure anything will be fine.' And to Gail, once the lounge door is closed on them, 'We're having fish.' Never one for preamble when preoccupied with the matter in hand, Lachlan begins, 'I've brought you here to talk about the boy.'

'Frank?'

'What do you know about him?'

'I've heard he's an evacuee. I've heard he hasn't spoken and that he's considered to be . . . well, slow is I suppose the kindest way to put it. Although it strikes me that any child uprooted from everything he knows may have reasons of his own not to speak. And from my experience, limited though it is, if someone is silent it doesn't necessarily mean their understanding is impaired.'

Lachlan strikes a match with a sulphurous burst, nodding

to himself as he does so. She believes he is agreeing with her. He is congratulating himself on the judiciousness of his choice in selecting her. She watches the ceremony as he rolls the cigar end, slowly lighting it in the flame.

'Angus is slow. Frank does not exist. Franz is a well. I threw down a stone when I first met him and I've not heard it hit the bottom yet.' He talks intensely for fifteen minutes as a cylinder of ash accumulates. She listens without interruption. Concluding, he waits for a response.

'Well, frankly, if you can't beat him at chess I don't think that academically there's much I can teach him.'

'To be quite brutal, I don't think you can either. But if not you, who else? He's too small for the High School. In any normal environment he would be moved up a few years as soon as he was properly assessed, but with his accent and size I think there's a fair chance he'd be bullied and I don't know if they could teach him either. I imagine you're more competent than the teachers there. He needs some kind of normal routine and to be near other children. There is more he needs to learn than lessons. Most things he'll pick up through osmosis. Just keep him around.'

19

Angus is stacking creels on the jetty. It is mid-afternoon, December, and he is working against the fading light. He works quickly. It will not do to be still for any length of time in this cold. He is young, and supple. He can carry out with grace tasks the older men grunt over. As he is stooping he feels a hand follow the curve of his spine down past the waistband of his trousers. He straightens in a sharp movement and spins round. Lucy is there. The wind is coming off the sea and he has not heard her approach. She is wearing her bib-and-brace overall and green pullover.

'Cold.' He does not respond but continues to stare at her. Having now met her on several occasions he is no longer completely mesmerized. As he looks at her now he appraises, the way she is used to being looked at and is comfortable with. 'Cold,' she repeats, as if not speaking but voicing her thoughts aloud.

'Cold,' he agrees, although he does not feel it. The response snaps her out of her train of thought.

'The thing I hate about this place is that there's no place to go.'

'What do you mean?'

'What do you think I mean? I mean there's no place to GO!'

'Are you working?'

'Whatever gave you that idea? I've been working since . . . dawn.' Dawn these mornings is eight o'clock. 'I gave myself a few hours off and came to see you.' He is dumbfounded. She guesses. 'What, never had no visitors before? Have you got anywhere to go? I live with those miserable bastards who would shoot a man within ten yards of our room. Do you have a place to go?'

'I have a room above the shop.'

'What shop?'

Any of the locals would have known. 'The shop' sells the kind of miscellany small places with a near-monopoly do. He tries to explain by giving examples. She interrupts.

'You don't get it. I'm not interested in what it sells but where it is.'

'Near the harbour.'

'That's fucking miles.' She looks at her feet and between the planking to the recess below. 'What's down there?'

'The sea – at high tide.'

'Well, it isn't high tide now. C'mon. At least it's out the wind.'

The rocks are slippery with flaccid seaweed that pops beneath their feet as the small bladders burst in tiny spumes of brine. She leans against one of the stanchions nearer the beach, the high-water mark coming to just below her shoulder blade.

'Come here.'

He moves towards her, his step steadier on the rocks than hers. In the failing light the two figures seem to merge and disappear into the upright she has her back to.

The observer moves from the lee of the wind-blown oak, sure of being unseen by the couple preoccupied with each other. Turning its back on the sea, it begins to make its way inland across the dull fields.

20

Giving time to Franz is not as difficult as she first thought it would be. Angus's attendance, always intermittent and dependent on the haphazard work schedule of whatever odd jobs he can pick up, has now fallen off almost completely. He turned up at the Campbells' the previous Sunday morning, without forewarning, standing in the middle of the kitchen floor, and needlessly apologized in a rehearsed explanation that degenerated into a torrent of stammers, prompted by the audience of the elderly couple he had not anticipated being there. Taking pity, she had silenced him by explaining that his attendance was optional and to come only when he felt he could. He left looking chastened.

She wonders if he was so simple as not to have foreseen the possibility of the Campbells being in their own kitchen. 'God forgive me,' she thinks, 'but there will be more stimulation in teaching someone who may not need me than in nursing that poor boy.'

The time she had set aside for Angus is used to accommodate Franz. She waits until the class disperses before inviting him to come up and sit across from her at her desk. He walks between the rows of children's desks, lugging the Gladstone bag. His arrival with it the first morning prompted laughter in the class. She had diverted their attention elsewhere. At the first break he seemed disinclined to join the children outside.

'You shouldn't be here, Franz. You should be out there, with them.'

Taking this as an instruction, he climbed out of his chair

without a word and walked out to stand in the middle of the playground, bag in hand, listing slightly with the weight of its mysterious contents. He stood like a stone in the midst of the flux around him. Several games were being played simultaneously. She watched him anxiously, her breath misting the cold pane. A ball ricocheted off his shin. A ragged circle formed round him, the bag being the object of curiosity. She could see questions being addressed. He mouthed responses. Attention spans being momentary, curiosity faded. Spectators moved on. Another ball hit him on the back. He was in the middle of two impromptu football games. One of the boys said something to him, pointing to a specific spot on the playground, currently occupied by the jumper of the pointing boy. He was being asked to put his bag down to mark one of the goalposts. The pointing boy was cold and wanted his jumper on again. She saw him agree and replace the goalie, their concession to let him be near the bag they needed as a marker.

When she sounded the bell he came in. For the first time since leaving home he looked like someone his age should, flushed and if not happy then animated. She looked forward to telling Lachlan.

'To be frank . . .' No pun is intended. She starts again. 'To be honest, from what Lachlan tells me, I don't know what I can do for you. You can have access to any of the textbooks we have here, but Lachlan tells me you read whatever of his books you want to. And I think the books you find at home will do you more good than anything here. What I thought would be a start would be if we introduced ourselves to one another. I tell you about me and you tell me about you. Do you think this is a good idea?'

'Yes.'

'Would you like to go first or would you like me to?'

'You go first.'

'Right . . . Having suggested it, it would probably have been advisable if I had thought what I was going to say. There's really not much to tell. I imagine your story is much more interesting. I was a teacher back home.'

'Where's that?'

'Winchester. When my fiancé enlisted I thought somehow I should be making a greater sacrifice than I was.'

'Why?'

'It seemed too easy, just comfortably staying at home doing the same things I had been doing when everyone else was doing so much more. A lot of the children I taught moved to more remote places.'

'Like this?'

'Perhaps not as remote. I thought working on the land would be a good idea. I looked forward to working with my hands, probably because my mother hadn't.' She laughs. 'It seems strange but I looked forward to getting dirty.' From his reaction he does not find her aspiration strange. She stops laughing, realizing they probably have no common experience to allow him to gauge the incongruity of this. If what Lachlan guesses is true, Franz has been through enough in the past year to relegate everything she has experienced to the commonplace. 'And here I am, clean hands, sitting in a classroom again.'

'You could always pick up some mud on the way home.'

'Yes. Somehow it wouldn't be the same.' They fall silent. She is under no obligation to justify herself to the boy but somehow feels she has done herself an injustice. The reduction of her life to this summary makes it sound banal; yet to embroider it with irrelevant facts to infuse interest would be worse. It would be pathetic. She comforts herself that she is much more than a summation of details.

'Your turn.'

'English, French or Russian?'

'. . . English,' she answers, perplexed. He slides from his seat and lifts the bag to an adjacent child's desk, set at a convenient height for his investigation. Opening the bag, he delves into it, like an entertainer into a beast's maw, his back concealing the proceedings. He straightens, holding some kind of packet, which he opens and methodically goes through till he finds the appropriate document. He turns, extending his arm towards her, holding the papers like a relay baton.

21

Angus's simple mind is in a blissful whirl. For the past two weeks now he has been seeing Lucy intermittently. She arrives when it suits, finding him wherever he happens to be working, or here. He cannot predict her arrival and lives in a state of anguished anticipation. When she is not with him he has no knowledge of her whereabouts. His movements are more predictable. She has a reputation for doing as little as possible on the farm. The times they are not together cannot occupy her with work and sleep. She seems to find him when she wants him. He has taken to reconnoitring around the Drovers in the hope of seeing her, without working up the courage actually to enter. But this evening she has told him she will be here.

His preparations have been frantic and ineffectual. He has spread the bed, left unmade since she last lay there, unwilling to erase her cherished imprint. He has cleaned his one-ring gas burner. The toilet off the narrow stairwell is shared with other desultory tenants. Having no cleaning materials, he has gone to 'the shop' for bleach and cloths and cleaned that.

Besides the bed and the gas ring the room has a small fire and is furnished with a deal table and two collapsible chairs. Linoleum that does nothing to cheer the prospect or conserve the heat had been laid on top of a previous layer and is now worn through in patches to reveal strata. The curtain covers half the window. There is nothing between the pane and the Atlantic; he has no need for privacy.

He was sure she said something about five o'clock and sits

perched on the edge of the bed from darkness onwards. She arrives around seven. He can hear her pant as she makes her way up. She is smoking a cigarette as she enters.

'Y'know, if you were on the game it wouldn't be the work but the stairs that would kill you.' He doesn't understand. He is prepared to take her coat. 'Not just yet, dearie. Wait till I heat up. What's to drink?'

'Tea.'

'No gin? Beer?' She is touched by his confusion. Fishing in her purse, she pulls out notes. She is as lavish with her money as with her body. 'Here, nip down to the Drovers and get half a dozen bottles of stout.' He is nonplussed. 'What're you waiting for?'

'The Drovers. It's not allowed.'

'And I am? I've been on my feet all day. My back's killing me . . .' His confusion deepens. Seeing this she stands, stiffly.

'No. It's all right. I'll do it.' He leaves her stoking the fire, one hand massaging the small of her back.

His entrance provokes a ragged chorus of greetings and good-natured jokes. Looking round, he cannot see the obvious iniquity of the place. He has carried out casual work for almost everyone here except Graham MacKenzie, the landlord, who leans on the other side of the counter with a quizzical smile.

'Seen the light, Angus?'

'Six bottles of stout please.' He proffers the money in a single crumpled handful. Graham takes what he needs, handing the bottles across with the change.

'Having a party, Angus?'

'Something for the weekend, Angus?'

'She'll eat you raw, Angus.'

Douglas Leckie and any of the other half dozen men Lucy has worked her way through would have made a show of accepting this banter in the spirit of randy camaraderie with which it is intended. Angus begins to reverse out, looking as if he expects to be shot if he turns his back. His head bangs against the doorjamb and he drops a bottle, eliciting a titter that runs round the room. In his confusion to retrieve the bottle he drops another, which bursts open in a foamy plume, provoking a guffaw. Help comes from an unexpected quarter. Murdo, dart poised, stoops down and picks up both bottles in his hand. He speaks at a volume to be overheard. 'Never mind them, Angus. They're just jealous. At least you've got something warm to go home to that doesn't look like a farmyard animal in curlers. Not many of us here can say the same.' The deflection is adroitly done, too subtle for Angus to notice. Murdo turns to the bar. 'It's been so long for most of you bastards that you'd come off quicker than the stout.' There is a general shout of laughter that has nothing now to do with Angus. Murdo lays the open bottle on the bar. 'Graham, give him another. Put it on my slate. I'll drink this.' Angus accepts the replacement wordlessly, exits staring fixedly at the floor and runs up the stairs, bottles clinking. When he goes in she has lit another cigarette. She sees on his face more than confusion.

'What's the matter, love?'

'They made fun. Of me. Of us . . .' He cannot explain. Despite all the things he has been told about innate evil and our predisposition to sin, this is the only sacrosanct thing he has ever had and it is held up for public ridicule.

'Fuck them. They're just jealous.'

'That's what Murdo said.'

'The big bloke?'

'Yes.'

'Well, he's right. Forget them.' But she sees this casual dismissal will not do. 'Come here.'

She has never yet met a man who is not consoled by sex

and she has met many men. This is earlier than she intended. She wanted a sit-down and a drink first. Not much chance of anything to eat from the look of this dump. She has never come across anyone so pathetically grateful for the smallest of intimacies. There is something touching in his gratitude, his eagerness to learn and to please, the embarrassment of his almost instantaneous climaxes, the stamina of his youth, the persistence of his desire again and again till she really must go. She abandons her cigarette to the hearth and stands.

'You must be upset.'

She is surprised at not being presented with the automatic erection she is usually confronted with when sliding her hand down his trousers. She coaxes the blood easily in rhythmic clenches. It was well practised before she came to Rassaig. She laughed at the ease with which she milked her first cow. Watching from the shadow of the barn, Ewan McHarg over-heard her make the comparison to Harriet. He intended cough-ing to make his presence felt but somehow forbore, and stood in aroused silence, listening to the drum of milk on tin.

She undresses and kneels in front of the fire. The room is cold. Glowing coals warm her nearest side. There is a narrow strip of rug. One knee rests on the flattened pile. She can feel the grit of coal dust beneath the other knee on the linoleum. Obediently he kneels behind her. The first time she told him to do this he told her it must be wrong because it was 'like the beasts'. On the occasions they have been together she lets him enter her quickly, getting his first orgasm out the way so that she can enjoy him at her leisure, controlling his position and speed at their next coupling. She anticipates the same now, but his upset causes some delay. He remains erect, rhythmically pumping. His explosive climax deferred, she feels herself float. Her hanging breasts bob slackly, rocking with expanding waves that radiate out from between her legs. She climaxes before he does, the snort from her nostrils dispersing grit. He continues. With surprise she climaxes again, and moments later feels herself rising once more on the upward slope. Young men are better, this one better still. His pubes and thighs are slick with her juice, she, his marvellous ripe, ripe fruit. She pants, exhaling words between thrusts, 'Don't ... stop ... let's go ... for the ... hat-trick,' and gives a strangled laugh at her own humour. He leans forward, turning his face sideways to rest his cheek in the hollow between her shoulder blades. Both are sweating. She is too preoccupied to feel the tears trickle on her spine. Adoringly he kisses the mole on her back – his beloved has a blemish that complements her perfection – and reaches round to cup her dangling breasts. As he squeezes she spasms, pushing back to force him in, and contracts. Moistly socketed, he comes in a surge that clouds his vision and prompts a scream from her. She rests her forehead on the dirty rug till her breathing subsides.

'Angus. What a talent. What a waste till I got here. Aren't I lucky?'

'I love you.'

22

Since reading the letter Gail has had to restrain herself from putting her arms around Franz each time she sees him. Most mornings he is hunched attentively over his desk reading whatever absorbs him as she claps her hands for general attention and the register. No matter how preoccupied he is, he does not need telling twice. The large book disappears into the larger bag. He brings his full focus to bear on problems she knows he must find puerile. If he is bored by the simplicity of the lessons, no trace escapes him. She is grateful for this courtesy, knowing from experience how unruly bored children can be, particularly boys.

Despite the isolation of this community his idiosyncrasies haven't marked him out. His accent, the care Agnes has taken with his clothes, his notorious bag, his reserve in lessons, only ever volunteering the answer when it is apparent no one else will and she is getting exasperated by the general uncomprehending silence, all the traits that could have identified him for victimization go unremarked by the motley assortment of his schoolfellows. She is relieved. Children will adapt to anything. She thinks the parents could learn something from this.

Just as they have accepted his clothes, accent and bag, they have accepted that he stays when they leave. It occasions no comment. He is different, and staying behind is simply part of his difference.

The limited experience she has had teaching precocious children is of little help to her here. Previous experiments have involved finding out how much the children know, gauging their advancement on the curriculum and taking it from there. With Franz she finds herself at a loss. The curriculum is of little help in calibrating the intelligence of a boy who presented a letter in three languages, all of which he no doubt understood. In private she will not insult him with the rudimentary arithmetic sufficient to teach the sons of fishermen and farmers not to be short-changed at market. So mostly their lessons begin with something he effortlessly absorbs and become conversations. Given what she knows, she thinks the best thing she can do is to befriend him.

His father encouraged all the children to question and to speak. He would have been prepared to discuss almost any topic with them. Her faith taught Natasha greater circumspection, but she too encouraged conversation. Of all the children Franz availed himself most of this advantage, and it was he who felt it most when the privilege was withdrawn. He never spoke about anything personal after he left Prague, and eventually he never spoke about anything at all. Natasha had been careful to write to male relatives, reasoning that the battle would more easily be won if she could persuade them. The women Franz has had any experience of since leaving home have been limited to the wives of the men who took him. They had their own commitments. And he was astute enough to know that nice as these women might be, they saw him as someone who could come to jeopardize their families. Irene was the exception. She had only seen him as an encumbrance. Confronted by his impenetrable silence, she had drawn her own conclusions. She was not a bright woman and Franz had ascribed to her the limited intelligence she thought his silence betokened.

And now here he was, his slow recuperation being fostered by Lachlan and his library of facts up the hill, and this attractive and attentive young woman in the schoolroom, people who do not see him as a liability or an imposition.

It did not take Gail long to notice that he said almost nothing in public, besides putting her out of her misery when the correct answer refused to come from the class. He was more forthcoming in private. She was in a quandary, wondering how much of a professional distance to try to maintain. But then, she reasoned, there is little she could actually teach him. She could not envisage circumstances where he might exploit a friendship and become rowdy in the classroom. So she asked him if, Lachlan's agreement permitting, he would like to come with her the following Saturday to Oban.

Lachlan didn't object. There was nothing remarkable in the outing. Franz followed in tow while she window-shopped. They walked up to McCaig's Tower, the Coliseum-like folly overlooking the bay. The sea was membranous under the low cloud base. From their vantage point they saw columns of light puncture the canopy, daubing luminous spots on the shifting water.

'Those shafts of light. We called them Jacob's ladders when I was a girl, from Jacob's dream in the Bible when he sees angels climbing to heaven. I don't know if the expression translates.'

He did not reply but looked from her face back out towards the spectacle she was pointing to, beyond the island of Kerrera, out towards the Inner Hebrides, where the weather front was congealing. They could see opaque curtains of rain or snow being driven landwards. And all this, the Victorian solidity of the uncompleted folly, the brindled sea, the approaching storm, her at his side leaning into the wind, traffic in the harbour below, raucous cries of the gulls circling the returning smacks, all poured in to be indelibly committed to his memory.

'We should go down, beat the weather.'

They make the tea room with seconds to spare, the first pattering of hail on the awning driving pedestrians off the street. Others have had the same idea. They stand together waiting for a table while she reads selectively from the menu. Finally seated at a window table he is allowed to choose, he uses his cuff to rub out a circle of condensation from the misted pane and from this blurred porthole watches pedestrians emerge as the weather lifts. She presses her face against his to share the view. He wonders if she can also hear his heart.

'Look at the harbour. The water is churned into peaks. I'm sure my mother would think of meringues if she saw that.'

A three-tiered cake stand, complete with tongs, arrives with the tea.

'Posh,' she comments.

Hostile as Lachlan is to the teachings of the Viennese witch doctor, he understands the concept of transference, tacitly subscribing to it by the use of layman's terminology to describe the same thing. When they return from their jaunt to Oban, Gail comes to the house to deliver the book Lachlan asked her to buy. By prior arrangement they all eat together. Talking to her across the table, Lachlan observes Franz throughout the meal. He watches him formally thank Gail in the hall as she takes her leave. He watches him in the lounge afterwards, toying distractedly with the pieces of a model Lachlan has given him to assemble. Brief as his acquaintance with the boy is, Lachlan believes this to be out of character. And he watches him as he says goodnight and takes his leave early to read in his room.

Tomorrow is Sunday. Franz imagines the schoolroom in the darkness, the inert furniture, like him, awaiting her arrival. For the first time Sunday will be as long for him as it is for the Presbyterians.

23

My dearest Arkadi,

If this letter goes no further than you then there is really no need
of it. You do not need me to ask you to care for my boy. I know
you will treat him as one of your own, and bring him up in the
faith we share and which I have been careful to have him
instructed in.

Having denied to himself the seriousness of our position, my
husband, now accepting it, has given himself over entirely to doing
what he can to better our circumstances. And having accepted this
state of affairs he has, as with most things he turns his attention
to, seen more clearly than I have what the outcome might be. And
he has concluded that it may not be possible for Franz to stay with
Arkadi.

So this letter is to you, whoever you may be, who now have the
care of my dear, dear boy in your hands. This letter is so very
difficult to write, and I have left myself so little time to write it.
Were it longer it could not begin to do justice to my feelings or
those of my husband.

Franz is an extremely intelligent child. I am aware that this
may sound like listing one of the advantages of a piece of
merchandise I am trying to sell. I am writing this only to explain
that he has the kind of sensitive nature that normally accompanies
one of his gifts. He is reserved at home. If he has found his way to
your care by who knows what path, he may be more reserved than
ever. Please do not mistake this for coldness. He is a very loving
boy and for all his intelligence he is just that, a boy.

Please care for him. Be kind. I cannot begin to guess what he *must have been through if this letter is being read by someone who is strange to me, and I cannot begin to express the gratitude that I and my husband feel towards you, this unknown person to whom we have entrusted the most precious thing we have.*

My life now is a constant prayer. I pray for my boy and I pray that you, whoever you may be, will have the decency and fortitude to bring him up to become the kind of man he would have been, had circumstances allowed him to stay with us. And I pray that somehow, somewhere, his father and I will be given the opportunity to thank you in a way that this inadequate letter cannot.

Please do this thing for me. You cannot know how terrible it is to consign your child to the unknown, and to depend on the kindness of people you have never met.

My greatest hope is that this letter remains unread. If you are reading this, if you have my boy, if you are doing what you can to keep him safe, you have more than my thanks. You have my love.

Natasha Brod. Prague. 20 March, 1939.

It is very late. The rest of the house is in darkness, the rest of the world asleep. The only illumination in the study is provided by the glow of dying embers from the hearth and the desk light. The curtains have been carelessly drawn, casting a vertical bar of orange over the short expanse of garden. Snow is falling again. Within the visible slit large flakes loom out of the heavy sky to drift down, disappearing noiselessly into the white carpet. Lachlan removes his glasses, squeezes his eyes closed and massages the bridge of his nose, pinching the red crevices that years of wear have eroded. Replacing the glasses he reads the letter once more and places it, face down, within the luminous pool of his desk. Gail handed it to him this afternoon without comment, asking only that he return it to Franz once he had read it.

If possible this has drawn him closer to the boy. We are all born to be orphans but now he knows that he and Franz have something additional in common: they stand at the bow-wave of the present with nothing remaining in their wake. Franz cannot fail to know that the author of this letter, her husband and daughter are obliterated. Aside from the tragedy of the situation, what strikes Lachlan most forcibly is the irony of the fact that this is an indirect appeal to faith, the faith that earmarked Natasha and her family to be consumed by the inferno aimed at them, and of all the people to whom an appeal of faith could be addressed he feels the least qualified.

He made a silent pact with the boy that first freezing night on the clifftop. Irrational though he knows it to be, he now makes another with the dead woman.

From the garden the curtain chink is a narrow column of light. From a distance this is a tiny strip in the immensity of the surrounding darkness, as snow continues to fall softly into the void.

24

School has finished for Christmas. As Gail dismissed the children, chairs scraped back and the class was cleared with an exuberant rush. Her desk is dotted with presents, mostly home baking, which she feels her short tenure has not entitled her to. She lists the names with the intention of writing thanks to the parents. Looking up, she finds that Franz has waited behind.

'Lachlan's celebrating Christmas,' he says.

'So I hear.'

'Agnes says it's a miracle. Do you believe in miracles?'

'I don't think Agnes means it literally. I think she just means she's surprised.'

Previous Christmases have involved Agnes demanding money from Lachlan that he hands across with a histrionic groan, reminding her that 25 December was a pagan festival whose date has been arrogated by 'her mob'. The truth is that he allows her to cajole from him the virtues he would otherwise practise in secret. She would order the tree and buy presents on his behalf for whatever members of his small clique she believed deserved it. This usually comprised those who bought for him. His only concession was to make a secret foray to Glasgow or Edinburgh and walk mystified among the Christmas lights until something sufficiently garish seized his attention, that he would then buy for her. The standard routine comprised her attending midnight mass on Christmas Eve, returning to find him still up. They have a drink, exchange presents, with her invariably thanking him and asking for the receipt. On Christmas Day his small circle of intimates from the Drovers come round for a late-afternoon dinner. He pays lip service to helping and stands redundant in the kitchen until dismissed. Despite being the only atheist present he is a magnanimous host, and enjoys reading labels, dispensing parcels whose contents are a mystery to him and receiving thanks for presents he has only paid for.

Last week he astonished Agnes, pre-empting her arrangements by turning up with an enormous tree he had had Angus drag up to the house.

'I've already ordered a tree from Kyle.'

'I bought this from Kyle.'

'It's too big.'

'You've no sense of style.'

'It won't fit.'

She is correct. Help is summoned. After two abortive attempts Angus, in the middle of the lawn, saws four feet off the top. The truncated version now dominates the lounge. Each slammed door dislodges a green halo. Viewed from the garden, a tree appears to be growing through the interrupting ceiling into Lachlan's bedroom. Agnes is obliged to buy more ornaments. Adorned, the thing looks even more monstrous.

'Any more surprises?'

Unasked, he passes her a wedge of notes. This is far more than she would have demanded. 'The usual and . . . be good to the boy.'

'Does he celebrate Christmas? Being Jewish, I mean.'

'Would you have him excluded?'

'Of course not. What a thing to say, Doctor McCready.'

'I believe in Yahweh no more than I do the Holy Ghost or the tooth fairy, and I celebrate Christmas. I'll support anything that promotes good will, no matter how specious. And anyway, show me a boy who doesn't enjoy getting presents. And by the way, before you try and convert him, there's a Jewish gentleman will be coming over from Oban from time to time. I've asked him to come and talk to Franz. I said we'd be happy to put him up here if it's more convenient for him to stay the odd night.'

'You've traced a relative!'

'Not exactly . . .' She has not read the letter. Lachlan complied with Gail's request and handed it back to Franz with as little commentary as he received it. 'I'm having him instructed in his faith.' He has confounded her. She absorbs this in total silence and goes away to consider its repercussions.

Gail has been invited to Christmas dinner at Lachlan's and been obliged to turn this down due to other commitments. Gracious as ever, Lachlan has told her that Agnes cooks for a battalion and that the cold remnants will be available for days. 'So if you come back earlier than you intend, don't be a stranger.' As ignorant of his history as everyone else, she cannot know that the invitation comes from personal experience.

So she packs. It is an embarrassing departure. Now that she no longer works on the farm she feels she occupies her accommodation on sufferance. The Campbells have been kind enough and now give her a departing gift. Having nothing to return the unexpected courtesy, she kisses them both, unexpected tears welling. She tries to cover her confusion by lifting her bags and abruptly walking out to the waiting van. Lucy has called in favours, or bestowed more, to have Douglas Leckie agree to drive her to the station.

On the swaying trains south she has time to contemplate her situation. Her tears were not just caused by the Campbells' generosity. She is apprehensive about meeting Clive. Her anxiety is not lessened by the journey. Rural darkness is replaced by the muffled lights of cities. Here restrictions are imposed. She is moving towards the war. The plan is to spend Christmas and a few days afterwards with her parents before going up to London to meet Clive.

Her mother is delighted that she has abandoned the farm for the classroom. She has never understood her daughter's motives. To move to manual labour seems to her a retrograde step. Dirt is degrading. If she had to do it, why not somewhere more accessible, why Scotland?

Of her parents Gail more closely resembles her father. She has his intelligence, if not his complete reticence. She knows her mother feels excluded by the intimacy she enjoys with him. What her mother fails to appreciate is that she excluded herself. Gail's respect for her father's judgement is tempered only by her failure to understand why he chose to marry a snob. But ironically, if Rassaig has taught her anything it has taught her tolerance. The determination that ordered Gavin Bone from her classroom was not her father's. She now knows that. She also observes that even in the brief interval of her absence, both parents have noticeably aged.

She is solicitous towards them both. Something has happened to them that she has noticed happen to others: adversity, or perhaps simply acceptance of compromise that age brings, has reconciled them to each other. Foibles do not seem to grate. They are kinder towards each other. This kindness puts an end to her role as go-between, a position she reluctantly adopted from her late teens.

For the first time she encounters powdered egg, interminable queues and the national loaf. Her parents are proud of procuring half of a turkey. She makes a mental note to try to be more diligent in sending food parcels south.

She goes to London two days before the New Year. Clive held on to the flat in Bayswater. Before leaving home she used to apoplex her mother by coming up to stay with him for the weekend. She arrives before he does. It is late afternoon. Slanting lemon sunlight drenches the dormant furniture, awaiting her arrival to bear witness. The silence is eerie. She sits in a familiar cane chair and is startled by the fusillade of cracking. She opens all the windows: cold is preferable to stagnation. The place is a corridor of air for ten minutes. She closes them, prematurely draws the blackout blinds and sets the fire. The queues here are worse than in Winchester. She does not want to shop. The cupboards yield unexpected dividends, the residue of purchases before rationing bit. There is beer and tea. There are tins of chopped pork, each with the key attached. She breaks a nail prising a key off, unwinds a metallic spiral and upends the tin over a plate. The meat is mottled, like a cold thigh, and emerges with a sucking sound, surrounding jelly retaining the internal contours of the tin. The rattle of the key in the lock startles her and she stands erect, her heart hammering, as if caught in the act of stealing.

The conversation is stilted. Perhaps, she thinks, he is as apprehensive as she is. They have written to each other so diligently, anticipating the meeting, that the moment has been invested with a significance that kills any spontaneity. On previous meetings, after a period of separation, they have simply undressed and had sex where they stood. She has lain, or sat, or crouched on every appropriate surface. The flat is fraught with mementos of their importunate lovemaking. Now, when he enters, he sees the makeshift meal and a desultory conversation circulates round dinner. They drink warm beer. He eats voraciously. Not hungry, she hands him hers.

Despite the awkwardness neither is willing to suggest going out. Their correspondence has hinted at satiation, to be together all night. There has never before been a question of taking the initiative, it had always been a mutual urgency that dictated the pattern of behaviour. Knowing somehow that he will not begin, she goes into the bedroom and takes her clothes off, calling him through, reflecting, as she does so, that her mother may have done the same to her father. He walks briskly into the room and begins to undress. He has not looked at her. Previously he has always watched her undress. The motions of his hands are violent and precise, as if dismantling a weapon under drill inspection. It is obvious from the first instant that there is something different about the two of them. She wonders if the weight of this change is due to either or both. She lies down, putting a pillow just below the small of her back to raise her buttocks. Despite the lack of preamble she is moist and anxious for him. They have made love many times before in this position, him kneeling above her with her calves resting on his shoulders. It is not until he kneels between her parted thighs that he fully looks at her for the first time since entering the flat. His gaze wavers. There is something dreadfully different that she cannot place. Has he been with someone else? Before she can conjecture further he enters her in one progressive, slow thrust, pushing her legs from his shoulders to lie on top of her, his face buried in the rope of her hair looped on the pillow.

The action of his tilting pelvis seems independent from the rest of him, which clings. She realizes what is wrong: he is frightened. He is going to war and he is terrified he will die. His fear is palpable. She kisses his neck and whispers to him that it will be all right, that she is here. His grasp tightens. His fear is more real to him now that he has silently admitted it to her. She knows she will not come and strokes his back till she feels the muscles spasm with his soft outpouring.

In their present mood it is too early to stay in bed. They return to the lounge to drink more beer and listen to the radio. Suddenly hungry, she opens a second tin of meat and begins to gorge, both relieved and guilty that it is he who has changed more than her. She tells him it is nothing to be ashamed of, that everyone must be terrified and not admit it, that she would be paralysed by the prospect of seeing action, that it is so much easier for her and she can only imagine what he is going through, that it is more laudable to go if you are frightened. Having unburdened himself he feels like a schoolboy who has voluntarily admitted to shoplifting, his guilt alleviated by confession. At the first sound of news on the radio he grabs for the dial, warbling through static till he locates some more music. She touches his hand.

They spend the next three days and nights almost exclusively in the flat. She goes out to shop and stays in the fresh air as long as she can, for the first time feeling no irritation with the queues. To listen to the complaints and conversation of others is a form of communion. Any contact is welcome. They both know he is not relaxing but hiding. He rouses himself only when the sirens sound the second night. Fascinated, she stands in the street, loath to exchange the flat for the confines of the Anderson shelter. He insists. At the first sound of the all-clear he scuttles up the stairs as quickly as he can.

They hear in the bells of the New Year over the radio. She is stifled. After their first encounter they make love frequently at his insistence. There is something frenzied in his performance. It is as if he is trying to wring an epiphany out of every sensation, greedily manufacturing memories, ballast for stability against a turbulent future. Previously he had always been a considerate lover. For her this has degenerated into a kind of captivity of intermittent sex, with him totally preoccupied, keeping fear at bay with stimulation. She climaxes despite his disregard of her reaction.

He sees her off at Euston. He is rejoining his regiment a

day early to allow them to leave together. She suspects he needs the impetus of her departure to make him move; if he did not leave with her he would not leave until fetched. She tells him not to wait till the last moment, till the receding platform separates them. He nods wordlessly in agreement and despite the absence of blowing whistles and slamming doors kisses her with an intensity that anticipates the train drawing them apart. She can feel the desperation in the embrace. She doesn't know what to say. Anything sounds trite. Perhaps this is a time for unspoken promises to be articulated, but neither succeeds in saying anything. He lets go. Manufacturing a jaunty air to lighten the moment, he sets his hat at a rakish angle and walks off the platform. The parody only distresses her. It has not been a good parting.

She is numb, swaying north, up into colder, darker, welcome Rassaig. If their time has convinced her of anything it is that she loves, without being in love, with him. He has been in love with her now for two years. There has been no declaration but both know this. She has been waiting to feel the same way and has managed never to exploit the advantage which the discrepancy in their feelings for each other conferred. Part of him has resented her tact.

They became engaged in preparation for her making the leap of faith. Her mother hoped the war would accelerate their plans. Instead it succeeded in deferring things indefinitely. She refused to be a war bride, at home with an absent husband, coerced into a marriage she might otherwise fight shy of in civilian life. So they settled for cohabitation and recreational sex till his call-up papers arrived and she enlisted in the Women's Land Army.

She watches the darkling landscape slide past till the train is shuttered against the Luftwaffe. She feels she has failed him. Emotionally she has kept him at arm's length and in the past few days her only response to his fear was to lend him the use of her loins. Given on these limited terms, who can blame him for his preoccupation?

She spends the night in the Central Hotel in Glasgow. The following morning she has two hours to kill before her train. She shops, enjoying the flux of people and her sense of distance from them. She buys Lachlan a half Corona, Franz a fountain pen and Agnes a scarf. She is in Rassaig by late afternoon. The thought of going directly to the Campbells' depresses her. She goes to Lachlan's house to take up his offer. Agnes and Franz are in, Lachlan out, probably at the Drovers. With luck Lucy and Harriet might be there too. She stops long enough to deliver the presents and makes her way down the hill into town. Someone is leaving just as she is about to enter. Spilling out with the light flows a wave of sound: the thud of a dart and a genial hubbub. Her heart lifts for the first time since she left the village.

The departing customer has held the door open for her. His enormous shadow blends with the dark recess. It is not until she gets closer that she can see it is Murdo.

'Nice to see you back.'

She had no idea he knew she had gone. She is not sure whether or not he is being sarcastic. She thanks him and stoops under the outstretched arm holding the door open. He exudes a smell of clean cotton and fresh sweat. Evidently changing his mind, he follows her inside. Without even looking back she can feel the full vitality of him, the sheer animal health he radiates like heat on her thighs and buttocks and back and neck. Telling herself not to, she glances round. He is waiting for this and levelly meets her gaze. It is glaringly obvious he isn't frightened of anything.

In the privacy of his room Franz is still staring intently at the fountain pen, as if trying to distil some meaning from its darkly lacquered surface. He has other pens he can write with. Finally he wraps this in a handkerchief that is then wrapped within another and placed with other cherished paraphernalia in his Gladstone bag.

25

While Gail sat half naked with her fiancé, eating from tins, listening for Big Ben to chime in the New Year over the radio, Lachlan stood at his hearth, glass in hand. Hogmanay at the magnanimous doctor's house has become something of a recent institution. Half the clientele left the Drovers at early closing to climb the hill and avail themselves of Lachlan's alcohol. It is the one time of year he extends his hospitality beyond his own small circle. The crowd is always boisterous and good-natured. Agnes is vigilant against burns and spillages. He finds her armed with a cloth and empty ashtrays, confiscates them and orders her to enjoy herself. Franz, having satisfied himself that his bag is safe in his room, threads his way through the adults, enjoying the novelty of the scene. He will only instigate a conversation with Lachlan, Agnes and Gail, but will now talk back to others if addressed.

Lachlan has been watching him keenly all night. The boy has metamorphosed from the traumatized, underweight child he brought home. The letter comes back to Lachlan at every unoccupied moment. He thinks frequently of his pact with the dead woman. He also thinks of the odds of Franz being here, now, and believes the variables defy calculation.

Since the death of his wife Lachlan has ceased to look for equity or signs of benevolent purpose. But somehow the sight of the boy and the thought of the concatenation of unknown circumstances that delivered him here, to Lachlan's hearth as opposed to all the others in Europe, stirs something long dormant in him. Why has Franz, of all children, been preserved from the obliteration to which an unknown proportion of his race have been consigned? He has heard of Comrade Stalin asking how many divisions the Pope has, deriding God's proxy warriors, and of Mussolini's calculatingly profane ultimatum, slapping his watch on the podium and giving divine providence a minute to intervene. But the God who has presided over a race with a history of atrocities to its credit is not likely to be goaded into revealing Himself by the predictable antics of a demagogue. Lachlan has read enough to comprehend the meaning, if not imbibe the message, of the leap of faith. The incremental progression of logic stops at the abyss. Such a leap is an emotional, not an intellectual jump. Why should faith require a plunge into the unknown when love and every other crucial transaction of the heart do not? Does everyone in this room know something he does not? He has always considered the gift of faith a lack of healthy scepticism by any other name. It is a long time since Lachlan was assailed by any doubts. Perhaps he left himself open to the possibility. He is not asking for much, not an apocalypse, perhaps a billowing of the curtains, something private, cryptic, unobtrusive but inter-pretable.

He waits, perhaps five minutes, perhaps ten, smiling at the hubbub, to all appearances pleasantly abstracted, his large mind at intense full stretch. Finally giving up, he smiles, rebuking himself for his private folly. Franz, concerned at the old man standing alone, looking at nothing, comes across. 'My intelligence has gone porous,' Lachlan explains, taking his hand. 'Old age. It comes to us all.'

'No. It does not.'

'No. I'm sorry. You're right, it doesn't.'

'Are you enjoying your party?'

'Very much. But I don't think I'll get to Damascus tonight.'

26

This time he has awaited the dismissal of the class and Franz's tardy departure before making an appearance. She is arranging the books for marking. She does not hear him enter. His shadow across the page is the first indication she has of him and she starts back, the chair scraping loudly in the echoing space.

'Get out!'

'Not before I have a word with you.'

'Get out!'

'There is no one to send for the constable.'

'I will go myself.'

'Not before I have a word with you.'

She is already on her feet. The position of her desk in the top corner of the classroom is such that one side is against the wall. He is directly across from her. When she moves to the open end he moves in parallel. For the first time she is frightened.

'Are you threatening me?'

'I understand that there are certain things you are teaching the pupils.' It is not a question, although he pauses for a response. She is unwilling to engage in a discussion about anything. She feels her only protection is the desk between them. He is prepared to go on without a reply. 'There are certain things that you may believe to be true but that I, and the congregation I am a member of, do not. Nor do I want them presented to the children of our Church as accepted fact. Let the papists have their children's minds filled with what they will. There will be a reckoning and they and you and everyone else will find out how old the world is and how hot hell is. I do not want discussions about pieces of coal and animals older than the world of His creation.'

'Don't presume to tell me what to teach. If you do not move out of the way I will throw this chair out that window and begin to scream.'

'I will have said what I have to before anyone arrives. I have not touched you. I have committed no crime.'

'I will tell the constable you detained me.'

'Angus detained you every night for weeks.'

'Don't be absurd.'

'But he does not detain you any more, does he?' She refuses to answer. 'That is because your friend detains him. That hot bitch spoiled him under the jetty. She copulates like an animal in the fresh air. Perhaps she thinks her actions go unnoticed. Perhaps she does not care. I don't care about her. She is hellbound anyway. I don't want her polluting anyone else. Tell her—'

'Tell her yourself.'

She has not moved but he is now circling the desk towards her. 'You come here with your whorish friends and your filthy theories. One more word about men standing up from four legs and I'll have our children taken away. It is almost believable that that blonde harlot came out of a beast. She certainly takes it like one. And meanwhile you presume to teach. You don't teach, you contaminate.'

She has lifted the pointer. She wishes she had kept the belt. She can imagine the dull slapping sound it would make on his face. The front door opens. Murdo walks in. He takes in the scene at a glance and walks slowly between the desks towards them. Gavin seems unconcerned till he sees the look of relief on her face. He is trying to remember the other man's affiliation. He is not of any Church as far as Gavin is aware.

Murdo looks at Gavin only long enough to take a grip on the other man's jacket. Turning his attention to Gail, he rotates his grip until the material corkscrews round his fist. The jacket now too tight to shed, Gavin is held.

'I saw a light.'

'Mr Bone here objects to the teaching of evolution.' She is both relieved and frightened. There is something even more alarming in Murdo's stillness than there is in the older man's fanaticism. Gavin can feel it too. Despite his sense of righteousness he suddenly wants to urinate. The unfair odds would be of no more account to Murdo than they would if he was confronted simultaneously with all the men of Gavin's congregation. If he deems it appropriate he will beat Gavin with as little compunction as he dispatches palpitating fish. Turning away from Gail, he focuses his full attention on the older man.

'I've never made a threat. I don't see the point in telling someone what I'll do. This isn't a threat but I'll make an exception and tell you what I'll do.' He clamps his free hand on the top of Gavin's head and rotates this until he is forced to face Gail. As Murdo speaks his voice gets quieter. 'If you come here again . . . No. Start again. If you come near her again, wherever she is, I'll club you like a lame dog. It doesn't matter if you're wherever it happens to be first. If she arrives, you leave. I won't ask you if you understand because there's nothing not to understand. If you want to go and fetch the constable, go now. Once he's taken statements and gone to bed I'll come and find you.' He releases the head and unwinds the fist almost gingerly. His voice now is almost a whisper. 'Get out.'

Gavin automatically straightens his clothes before turning and walking out. There is a list to his stride and he totters slightly, as if light-headed. With a genial nod to her Murdo follows. For a moment she thinks he has gone to check on

Gavin's departure. A minute elapses and Murdo has not come back. She realizes that he too has gone and that no force this side of hell would coax Gavin to return. She is still standing, holding the pointer defensively before her in a raised diagonal shielding her body. She drops it on the desk and sits limply in the chair.

27

Gavin has been as good as his word. When in the course of the next free period she took down the butterfly case from its mounted bracket, several raised hands confronted her as she turned to face the class.

'Morag?'

'Miss. My father says if you say anything to us about animals I'm to leave.' From the other hands still raised and the homes she sees them depart to she knows they have received the same instructions. She finds herself in a quandary: continue for their own good and find her lessons boycotted by a substantial fraction of the class, or abandon this theme altogether. She replaces the case on the wall and goes back to *Alice in Wonderland*.

That night she sits in front of the fire, gratefully accepting Hamish Campbell's offer of a drink, and gives herself over to thinking about the options of the situation. She is under no obligation to teach the rudiments of science. To stop doing so deprives everyone. Besides which, what might Gavin object to tomorrow? A fanatic cannot be allowed to determine the curriculum. When she considers the children under his tutelage she thinks it is a shame that those most in need of learning are denied it. But she cannot allow them to be taken away to rot in complete ignorance. The compromise she reaches with herself is announced next day.

'Anyone who wants to stay after hours on Tuesdays and Thursdays to talk about the coal and the butterflies and the lizards and all the other things we've been talking about during the recreation period should ask permission from their parents. If your parents don't want you to talk about these things you can go home at the normal time. Can you make sure your parents know we won't be talking about them at all during normal school hours. If any of your parents are unclear about any of this tell them to come and see me and I'll be happy to talk to them.' The last sentence is a lie. She has no desire to defend herself to more of Gavin's ilk, if they exist.

A gratifying complement stay back the first Tuesday. This means more work for her, which she is happy to accept. Theoretically it also bites into the time she has privately to tutor Franz, but he needs company more than tuition, and he can get it if he stays behind too. Lachlan's predecessor, who sold him the house, bought books by the yard, not to satisfy intellectual curiosity but to fill the shelves of a study and give the impression of learning he had no right to. Lachlan has dipped into these books, morocco-bound editions of the Waverley novels, Dickens, Hansard, the King James Bible and a motley assortment of others. He has told her that the boy started with *Little Dorrit* and is inexorably working his way forward. Gail has consistently to remind herself what that poor woman said in her letter: for all his intelligence he is just a boy. She wants him to continue to attend school because she feels the best thing she can give him is the comfort of a routine and the company of his contemporaries. She has explained all this to Lachlan, who agrees.

She has also given Lachlan an edited version of Gavin's visit. She told him what Gavin said without relating the menacing way in which he said it, because to explain this more fully she would have also to explain how the threat was removed, and for reasons she cannot explain to herself she wants her brief interaction with Murdo kept out of it.

In Lachlan's view there is no stigma to being congenitally

stupid. But for a person deliberately to restrict the scope of their own natural intelligence is, to him, blameworthy, and to curb the potential of young minds by forcing on them a blinkered theology is infinitely worse.

It was with some satisfaction then that Lachlan emerged from his surgery to see Gavin next in the waiting room. Lachlan held the door open. Gavin preceded him to sit in the chair and look suspiciously around.

'What can you give me for a persistent cough?' His manner is aggressive enough to suggest Lachlan gave him the cough. One of the reasons Lachlan let Gavin in first was to get a side view of the head against the scale on the wall behind, as he passed. Sitting down, he views the head from another angle and reaches down to unlock his bottom drawer.

'I imagine you will have exhausted every other remedy you could find before placing yourself in my hands.'

'I am not here for a discussion.'

'No. You are here for the help of medical science to alleviate a cough that old wives' remedies could not.'

'Give me a pill.'

'That would be a pill produced after extensive tests on animals then?'

'You're the doctor.'

Squinting at his cranium, 'Tested on animals whose physiology is sufficiently similar to ours to allow us to infer that if it does them good it might help us too.'

'What language are you speaking, doctor?'

'The language of common sense. It would appear to me, Mr Bone, that you seem to believe in the proofs of science when it suits and deny them when it does not.'

'If you're going to talk about that heretical mumbo-jumbo that so-called teacher spouts, then save your breath. Do I get a pill?'

Lachlan momentarily toys with the idea of a volcanic laxative. But the linkage of cause and effect would be too direct. 'Yes. You get a pill. And by taking it you admit, whether you like it, or not, your common ancestry with the animals who tested it for you.'

'Keep it!' He stands abruptly and walks out, slamming the door behind him.

'Always glad to be of assistance,' Lachlan calls after him.

The same evening of Gavin's visit to the doctor, Gail makes an unscheduled visit to Lucy and Harriet. She has only visited them once before at the McHargs' house. The atmosphere was so strained she did not return. Ewan answers. He takes an inordinate amount of time looking at her on the doorstep before shouting over his shoulder in the direction of the girls' room. Harriet comes into the hall and gestures Gail in. Ewan stands grudgingly to one side. The doorway is wide enough but he has positioned himself in such a way that she is obliged to rub past him. She walks straight past them both into the room. Harriet follows and closes the door behind them.

Despite a low ceiling, the room is surprisingly spacious. The curtain looks small, covering, she supposes, a smaller window. She suspects that this place would require artificial light even in the height of summer. A fire burns in the small grate. There are two beds, a plain bureau and an old leather suite. The girls have tried to soften the austerity with various ornaments and a swathe of material over the battered sofa. Lucy is lying on this, smoking a cigarette. Harriet has obviously been reading, her seat angled near the standing light. At the sight of Gail, Lucy claps her hands.

'A visitor! I'll get tea.'

'No. I'll get it.' Harriet can guess that Gail would not come here without a purpose. She infers it has not been to visit her. She goes to brave Mrs McHarg in the kitchen.

'Can we be overheard here?'

'This place is medieval. Like the McHargs. The walls are two feet thick.'

Gail takes off her coat and settles herself on the seat Harriet vacated. 'Gavin Bone came into the schoolroom the other afternoon.'

'I didn't know he had kids.'

'I don't think he has.'

'I heard there's a Mrs Bone. Can you imagine that old grunter climbing on, puffing away between prayers?'

'He mentioned Angus to me.'

'What about Angus?'

'Bone is doing everything he can to make things difficult for me at the school. And when he wants to score points he mentions you and Angus.'

'The boy is gifted. I'll say that for him.'

In her frustration Gail has an impulse to reach across and slap Lucy. 'You're missing the point.'

'To tell the truth, dearie, I'm not really that interested in Gavin Bone's opinion.'

'It's not just his opinion. If he makes it his business he can make it the opinion of lots of other people too.'

'There's a war on.' She stabs the cigarette out prematurely in a little incandescent collision, a look of irritation clouding her usually cheerful face. 'You have to find your fun where you can. Who cares if it upsets some dreary bible-thumpers?'

'It's not just about fun.'

'You're beginning to sound like one of them.'

'And it's not just Gavin Bone.' She thinks of her first day in the classroom, of how the boy referred to Lucy. 'Your reputation extends wider than one congregation around here.'

'So I'm well known for having fun. It was the same back home.'

'If it was just your fun I wouldn't be here to talk to you. But your . . . behaviour rubs off on the rest of us, me and Harriet I mean. We're all being tarred with the same brush.'

'You want to get out a bit more then, have some fun yourself to justify the label.' Harriet enters with the tea tray. Her manner is almost apologetic. She has guessed Gail wants privacy if Lucy does not, but short of standing in the freezing barn there is nowhere else for her to go. From her prone position Lucy launches her next remark across the room. 'Hey, Harriet, Gail here says that the two of you are being tarred with the same brush as me. It seems that you two get some of the reputation and I get all the fun. What do you think?'

'I think that you should keep your voice down.'

'The walls are two feet thick.'

'The door isn't.'

Gail makes the point again, as much for Harriet's sake as in the hope that repetition might cause it to sink in. 'It's not the reputation rubbing off, it's the fact that your behaviour is making my position teaching here more difficult than it already is. Gavin Bone objects to me being in the classroom and he's using you and Angus against me.'

'I'm not a fucking nun, you know. I always thought that was why they were called nuns: they get none.'

'And it's not just additional difficulties in the classroom. It's Angus.'

'I saw him first.'

As a matter of fact she didn't, and Gail has to prevent herself from dragging the conversation down by saying so. 'Lucy, he's a child.'

'Well, he certainly doesn't perform like one.'

'He doesn't know anything.'

'He didn't know anything. At least after meeting me he knows a lot about one thing.'

'Lucy . . .' She is at a loss. It occurs to her that Lucy's moral development is as retarded as Angus's literacy. 'You can't just take up with him because it suits . . .'

'Why not?'

'What will you do afterwards?'

Lucy tilts her head slightly as if trying to rid her ear of bath water. Her normally animated face is momentarily vacant, as if being presented with a mathematical problem wildly beyond her capabilities. 'I don't know . . . Something else. Who knows? We might get invaded tomorrow.'

Gail leans over. Her voice drops. 'To be honest, it's not you I'm worrying about. You'll always get by. It's him.'

Lucy's expression immediately brightens. The solution was obvious all the time. 'You're just jealous because he chose me,' she says without rancour.

'Lucy, he didn't choose anyone. He isn't capable of choosing anyone. You chose him.'

'All right, I chose him before you got the chance to. No hard feelings. Let's have the tea before it stews.'

The Day of Judgement is unknown to us so that we must desist all carnal activities and be perpetually vigilant. In anticipation of that day we must purge the leaven that might affect the whole lump.

There is an attack of iniquity in Rassaig. For years now we have had the misfortune to have one of the unregenerate as a doctor, a man dead in spiritual faculties. He is now abetted by these foreign women, one who defiles young men in the fresh air and another who attempts to teach impious nonsense to children who are not at an age to know better.

These three have executed a pincer movement—

Gavin stops. Can a pincer movement come from three sides? Isn't the whole point of pincers that they are two-sided? He scores through the last line and is now irritated. In his heart of hearts he would have to admit that this journal is being kept for posterity and now the whole effect of the page is spoiled. These heretics: they sow doubt with their spurious medicine, pollute the minds of our children with their profane theories, despoil our young men with their bodies and now ruin the effect of the pages of our journal. No detail is too inconsequential for the hellish machinations of the dark forces. Always in a state of simmering rage that he intermittently stokes to feel the pleasure of righteous anger, Gavin is determined he will not let this blemish stop him.

These three have executed a three-pronged attack. I have warned the parents. Angus is another matter.

Since his intervention in the schoolroom Murdo haunts Gail's thoughts. He arrives unbidden in the slacker moments, when the corrections have become too tedious to persevere with, when falling snow compels introspection, when the wobbling oval of her bath is punctured with an exploratory foot, when she lies alone in her farmhouse bed, a conscious speck in the cavernous silence of the Glen. She has thought back and does not remember the same preoccupation in her earlier days with Clive, and catching herself having given space to the comparison feels a stab of self-reproach that dispels the image of Murdo till his next interruption.

He has not come back to the schoolroom. Aside from the evenings she stays back with the children, she is accustomed to remaining two other evenings. These are usually spent alone while she plans future activities, reduces the stack of corrections or contemplates how it will all end. A letter from Clive arrives, tersely circumventing an apology. What has he to be sorry for? Without the immediate absolution of her presence and her loins he is too embarrassed to admit to fear. She knows him well enough to know that his former candour now embarrasses him and now, again, he will resent her tact. Instead, by a cautious vocabulary that escapes the censor's pen, he hints at future activities and foreign travel.

It is while reading this letter in the deserted schoolroom that she hears the door click open and her hope rises. But it is only Paul, the constable's son, and she is shocked at the infidelity of her trapped heart, that it could be so unsettled by a forgotten muffler and a returning child.

She has the courage to force herself to face the possibility that she may not be as good as she thought she was. Her imagination, she knows, she has almost no control over. Her actions are a different matter.

When he comes to her in her dreams, or daydreams, there is no dialogue. Nor is there any marked transition from the initial meeting to his penetration of her. Her imagination requires no context for this coupling, just an urgency that transports them instantaneously from wherever they happen to be to this bedroom, undressing them en route. Perhaps she credits him with no dialogue because there is nothing he could say that would augment his function. A week after he evicted Gavin Bone she woke from a dream disturbed by the fact that the thought of Murdo has succeeded in arousing her more than the presence of Clive ever did. This gives more cause for self-reproach. She thinks that perhaps she has credited Murdo with erotic qualities he does not possess. She still has the good sense to be frightened of him.

For two weeks, again to possess herself, she forgoes any outings to the Drovers or elsewhere, with the exception of a dinner invitation to Lachlan's, one of the few places she can be assured of not meeting Murdo. Every night, after she finally leaves the abandoned schoolroom, she walks to the little harbour and stands at the extremity of the sea wall, gulping down lungfuls of freezing air. She stands till the wind has numbed her face, listening to the suck of the backwash, watching seaweed flail in the moonlit swells, the reverberation of ceaseless pounding shuddering up through her boots. She stands till she feels purged and coldly vacant, till the Campbells' kitchen will feel like a welcome reprieve, not a bolt hole she has retreated to straight from work.

This becomes her favourite part of the day. By the end of the first week she is aware of him watching her from the door of the Drovers. It was foolish not to foresee that they would meet here. This sea is his living. But she is unwilling to forgo her exposure at the promontory. There is something in her willed isolation that deters. He has the tact not to approach as she stands alone and for this she is glad. But she is obliged to walk past the pub on her way back to the farm and he has begun to notice the predictability of her timetable. When not out in his boat he has taken to abandoning his drink at the bar to stand within the shadow of the doorway to watch her pass. He says nothing but has begun to follow her a hundred feet behind as she threads her way through the few brief, half-lit streets into the surrounding gloom as she finds her way to the farm.

Without looking back she is aware of his presence. Besides the vague fear she feels something else. She is aware of his reputation, but then he had her alone after evicting Gavin Bone, and he left without touching her. All the sinister rumours can't be all the truth. She knows he helped to extricate Angus from his only foray into the Drovers. None of the gossip she has heard about Murdo ever hinted at compassion. He still carries obvious marks of the beating he received at the Trongate and she has come to believe that this is an indication of some inner mutilation. She asks herself if she is inventing extenuating circumstances and then reflects that she does not know what there is to excuse. He is just the focal point of rumours, as is she, and they may be as groundless in his case too. She cannot imagine he has been so badly maimed, both inside and out, without imagining a role for herself in his recuperation. Illogical though she knows it to be, the more damaged he appears the more attractive he becomes.

She carries a torch that she turns on intermittently, in the five-minute dark expanse between the edge of the village and the farm. She has never turned round and directed the beam back. Just as she can sense his presence she knows he stops at the end of the village, within the little island of light. Paradoxically, it is in the dark that she feels safest.

She is not the only one to notice his intermittent presence behind her. Having kept Lachlan company on an evening house call, Franz, sitting in the passenger seat, sees a figure, swathed against the cold, glide past the side window. Within the fraction it takes him to deduce who it was the headlights illuminated they have also picked out Murdo, walking in her wake. Suddenly animated, Franz persuades Lachlan to turn round and pick Gail up. As they pass Murdo the second time Franz notices him peel away, looping backwards in the direction he has come from. Nevertheless, Franz is gently insistent to Gail that they take her home. From behind the wheel, looking from one to the other, Lachlan gently nods, and from this she infers he wants her to humour the boy.

Lachlan's house commands a view downhill of most of the village, a prospect of steeply tiled roofs receding to the surging expanse of sea. A stunted beech obscures the view from all but a disused and unheated room on the top floor. It is here that the boy goes each night after class, climbing the stairs without taking off his coat. Stamping to keep warm, he alerted Agnes to a presence in the uninhabited room. She found him in his outdoor clothes, standing on an upturned tea chest, straining to look at something down towards the village. Noting her presence, he returned to his task without further acknowledgement. Something intense in his vigilance caused her to retreat. She thinks it may be some imagined horror of his past come to haunt him. Lachlan had given her a summary of the details he has gleaned of Franz's recent history. In Agnes's mind Europe is simply a confused morass of foreign countries whose current disagreement is threatening to spill over into England. All she has taken from the résumé is that Franz's arrival here is a merciful escape. Perhaps he is staring down the hill in anticipation of imagined persecutors eventually arriving in Rassaig. She has not yet told Lachlan of the boy's evening vigil, thinking it may be best to allow the thing a chance to work itself out.

Between the descending tiers of white roofs Franz can just make out the chink of the crossroads that will allow him to mark her passing. On three consecutive days her swathed figure, leaning into the wind, has galvanized his already strained attention to intense pitch as he awaits her accompanying shadow. He appears on the fourth. Pre-armed with his written slip, and noting the time of his descent, Franz runs downstairs and frantically awaits the estimated period of her return. The Campbells are among the privileged few in the village to have a private telephone installed. Clumsily dialling Franz asks to speak to Gail, and at the sound of her puzzled voice relaxes sufficiently to make the pretext of the call not quite as ludicrous as it appears on the written sheet before him. These conversations occur three times in two weeks. Only in retrospect does she make the connection between Franz's calls and the attentions of her shadowy admirer.

30

For the first time in his conscious memory Lachlan calibrates the passage of time differently. This is no longer the daily rote, extending into the cyclical transition of seasons with him and Agnes winding down in tandem like old clocks. Since he and Agnes and all the older people of their acquaintance age at the same pace, no one notices.

But now, time, for Lachlan, is calibrated by the boy's progress, his reserved but growing confidence, his independence and the still closed books of his past and full intelligence. Lachlan has become absorbed with the child he never had, trying to familiarize himself with the boy's history, as if mentally making marks on the doorjamb calibrating heights Franz has grown beyond to occupy his present proportions.

January slips into February. The cold does not abate. Although the novelty of teaching him has paled, Lucy continues to visit Angus, although she now admits to herself she is bored with him when not joined in the act. She has begun to realize that nature is relentless and all the tasks she was forced to carry out on the farm will become necessary again when spring finally approaches. What, she asks herself, is the point in that?

Murdo continued intermittently to shadow Gail. From his eyrie Franz saw the two figures finally meet at the chink of the crossroads. Superimposed, two became one, became two, who continued in the direction of the farm separated by a sliver of streetlight that suggested neither surveillance nor strife but companionability, until absorbed by the diagonal white blanket of the foreground roof. Her exuberant response to Franz's call that night did nothing to allay his fears.

The 'Jewish gentleman' Lachlan alluded to in his conversation with Agnes has paid two visits, admitting his provenance by carrying under his arm a copy of the *Oban Times* Angus aspires to read without dissembling. For the first time Lachlan finds himself on the other side of the exchange, anxiously awaiting a prognosis of a kind. His instructions to Agnes about the food to be prepared have been precise. Having unhelpfully described Franz as a 'delightful boy', Mr Levine surprised the doctor and his housekeeper by donning his coat and picking up his portmanteau again to brave the elements. It seems he is staying with an elderly couple on the other side of the village who keep themselves to themselves, who most people believed suffer the same unfortunate scepticism as the doctor because they belonged to neither indigenous congregation but who now, after years of apparently languishing in a spiritual vacuum, cynically turn out to be Jewish. Having discovered the persuasion of this couple, Lachlan wonders aloud in front of Mr Levine if there would be any point in Franz visiting them. Mr Levine opines aloud at equal volume that he doubts it, that the couple are very elderly, that in a village of this size they must know of a Jewish boy in the environs and that if they have not already volunteered their services they must have their reasons. Lachlan helps Mr Levine on with his coat and expresses his regret that the other cannot stay to sample the food 'specifically prepared in expectation of his accepting their hospitality'. Mr Levine expresses regret with sufficient grace to charm Agnes and irritate Lachlan. He does however return the following morning to apologize for the misunderstanding with a promise to stay on the next occasion. Agnes warns Lachlan not to indulge in the same gentle goading with Mr Levine as he does with 'Father Keenan'.

'Brendan is not my father, Agnes. But you are right. I would have to know Mr Levine better before I know what liberties would not give offence.'

Mr Levine, 'Morris' at his amiable insistence, is as good as his word. At his next visit two weeks later the dinner is a genial affair. Breakfast the following morning is as protracted as Morris's timetable allows. Lachlan has cleared his diary and Franz is at school. In response to further questions from Lachlan, Morris suggests it would be to the boy's advantage to visit a Rabbi in Glasgow. He hopes he does not mind but he has taken the liberty of mentioning him, nodding downhill in the direction of the school, to the Rabbi, nodding in the direction of Glasgow, a personal friend. Lachlan is far from minding. He needs all the help he can get if he is to keep his pact with the dead woman.

Another handshake on the doorstep, another donning of the coat and picking up of the portmanteau, a promise of telephoning to finalize arrangements once he has spoken to his friend, a blast of outdoor air as the door opens and closes, and Lachlan, a man not easily impressed, has been as charmed with Mr Levine during his second visit as Agnes was by his first. And asking himself why, he realizes that the man captivated him the more complimentary he became about Franz. Now he knows he has a blind spot to add to his bald spot. 'Old age,' he says aloud to the airy lobby, 'it comes to us all.' And remembering Franz's correction, tells himself to keep his platitudes to himself.

That night he knocks gently on the boy's door. Lying on top of the covers in his pyjamas, Franz is poring over yet another of the doctor's anatomical textbooks.

'Lachlan, don't you find the body interesting?'

Lachlan considers. Agnes would never ask the same question, being too old and too conscious of impropriety. If she did Lachlan would say that the body is a fragile bag, easily punctured, and that the novelty of investigating its machinations eventually palls. But for Lachlan one of the wonders of the boy is his lack of cynicism, given exposure to circumstances that Lachlan can only begin to guess at. And in looking at him Lachlan remembers his own curiosity and naive optimism. It is this that is too fragile to puncture.

'Fascinating.'

'Is it true women have all their eggs inside them when they are born?'

'Even before they are born.' Déjà vu. He remembers the sense of wonder this realization gave rise to in him: unborn people containing potential offspring, progeny accommodating their successors like Russian dolls. 'Put down the book a moment, please.' The boy does so and looks at him gravely. 'How did you get on with Mr Levine?'

He smiles. 'As well as can be expected.' It is a euphemism Lachlan has told him he dispenses like placebos, their little joke. 'He is a nice man but I do not think he can tell me anything about my faith my mother has not already told me.'

This is the first time he has ever made mention of his mother without being prompted by a direct question. Lachlan suspects Mr Levine finds himself as unequal to the task of teaching Franz as Gail does.

'He has suggested that you visit a Rabbi in Glasgow. Would you like that?'

'I am always happy to learn.'

'I know you are.' Touching Franz's cheek, Lachlan stands stiffly to go. The preparatory cough as he turns away reminds him of something: the preamble to Franz's first word in this house. He turns back. The boy's mouth hangs open, but having drawn attention to himself he seems uninclined to speak.

'Is there anything you want to say to me?'

'No. Yes. Gail. We cannot leave her alone with him.'

It is not difficult to guess who he is talking about. Franz is not the only one who has noticed him catching her up after her evening detour to the sea. 'If she wants to be alone with him there is little we can do about it.'

Having delayed the doctor's departure the boy now appears to ignore him. He is engrossed in the counterpane, picking with increasing agitation at some invisible flaw, the hand moving faster like a pecking bird gorging before the others arrive. Eventually Lachlan stays Franz's hand with gentle pressure of his own. He is patient. His bedside manner is infallible. They sit in this tableau, the old man's hand resting on the boy's, almost unconsciously registering the pulse, until Franz is prompted to speak.

'She does not know him.'

'And you do? Is there something about him you want to tell me?'

The boy takes a moment to consider his response and blinks several times in preparation. 'Only that she should not be with him.'

Another closed chapter in a closed book. Knowing that at this stage there is nothing more the boy will say, Lachlan leaves it at that.

The following week Mr Levine telephones. The week after that Lachlan drives Franz to the station for the southbound trip. The written instructions are precise, laboriously set out by Lachlan in block capitals given the obscurity of his handwriting. He presents this to the boy in an envelope also containing a number of new banknotes. He cannot know that this only serves to remind Franz of previous paperwork in a previous parting. Standing on the platform, Lachlan hands Franz the inevitable Gladstone bag. The boy refuses to have it on the rack out of reach. The carriage is otherwise unoccupied. There will be no problem. Tapping the window that separates them, Lachlan watches Franz pull it down and hands him a handful of change.

'Just in case . . . Now, you've got your instructions, your sandwiches, money, the address . . .'

'Yes.'

'Our telephone number?'

'Written inside my hat.'

'It's only two nights!' Lachlan blurts. Having said all there is to say, he is thinking aloud now. Franz seems to be accepting the separation with disarming aplomb. Lachlan realizes why: young as he is, Franz is the more accustomed of the two to leaving familiarity behind. He wants to assure the boy that it is all right, that he will come back, that everything will be as it was – better, since Franz will have continued on the path that his mother intended for him and will know more about the subject she considered more important than anything else. But he doesn't say a thing. He just stands there, clapping his hands in the cold like solitary reluctant applause. At the first judder of movement the boy closes the window, takes an improbably large medical textbook from the bag and sits with this still closed like a shelf on his lap. He raises his hand to Lachlan to mirror the other's gesture as the old man begins to accelerate backwards.

Lachlan is frozen in an attitude of farewell till the train turns out of sight. As he drops his arm his old heart seems to be caught in a prolonged systolic squeeze, and he realizes, with apocalyptic certainty, that nothing in the world matters so much to him as the fate of that departing child.

31

Snow melts. Morning frosts persist. The gusts of late February presage a blustery March. If anything, Gail enjoys this turbulent weather more. In daylight, spume overarches the sea wall, forming transient rainbows for the benefit of anyone fortunate enough to see. Several times he has walked her home now. She has never invited him in. He has no expectation of being asked. She knows this is childish, like deliberately dropped schoolbooks to instigate a meeting. On the last occasion he walked with her Mrs Campbell was looking anxiously out the kitchen window, awaiting her arrival in the yard. He saw her before she did and retreated back into the dark with a muttered goodbye. She knows that if Eileen Campbell saw them walking home together the news will be common knowledge by tomorrow, but believes that they have got away with it this time. And she knows her relief makes her complicit.

His conversation is terse and sardonic, usually at someone else's expense, and almost always funny. She did not anticipate a sense of humour. Every instinct tells her she should disapprove of this man, but it is almost impossible to dislike someone who makes you laugh. At his first request to accompany her she told him it was a free country. She tried to placate her conscience later by telling herself that she could not stop him. But she knows that is not true. She knows she encouraged by not actively discouraging. Her reproach prompts her to write frequently to Clive, as if the thought of him is an antidote to the thought of the other, inane rambling letters that touch only on the superficial. She is too apprehensive to venture into the morass of their reciprocal feelings. Although guilt prompts her to write, she feels even more guilty sending these letters off, envoys entrusted with worthless trivia, destined to wander in search of a lost recipient.

The presages of February were correct. The beginning of March blows keen and dry. There is a sense of reawakening, an airy vigour few can fail to notice. The war, unable to stop the inexorable approach of spring, seems another world away. The sunsets are still early. Lucy arrives later and later at Angus's room, reluctantly keeping an appointment to assuage an appetite that was keener when the arrangement was made. There is a listlessness to her now and then. He is at a loss to understand and construes every one of her increasingly pronounced mood swings as an indication of their bond. His gift for misinterpretation is such that there is almost nothing she could do that would fail to corroborate for him what he desperately believes to be true, because the alternative is too awful to contemplate. The truth is that she is even more careless of his feelings when she is not in the mood for what she considers the only thing they have in common.

'I'm late.'

'It doesn't matter.'

She snorts. She could have predicted the exchange verbatim. She knew the misinterpretation he would put on the words. She lights a cigarette from his fire and tries to explain in words of one syllable what 'late' means. His gaze is so vacantly placid that in sheer exasperation she grabs her coat, pushes her way out into the narrow passage and clicks her way down the stairs. He stands bereft in the middle of the floor, conflicting emotions struggling as the full import of her words finally registers. Finally sitting, he is quietly exuberant. His least suspected solution has presented itself.

32

'You can put your clothes back on now.' She adjusts herself quickly. Lachlan believes this to be a matter of practice. Local folklore would have it she has had lots, getting in and out of clothes like a cormorant diving and surfacing. Looking at her, he knows she knows the result.

'I'm sorry, I can only confirm what you already suspected.'

'That's not all you can do.'

'Yes it is. You can't continue to do the heavy work that's been expected of you. You might want to consider going home.'

'For all I know home's a fucking crater by now!' She bursts into tears and huddles herself, her back rising and falling with the sobs. His hand hovers indecisively over her head till he finally sighs and strokes her hair. At the feel of his touch she believes she has sensed a concession and sits upright, almost cheerful.

'You'll help me then?'

He knows why she has come to him. Since his first emergency call out at Rassaig all those years before he has helped dozens of people prematurely conclude the remainder of a life consigned to pain. He has been as discreet as he could about this, but despite his silence word obviously got around. People from outwith the village came to consult, looking for the help they knew their own doctor would not provide. He has only ever aided a natural deterioration. He thinks it is one thing to ease someone out of this world, helping them to retain what faculties or dignity corrosive pain has left them with, but quite another to deny a human being the opportunity of ever arriving.

'I'll help you with your pregnancy. I won't help you end it.'

'What kind of life will it have?'

'The best you can give it, if you try.'

'Can you imagine me with a baby!'

'What did you imagine would happen if you persisted in having sex without using anything.' It is not a question. She makes no attempt to answer.

'For God's sake, there's a war on. Who can bring a child into this?'

This has occurred to him. Were he to follow his credo to its logical conclusion he might give her argument more thought. But he knows she is citing this as a convenience. The fact that there is a war on did not cause her to minimize the risk. And truth be told, awful as the circumstances are, life being held so cheap elsewhere simply makes what comes within his compass that much more precious to him. When he thinks of Franz's family that stayed to be consumed, and the fraction that they represent, he cannot bring himself to add to the aggregate of abbreviated lives. And Lachlan believes there is another reason, if one is needed, that he cannot even begin to explain to her. Unlike the war he saw active service in, he feels this war needs to be fought. If they do not prevail then all the humane values he believes in will perish with the dead. And to terminate a life for convenience insults the sacrifice.

'God knows there are enough orphans, but if you stay I will do what I can to find you accommodation and help you have the child adopted.'

'I'm not like one of these women you have around here who keeps digging up turnips or whatever and takes ten minutes off to have a baby in a field.'

'I will not help you end this pregnancy.'

He has stopped her, in the dark between the village and the farm. He has laid a hand on her and spun her round. Placing his flattened hand in the small of her back he has grasped a fistful of her coat, the way he did with Gavin. The latent strength she can feel is almost pneumatic. With the one encompassing arm, she feels he could lift her towards his mouth. But he does not. Her heart is hammering.

'I can't just go on walking you back.'

'You don't have to. I never asked you to.'

'That's not what I mean. You know that.'

'Yes.'

'I want more.'

'I have no more to give.'

'That's a lie. You have more and you want to give it.'

She looks towards the dark, fluid expanse. At this distance its sighs and swells are reduced to an ebbing murmur. How awful to think men are out there, crouched in steel cylinders hunting one another in the blackness of its depths.

'Whether I want to give it or not does not matter. I will not give. I should not have encouraged you this far.'

'But you did.' And letting her go, he turns away and in the darkness the two figures go their opposite ways.

Half a mile away from the separating figures Lucy stands on the jetty, listening to the slap of the water Gail heard from a distance. She has assembled what she needs. Looking at the water Gail contemplated, she experiences a similar sense of dread, but for an entirely different reason. It is not in her makeup to consider the fates of the unknown out there who seek to invade or defend, who perish while she equivocates.

There is a horror at the dark mass that swells up towards the planking. She feels she is tottering, and it is the platform she stands on that rises and falls towards this seething abyss. And staring down into the dark water she feels a dreadful sense of vertigo while her mind rehearses the sequence of events: twisting in the darkness as she is pulled further down, flying tendrils of hair as the final blurt from her lungs erupts in a postponed bubble, then seawater surging into her lungs. She knows that people who do this do not rehearse such consequences, do not dwell on scenarios of their absence. And she knows not only that she loves life, but that she loves herself more than the life inside her.

35

A tread on the stairwell. Angus is all attention, hoping it will proceed beyond the entrance of the other tenants. He is at the end of the narrow passage. The tread continues, but is too slow, too heavy and measured to be hers. He has only ever locked the door when she is here with him. No one here steals. Even if they did, he has nothing worth taking. The door is pushed slowly ajar. Gavin Bone admits himself and softly closes the door at his back. Sitting near the fire, Angus does not speak. Gavin stays where he is, seemingly happy to conduct this interview from the threshold.

'Is she here?' Everything is visible, from the bed to the open tins beside the gas burner. The question is facetious. Failing to realize this, Angus shakes his head. 'Has she left you?'

'No.'

'I have felt for you, Angus. I have thought that perhaps it is not all your fault. Since you were a child your mind was open to confusion. I think perhaps it always will be. It is like earth awaiting a seed. I thought it had been planted with a good seed.' Contemplating the tangle of the bed sheets, 'I see I was wrong. I do not consider myself blameless. I should have stopped that schoolteacher earlier. I should have known when she had you chasing her hat like a dog. To allow a woman like that to poison your mind—'

'She didn't do anything wrong.' Angus has never interrupted anyone before.

'To allow a woman like that to poison your mind was one thing. When I found out I took the necessary precautions. But the next choice you made yourself. It was not something you passively took in just because you sat in a class and listened. You acted. Oh, Angus, Angus . . .' his tone has dropped an octave and is almost tender, 'to go with that whore—'

'Not!' He has shouted. He has interrupted and now he has shouted. This explosive syllable has shocked him. He stood to shout, jerking upright as the sound erupted out. Conscious in the startled aftermath, he sits slowly down again looking towards the fire, his voice collapsing in on itself. 'Not . . . No . . . She is not what you said. We love one another. We are to be married.'

'Your marriage bed is stained before you get into it. Tell me, Angus, is this your idea or hers?'

'It is ours.'

'And why would she want to marry when she has had what she wants without it?'

'We are to have a child. We will be married and she will have our child.' He repeats this twice more in a kind of litany.

'I don't think so. She will leave.'

'No she won't.'

'And one bastard begets another. It is the way of things.' Angus looks up from his preoccupation with the fire. 'Where did you think you came from, Angus? Your mother was like her. She came with a story of a dead husband, taken by the sea. We might have believed her if she had not behaved the way she did. And now you and your trollop. It is the cycle of sin. You will meet your bastard in hell, Angus.'

36

Of all the places she might be Angus finally finds her on the jetty, their first trysting place, the bolt hole of his childhood. It was here he would run to in all weathers, after the arguments between his mother and the succession of men who drifted through their house, after persecution at school. Larger stones revealed by the low tide give way to shingle in the steep upper part of the beach. Even at high tide there is a sheltered alcove beneath the jetty above the watermark, the shingle floor rising to meet the level roof of the planking in a constructed cave he always thought of as his. He has lived his life with the constant tidal ebb and flow, with the incessant hissing of dissipating waves. Here he has lain curled on dried seaweed finding comfort in the rhythm, a foetus mesmerized by a larger heartbeat.

At the sound of footsteps she kicks sacking over the pieces in front of her, embarrassed by the evidence of an intention not followed through. When she turns to see that it is him, a flicker of something moves across her face. She turns back to face the sea. He puts his arms around her, alarmed at her proximity to the dark water, standing as she is on the extremity.

'Gavin Bone came to my room.' She says nothing but accepts his embrace like a coat, her mind still sucked down beneath the swell to where her imagined histrionic self twirls at the end of the rope. 'I told him you were going to have a baby.'

'That's marvellous.' She is still too listless to be angry.

'It's all right. I've worked it out.'

'More than I have.'

He struggles to articulate what he has worked out. He was prepared to believe the two of them together, enjoying one another, was wrong. He has grown up with a theology that penalizes pleasure. Anything carnal carries a debt. But he cannot believe that what they now feel for one another can be wrong, or that the baby they will have will be wrong. He is prepared to gamble everything he has been taught against the realization that has dawned on him. Everything will be all right: they are redeemed by love.

But he doesn't articulate this. A collision of confused thoughts distils the sum of his reasoning to a single statement: 'We will go away.'

'Away where?'

'Anywhere. They won't know we were not married before you were expecting. We will get married somewhere and then go somewhere else.' He has never been inland. He has in his mind some rural pasture with an idyllic cottage awaiting their occupancy. 'To the new people we will just be like anyone else – married people having a baby.'

She no longer finds any comfort in his embrace. She realizes how far this fantasy has been allowed to run and slowly disentangles herself from his arms.

'Look, Angus, we've had some fun . . .'

'We can have more fun.'

'No, dearie, I don't think we can. People get just so much fun out of one another and that's it. I know. I think our fun is all used up. The only fun either of us is going to have now is with someone else.'

He blinks several times in quick succession, perplexed. 'But we love one another.' His eyes remind her of a cow's.

'No we don't.' She is irritated at the look of wounded imbecility as the gulf of their feelings and expectations begins to dawn on him. He begins to breathe rapidly.

'We . . . you could learn, when we go somewhere else.'

'You've never been anywhere else. What do you know? What would you do? How would you survive anywhere else?' She has been manufacturing anger to overcome her feelings towards herself. She knows herself just well enough to know that she is behaving badly. At the look on his face she begins to cry. 'Oh, Angus. You haven't a clue. This place keeps you. You get odd jobs from people here to help you. If you went somewhere else you'd be lost. You can barely read. I have trouble managing myself at the best of times, and they aren't now. I can't manage us both . . .'

'. . . the baby.'

She flares up in genuine anger. 'The baby! The baby! Everyone keeps talking about the fucking baby. No one talks about me!'

He feels a physical pain in the centre of his body. His legs slowly fold like a collapsing chair and he sits, cross-legged on the planks, trying to make sense of the water below. There must be a purpose to divine in this lapping against the piles, this ceaseless Morse. He had imagined wrapping her in his coat as he explained and her relief as the plan unfolded. He had imagined escorting her to the McHargs', standing vigilant at the bedroom door, deterring questions as she packed. Her case, his meagre bag, the morning bus, a convenient mist to obscure their destination from enquirers and the specifics he cannot envisage for a real departure.

She looks down at him. His disillusionment is another burden she cannot carry. Have some fun and look at the baggage. He is young. He will get over it, find someone more suited, some stupid farm girl who doesn't mind being ankle-deep in shit. And at least she's taught him how to please a girl. Not like some around here: boots off, dick out. His wife should thank her. They'll have a brood like themselves. Snowbound in delivery. Midwife arriving in a tractor. Placenta in the pig swill. Baby bathed in the front room. Three of them by the fire, just what the doctor ordered.

At least he enjoyed a taste of the exotic while it lasted.

Without looking down she tousles his head as she passes, already looking on to the next thing.

37

By the time Gail arrived at school that morning she had
decided to go straight home after lessons. If the end of the day
leaves her with additional work to do she will take it with her,
at least for the next week or so. They can spare her a corner
of the kitchen table to spread her paperwork out on. She does
not want to repeat the encounter from last night. He was right
in saying that she wanted to give more.

Since the only exercise she will get will be walking the brief
distance between school and farmhouse, she walks out at
lunchtime. Normally she sits in the class, keeping watch over
her charge in the small playground. The paved area is fenced.
She expected to walk out to interrupt the usual melee of
different games. But the children are all arranged round the
periphery of the fence, standing on the lower rungs for a better
view. Some balance precariously on the top. She shouts to
them to get down. At her approach they break a gap in their
ranks to let her through. There is a crowd of adults gathered
at the sea and several figures can be seen hurrying across from
the harbour end.

There is something ominous in the scene, in the stillness of
the observers. She orders the protesting children back into the
class. Paul, picking out the uniformed form of his father in the
distance, clambers over into the field and begins running. She
calls him back, but, like her, he has sensed the authority of a
larger event. Telling the children not to leave the playground,
she hitches her skirt and climbs over after him. She resists the

impulse to run, knowing that if she does they will follow, irrespective of her instructions.

Lachlan had not been telephoned. David Crawford, sent by Paul's father, walked through the waiting room. Authorized by the constable, he tapped on the doctor's door to interrupt the consultation. Observers were rewarded with a subdued exchange at the surgery door and then the sight of Lachlan snatching up bag and coat to follow the man out to the waiting car.

By the time Gail gets close there is a semicircle of backs Paul is trying to penetrate. At the sound of her voice shouting the boy's name his father emerges from the midst of the group looking grim. He picks the boy up.

'I'm sorry, Michael. He ran away. I'll take him back.'

'Don't bother. He's going home.' He puts the boy down, and on an impulse picks him up again and kisses him. He puts him down again. The look of his father coupled with this unprecedented display of public affection is enough to convince the boy of the gravity of the situation. Without looking for any further concession he turns in the direction of home. Drawn by macabre curiosity, Gail moves between the figures toward the nucleus of the group. Angus is lying on the pier. Lachlan has covered his face with sacking he found lying here, hiding the spectacle from public display as he tries to sever the cord that has been tied in a running knot around the neck. Low tide discovered him. By the pallor Lachlan estimates he has been in the water since last night. Any longer and the soft flesh would have begun to be eaten. The tongue is swollen and protrudes obscenely. The rope is deeply imbedded in the congested purple flesh of the neck which bears the indentations of Lachlan's fingers attempting to tug some slack. He turns to David. Since fetching him he has shadowed the doctor.

'Do you have a knife?'

'What for?'

'To cut the cord.'

'Don't you carry a scalpel or something in your bag?'

'Why would I? I'm not a surgeon. If you don't have a knife can you ask?' He nods grimly towards the assembled crowd, held back by the two or three Michael has deputized to throw up a cordon. 'They're fishermen. One's bound to have a knife.' He sees Gail looking askance at him from the other side of the impromptu barrier. She has shown more compassion and understanding towards Angus than anyone else of late. He gestures her forward. Witnessing the exchange, Michael orders her to be admitted.

She has already guessed as she approaches. David returns with a clasp-knife and stands a few paces back. Lachlan pulls back the sacking. She stands.

'Are you all right?'

'Yes.'

'Hold this up so they don't see.' He has to cut into the flesh of the neck to sever the embedded cord. She is surprised at the lack of blood, and is in turn surprised at the impartiality of her reaction. He puts the sacking back. Someone comes through with a blanket. They cover Angus. From his kneeling position Lachlan extends his arm towards Gail. She helps him to his feet, his knees cracking as he hoists himself erect. He takes off his glasses and pinches the bridge of his nose, a gesture normally confined to late evening after a day of reading. The canopy of clouds is lit by an unseen sun, suffusing the dome beneath in a metallic glare. In the harsh light she suddenly notices how old he is, the cross-hatching of creased skin on his neck, the network of broken veins ramifying like a rash.

The cord runs from under the blanket to two large rectangular blocks, tethered together at the other end. With his foot Lachlan nudges some random-looking piece of smaller machinery. He cannot know this is the only remaining evidence of Lucy's aborted attempt, besides the rope that Angus put to the use she pretended to contemplate.

'I don't know why he would bring this. Insufficient ballast.' Nodding towards the rectangular blocks, 'Car batteries. Didn't make any mistake there. Michael says he got one of them from the harbour. Thrown out. No one took the trouble to get rid of it – until now. We don't know where the other one came from. He was always tinkering with things. I don't know why. He never got things to work. As much mechanical aptitude as I have. I suppose you're in a better position than anyone to say what aptitude he did have. Either you or your girlfriend, the bottled blonde.' They are at the extremity of the pier, where Angus found Lucy last night. Lachlan turns in the direction of the sea and inhales sharply half a dozen times, as if intending to dive.

'I got him to throw the belt off here only months ago.'

'What?'

'The belt. My predecessor's. The man you described for me. I got Angus to throw his belt into the sea from here.' To cover his head adequately the blanket has been pulled up short, exposing his feet. Looking down, she sees that one shoe has been somehow lost. The sock is threadbare. She thinks this the most forlorn thing she has ever seen.

Lachlan takes one last sharp breath for the plunge. 'The thing is – the thing is . . .' He stops and speaks each word separately. 'The. Thing. Is –. he had to make two trips to get them here. From here to the harbour and back twice. Can you imagine what must have gone through his mind walking that distance, with that weight, knowing its purpose . . . ?'

A stretcher arrives. The road ends two hundred yards from the jetty. They will be obliged to carry him the distance to the waiting vehicle. The crowd separates for his departure.

Lachlan is about to follow. One of Michael's deputies crosses to the tethered batteries and attempts to lift them. Grunting, he manages to straighten with the load and puts it back down. David returns with the knife and cuts the rope binding them. They lift one each, staggering through the ragged gap left by the departing stretcher. 'Evidence,' the other one needlessly explains to whoever will listen. Aside from the strain of lifting he looks quite cheerful at the novelty of the situation.

Turning round and looking at her before he leaves, Lachlan takes Gail's hand. He calls Michael across.

'Can you have someone go across and dismiss the class.' It is not a question.

'I'll be fine.'

'You're the same colour as him.'

Michael nods. The stretcher is half-way there, the crowd beginning to disperse.

'Walk with me as far as the van.' They link arms. Who is supporting whom? Having asked for her company, he seems unwilling to talk. And suddenly, with barely suppressed anger he says, 'No doubt they'll have a ceremony of some kind for him.'

She helps him clamber into the improvised ambulance. She sees him perch his buttocks on some kind of welded ledge, contemplating the prone figure, seemingly immune to discomfort in his preoccupation. The doors close on this tableau.

She watches the van's slow progress across the rutted surface till the proper road begins. She imagines Angus, without the suspension of conscious restraint, juddering, the threadbare foot lolling. She looks around for something to lean on, a fence post, anything. The nearest upright is the playground fence. It is too far. At the realization of his absence she sits down on the ground, the way he did when Lucy left him on the jetty.

38

She has no desire to see Ewan McHarg. She has even less desire to be alone and another woman nearer her age seems more suitable company than Eileen Campbell just now. When she gets to the girls' farm she is admitted by Harriet. There is no sign of Ewan or his wife. Harriet simply says, 'She's in there,' as if having guessed the purpose of the visit. News travels faster than Gail anticipated. Lucy is sitting in the same position as on the last occasion but this time crying instead of smoking.

'Would you like tea?' Harriet asks.

'I . . . I don't think so. I can't think at the moment.'

'Why does everyone think tea fixes everything?' Lucy says. Her voice is nasal. She looks as if she has been crying for days. She moves her legs to make space for Gail. Harriet sits in her reading chair.

'I don't know that either. I've just come from there. I thought he'd just been found when I arrived. How did you know?'

'Know what?'

'That Angus is dead.'

The other two exchange a blank glance. In the prolonged silence the fire seems loud. Gail stares at the embers. She is only now understanding in instalments and only because she has seen for herself. Lucy's mouth hangs open. With her swollen eyes and red nose she looks momentarily imbecilic. Harriet is the first to rally.

'How?'

'He . . . he . . .' Gail is experiencing the same difficulty as

Lachlan explaining the logistics of the act. Someone is going to have to do this for the relatives. Are there relatives? 'He drowned himself.'

'Dear God . . .' It is Harriet who speaks. Lucy is still dumbly staring. She is so abstracted it does not seem rude to speak about her in the third person.

'What's she crying for then?'

'She's pregnant. She's been to see Doctor McCready. She says he refused to help.'

'There's been some misunderstanding. I don't believe Lachlan would have said he wouldn't help.'

'He said he wouldn't help me get rid of it.' Lucy has revived. She has dealt with the news the way she deals with most things. She understands that she understands this as much as she is going to, at this time, and she has put it to one side to concentrate on something else. She compensates herself with the thought that she might revisit this fact when the time is more opportune. But the truth is that she will not. The time is never more opportune. This thought will languish among the miscellany of other things she temporarily shelves till they disintegrate: forgotten fruit. Sometimes a bad memory is occasioned by something someone says, a smell, a fragment of music, but mainly there is only the flux of her immediate present. And talk of Lachlan has brought her back.

It is Gail's turn to look dumbly startled. She recalls Lachlan's remark about herself and Lucy being best placed to understand Angus's aptitudes.

'Is it Angus's baby?'

'Probably.'

'Did he think it was?'

'Probably.'

There is another long pause as she tries to digest the implications of this.

'Did you tell him it was?'

'What is this, twenty questions? I told him I was pregnant. I don't think he liked the thought of me with anyone else.'

'What did he say about the baby?'

'I didn't take notes. He was happier than I was.'

'If he was happier why did he drown himself?'

'I don't know! I'm not his fucking guardian angel!'

The anger is disproportionate. Gail realizes the other woman is prepared to allow herself a fit of temper to submerge what the conversation might otherwise disclose.

'You were happy to let that boy think the baby was his when the truth is that you don't know whether it is or not. And he was happy about it. What I want to know is, what happened after he was happy that caused him to make two trips to the harbour to find car batteries to tie round his neck and throw himself off the jetty?'

At the description Harriet turns her face away. Lucy, faced with the image of Angus twisting at the end of the rope that snared her fictitious self, the last bubble bursting from his lips, lets loose a wrenching sob.

'He wanted us to get married. Can you imagine? Me and Angus and a baby! He wanted to go away with me. He's . . . he was . . . not bright. Can you imagine him in a city? I told him . . .' As she slows her voice shrinks. She concludes almost in a whisper, staring at the ground, 'That we . . . he couldn't.'

Full realization of what occurred dawns simultaneously on the other two. Harriet turns back to exchange a look with Gail. Both read their own thought in the expression of the other. Between them there has always been an unspoken reciprocity. Lucy's lip is hanging down imbecilically again. A large thread of saliva droops towards the floor. She bursts out in a series of sobs, each preceded by a sharp inhalation. There is something histrionic and purging in these, as if everything will be all right by the time they have run their course. Gail does not believe them. She is too busy. A summation of Angus's life plays itself out in her imagination: ignored, bullied, brainwashed with an ideology that taught him he was in all likelihood damned; then he had the misfortune to meet Lucy.

'That boy . . . You chose him. He didn't choose you. He was willing to give up everything for you. Do you realize what that meant? For him to leave the familiar? For someone who's never been anywhere else? Not just a job or a room. Everything. He was taught to believe that going with you was going to hell, and he was prepared to do it for you and the baby. Everything. And I bet you didn't even thank him.'

The sobs have subsided sufficiently for Lucy to look up with a ready reply.

'How do you know he didn't just see me as a ticket out of here?'

Gail stands. 'You're not the first selfish person I've ever met, but I think you're the first one I've known who is incapable of understanding that people act from motives different from yours. And I don't want to meet another like you, if there are any.' She moves towards the door and speaks without looking back. 'I won't come here again. God help your baby.'

39

Angus is buried, his room let, his possessions disposed of, the few friends that attended to this last obligation struck by the meagre accumulation of a curtailed life. Nothing is left to mark his passing but individual recollections and a growing seed. After Gail's departure Lucy has turned remarkably discreet. Her condition is not common knowledge. Gail and Harriet keep their confidences to each other. Lachlan, the repository of countless secrets, is bearing up under the burden of yet another. Gavin's machinations are known only to Gavin. Lucy would be pleased had she known he kept his revelations for the posterity of the written word.

Gail has been subdued for the week. Franz's attempt at comfort after Thursday's lesson draws from her a rueful smile. What right does she have to indulge when he has gone through so much more? On his way home he runs into Murdo. He looks quickly back at the school. His inclination is to run back to her and stay to see out whatever happens. As Murdo bears down on him he finds himself unable to move.

'I'm not looking for her. I'm looking for you. I hear you're no longer a moron. I hear you don't talk much. Let's keep it that way. I wouldn't want talk circulating about anything you might have seen when you were our guest. Even more important, I'm looking for something that's gone missing. From my bedroom. You wouldn't happen to know anything about that, would you?' The boy is rigid with fear. This seems to mollify Murdo, confirm the boy's ability to keep a secret.

'I can't make up my mind whether or not it went missing at the same time as you left. If I think you've got something of mine and you're not giving it back, I'll come and see you. Do you understand?' Franz stands mute till Murdo, satisfied with the effect he has had, turns back in the direction of the Drovers.

The following day Lachlan again drives the boy to the station, for his second arranged visit to the Rabbi. Franz is silent in the car, debating whether or not to tell him of his encounter with Murdo. Eventually he decides not to. To mention the encounter would tease out other facts about his stay with the Dougans he prefers not to revisit. His main concern is Gail, but Murdo admitted he had been waiting for him, not her. Her evening visits to the harbour have stopped. And as Lachlan said to him on his last trip south, it's only two nights.

Again he sits with the Gladstone bag at his feet. Two other passengers already occupy the carriage, an old man half asleep from the journey's beginning, yet further north, and an anonymous woman who has precluded conversation by hoisting a magazine before her. Again Lachlan slides backwards on the platform, hand raised. This time Franz abandons his book to push down the window and shout into the watery midday sunshine, 'Watch Gail.'

The trip is uneventful. But arriving at Glasgow Central he already feels a sense of something more pronounced than on his previous visit a few weeks ago. The Rabbi smilingly awaits him at the barrier. When he hands his ticket across the old man gestures him to step aside to let someone behind pass. As he does so he sees Lucy stride past. There is no one else similarly dressed. She must have been the anonymous woman. She cannot have failed to notice him, especially since he shouted Gail's name out the window. It is clear from her speed and preoccupation that she does not want to talk. He shakes the old man's hand, politely refuses offer of help with the bag, and fascinated by the cacophony in this riveted space, walks companionably with his teacher out to the taxi rank.

That evening Lachlan stops while passing Gail to give her a lift. He tells her that Franz called to confirm his safe arrival. The boy also thought it curious that he saw Lucy coming off the same train. He said she couldn't have failed to see him but didn't make herself known. Confronted with these premises, Lachlan has drawn his own conclusion but adds nothing beyond what the boy has said.

With a sense of trepidation she cannot give reason for Gail breaks her promise and goes back to the McHargs'. Harriet is out. At the risk of running into Murdo she makes her way to the Drovers. He isn't there but she is.

It takes them several days to trace Lucy's movements. By the time they discover her destination the address has adopted a significance all its own.

Lucy's preoccupation when she strides past Franz at the barrier is genuine. Her speed is not. She stops at a paper stand till she sees the boy and whoever the old man is disappear into the departing throng. He was right in his assumption that she has no inclination to talk. After Rassaig the novelty of commerce and people on the move would normally buoy her naturally exuberant spirits. Crowds stimulate. Change of any kind excites her. But she is subdued, bent to a purpose that will not allow diversion. She stops at a tea room, flattening the piece of paper she has had as a crib note in her magazine, reading it yet again to commit to memory the arrangements she already knows by heart. She had not planned on the accents. She has no trouble with the slow musical cadences of Rassaig. Her first few encounters there made her realize the harshness of her own speech. Her accent is common currency. They hear it even north of Rassaig, listening to the music-hall comedies broadcast by the BBC to bolster the nation's spirits. No one has any difficulty understanding her, including the waitress who took her order and replied in an accent so thick Lucy has had to ask twice to understand, and nodded, still uncomprehending. She is not sure if what she gets is due to misunderstanding or rationing. She knows she has to understand, if she is to conduct the transaction she came here for.

It is dark by the time she leaves the station, lights all subdued in compliance with the regulations. She knows the name of the tram and the place to catch it, but the whole enterprise seems more difficult conducted in the dark when the street signs have been inexplicably removed. She swears softly. Do they really think they will daunt the Nazis by disguising the whereabouts of Sauchiehall Street?

She stops at a closed shop front in Union Street and in exchange for a light asks directions. The young man cups his hands, cradling the brief flare, smiling in that small illumination as he leans over to let the tip catch a glow. He blows out the match with a snort of smoke. His cigarette describes arcs in the gloom as he explains and she, inexplicably, begins to cry. Without a further word he takes her arm and begins walking. At the stop, while they wait, he offers to take her there. She says no, she must go alone. When the tram arrives he helps her up and says above her head to the conductor, 'She's looking for Ellinger Terrace. According to her directions it's just off Dumbarton Road.'

'It's next to the terminus at Dalmuir West. I'll keep her right.'

She understands most of this and turns back to thank the young man who, with a cavalier wave, has melted anonymously back. She thinks: 'Two weeks ago he would have been an opportunity.'

The windows are darkened. Headlights are blackened over, leaving only a slit to navigate by. She wonders about accidents. Unlike London, no one here has been bombed. By the time this is all over the darkness will have killed more people than the Germans manage to. Blacked-out tenements rise on either side. They seem to be passing down a gloomy canyon. She is cold. Passengers are laughing. How can people be happy? She falls into a reverie till she realizes the conductor is calling to her, 'Dalmuir West, dear.' As she shuffles off he points in the direction of Ellinger Terrace.

There is still a surprising amount of foot traffic, given the darkness. She supposes you can get used to anything, or, given her reasons for coming, perhaps not anything. The numbers above the tenement entrances are obscured by baffle walls, built to shield the closes from the blast of street explosions. In the gloom she is obliged to cross the street twice to work out the run of numbers and calculate the address. She knows she is there when she sees the number, but somehow she is compelled again to fish out the piece of paper and corroborate. The close is dull. Windows on the landings have been blackened out. Lights burn at minimum wattage. In this twilight the Victorian tiling gives off an eerie ceramic sheen. Uprights of the banister are carved with delicate spiralling flutes. Repeated polishing has rendered the wood the colour of jet. Despite everything else she stops briefly to admire the craftsmanship. People who built this chose to care.

Top-right flat. There is no need to corroborate the name on the brass plate: she committed this to memory the first time she heard it. The bell seems to sound from a deep inner recess. She hears no sound of approaching footsteps, just the mechanical jangle of dangling keys. The inner door is noisily unlocked, as are the solid storm doors she is facing, one of which swings inward.

'I'm—'

She is interrupted by a figure that brushes past her on the way out. It is a woman. There is a pantomime subterfuge in the combination of high-turned coat collar and low hat. She gasps the syllable of an apology. Holding the banister, the woman begins to make her way down the stairs as if they are covered in ice. Lucy feels a sense of shock when she realizes the movements are caused not by caution but pain.

A pleasant-looking middle-aged woman in carpet slippers and housecoat waits patiently in the hall. Prompted by her smile, Lucy walks in. Both sets of doors are locked behind her. The place is clean and well lit, the high ceiling creating an airy space which dilutes the unmistakable tang of disinfectant. No explanation seems necessary: anonymous women obviously only come here for one reason. The woman takes her coat. Several others women's coats hang on the peg. The sight of this somehow alarms Lucy. Her coat has established her place in the queue. The woman's dress suggests she is some kind of charlady but from the informality of her manner Lucy guesses she lives here.

She is shown into a room. The furniture looks almost municipal, the waiting room of an impoverished dentist. Everything is clean. A girl who looks no older than mid-teens sits on one end of a sofa with a middle-aged woman at her side. They are obviously mother and daughter. Although the mother wears a severe expression, she is sitting very close to the younger woman and from her perspective, as she takes her seat across the occasional table, Lucy can see they are holding hands. The otherwise sparse room is dominated by an enormous fish tank standing on a table against one wall, opposite the fire. It is backlit, diffusing a dim liquid glow. In front of it, and with his back to Lucy, a schoolboy still in uniform taps the glass to agitate the fish. The door opens again. The woman in the housecoat says something to the boy, a single-syllable reprimand Lucy cannot make out. He turns. His similarity to his mother is as striking as that of the wretched girl to hers. Lucy realizes that this boy lives here. It seems inconceivable that a family could live in this place. Perhaps for the first time she appreciates how little she understands.

The door is closed. The boy returns to his diversion. Lucy looks dumbly at the carpet. In the silence the incessant tapping of the boy's fingernail against the glass grates. At the first sound of keys approaching he jumps back from the tank. The door opens. The woman with the housecoat gestures to the girl, who stands. The mother also stands.

'I'm sorry. Only her.'

The mother sits. The girl goes through. The door is closed behind her.

The boy takes a ruler from his bag. Dragging a chair across, he stands and dips the ruler into the water. Lucy's eyes flick from the spectacle of the mother's wringing hands to the boy. The line of the ruler is distorted by refraction. Balancing on the chair, the boy looks at this from various angles.

'Looks bent but it's no,' he announces to the room, turning. Only Lucy has looked up. By default she is his audience.

'What?'

'Looks bent but it's no. Cannae huv a bent ruler. Wouldnae be a ruler if it was bent. Couldnae measure nothin'.'

'No, I suppose not.'

Having exhausted the novelty of the illusion, he diverts himself by stirring the water into a small whirlpool. Debris from the bottom drifts up. The water is becoming opaque. It seems he can continue this indefinitely. She watches, mesmerized. Any distraction is welcome. She does not know how long passes. The keys again approach. The boy jumps from the chair. Two desultory fish rotate in the roiled water. The door opens. The girl is leaning against the woman with the housecoat. Her face is drained of colour. She is crying. The mother runs forward and puts her arms around the girl. They stand in this pose for perhaps a minute, rocking slightly. The boy's mother stands patiently to one side till they compose themselves.

'She can wait here.'

'We'd rather go.' It is the girl's mother who responds. The daughter nods in agreement. She is dabbing her nose. The handkerchief can absorb no more. Six inches from her face a string of catarrh attenuates from her nose to the sodden bundle. The mother takes this from her and hands across her own handkerchief. The three make their way out of sight. In the rustling delay Lucy can hear the girl gasp. They must be putting their coats on. Then follows the elaborate opening and locking procedure. The woman in the housecoat reappears almost immediately. The turbid water is slowly settling. Without taking her eyes from the tank she expertly slaps the boy on the back of the head. As she moves towards the door Lucy stands.

'He's no ready yet. Cleanin' up.'

An image of a foetus in a bucket is conjured. A top-floor flat, a string of women: how do they dispose of . . . of . . . everything? Another image: smuggled with garbage, bloody linen, a confused heap of tissue. Left alone with the boy, she turns to him desperately for further distraction. He has taken the routine slap without complaint but obviously thinks better of stirring again. He has improvised a game of pressing his face as close as possible to the tank and mouthing in time with the larger fish. She wonders if he is in some way retarded. This last thought recalls Angus. Someone needs to speak to fill this gap.

'Why are there only two?'

'Used tae be mare.'

'Did they die?'

'Bigger ones ate'm.'

'That's awful.'

''at's whit fish dae.'

'That's brutal.' And having said this the immensity of her decision strikes her. Life is relentless. Life devours to perpetuate. She is here to extinguish a life and has just been horrified by the fate of goldfish. For the first time ever she experiences a sense of displacement. Had this occurred an hour ago she would not have climbed the stairs.

The woman opens the door. Motivated by a sense of being

195

caught in something larger that she has put in motion, Lucy follows her out. They cross the hall. She stops at the open door.

'This is a kitchen.'

'Whit did y'expect?' Aside from a kitchen table with improvised stirrups Lucy can see the paraphernalia of ordinary family life. There is a grotesque incongruity. This is all wrong. The table has been scrubbed down. She wonders if they eat off this afterwards. Among the strata of other odours she detects caustic soda. A large pot on the range is maintained at a rolling boil. The single blacked-out window drips condensation. The man who has had his back to her, administering to the pot, now turns. He is ceramically bald. His head reminds her of the eerie sheen in the close. He wears glasses which he removes intermittently to wipe free of steam. Beads of sweat stand out on his head and forehead. He wears a sleeveless V-neck jumper. The rolled-up shirt cuffs are bloodstained, although his hands and forearms seem clean. He looks like some kind of tradesman. She can imagine him helping fit out a Cunard stateroom as a liner takes shape on the Clyde.

She moves to take off her dress.

'We always settle in advance.' His voice is smaller than she expected, an academic drone. Perhaps not a tradesman. Some kind of inventory clerk? She hands out the exact sum, counted in advance. He laboriously recounts and hands the folded notes to his wife.

'Take off your shoes, pants and stockings. Lie down and lift your skirt up.'

A towel is laid across the table, more, she guesses, to protect its surface than to cushion her. She has to lie back exposed and lift her legs into the stirrups. Looking down the line of her belly, across her rucked skirt, she can see him between her thighs. He turns away from her to wash his hands and attend to the pot. With a pair of kitchen tongs he is lifting items from the boiling water, running each under the cold tap before leaving it on the wooden draining board. They seem rudimentary: an ordinary table knife with rounded tip bent at right angles to the remainder of the blade; some kind of skewer or perhaps a trussing needle; kitchen scissors. In her growing sense of dread she does not hear the distant droning.

He does. His back tenses. He exchanges a look with his wife. She taps the pocket containing the notes he just passed her. He nods back in agreement.

'Should I take the boy doon?'

'We should be all right here. If they're looking for anything it'll be the yards. This won't take long.'

He looks at the implements, taking inventory, selects one and turns to her. She has just noticed an open packet of tea on an adjacent shelf, spilled leaves radiating in a charcoal fan. Perhaps minutiae yield something. Perhaps purpose is divined in observation. Perhaps the world is just a vast accumulation of meaningless trivialities. Beneath the shelf is an oval galvanized tub, the size of a hip bath, covered with a cloth, large enough to brew hooch in, large enough to duck for apples as they did in her mother's house when she was a kid, large enough to . . .

The remaining moments of his life are a confusion of cause and effect. Her scream, her repeated. 'No!'s climax with a collapse of the ceiling. A portion of the floor, bigger than the table she lies on, disappears in the gap that separates them. Her vehemence has conjured a shaft through the flat. The air is full of swirling dust welling up from another collapsed floor below. He has just realized that something has fallen through the building when a bomb detonates in the street outside. The kitchen faces the communal back court. The blackened lounge windows explode inwards. The force of the blast catapults the boy through the glass tank. Perforated, he falls senseless on the floor with dripping glass fragments and two suffocating fish. In the kitchen his father is leaning over the hole. A dangling joist in the attic, freed by vibration of the street explosion, tilts to vertical as it falls to drive his bald head into his shoulders. He is already dead as he falls into the shaft. His trajectory is interrupted by the detonation of the dilatory bomb, embedded in the ground-floor kitchen. The last sight Lucy ever witnesses is framed by her parted thighs as a molten globe erupts through the shaft to expand in annihilating brightness.

42

The morning after Franz's departure to Glasgow Lachlan sits alone at the breakfast table. He breaks open his egg with unaccustomed violence, causing the yolk to explode on the slope of his waistcoat. This will require a cloth. This brings the number of things that have disrupted his usual composure to three: the boy, the paper and the egg. He missed the boy last night and now he misses their inconsequential exchange over breakfast. Given the brief time they have had together, he realizes the disproportionate attention directed at Franz. Even if he could have things otherwise, he would not. He misses his paper. Agnes always gets up at an ungodly hour, a habit of her farming upbringing she has never shaken off. She gets the paper before he does, scans this for human interest and disguises her perusal by ironing the broadsheet flat. As long as his paper awaits him at breakfast he pretends not to notice. It is a charade they have played daily for years. His quick reading of the paper is augmented by a longer examination before dinner, when he will read the editorials or look at a late edition. But his paper, ironed or crumpled, is not here.

And now this egg.

He crosses to the hall. The kitchen door is ajar. 'Agnes, a cloth, please.' It is not a shout. He has not raised his voice since an incident with a Catholic chaplain outside a field hospital in France twenty-six years ago. The rest of his remark is made over his shoulder as he returns to the table, as much to himself as her: 'I don't think it unreasonable to expect my paper with breakfast. I could even endure powdered egg, like those poor souls down south, as long as I have my paper. How am I expected to keep a grip on things without a morning read? Just because we live here doesn't mean—'

But he is interrupted by the sight of her entering. The paper is crumpled, her face ashen. Wordlessly she puts the paper in front of him and points to the headline. He never shouts. He never runs. But he runs to the telephone now.

43

As Lucy is on her tram, abortion bound, Franz is saying his goodnights. It has been a long day for them both. He has agreed with his teacher that they will spend most of tomorrow together. He will sleep here tomorrow night. This is sufficient excuse, if one is needed, for an early night. But one is not needed. He says goodnight to each of the family in turn and goes to the room set aside for him.

A few weeks earlier Agnes took him into her confidence and told him of her evening prayers, their intention if not their content. Now, in his mind he runs through an inventory of those he wants preserved, and prays for the repose of those lost to him. He always begins with the latter: mother, father and Nina. Next come his brothers. In praying for the boys he is shading into the living, his prayer an entreaty that they are among them. Then follows the mental list of those deserving who have sheltered him. Towards the end of this he prays for Isabel and Morag, but not Murdo. He concludes with a prayer for Agnes, Lachlan and Gail. In this last prayer his fervour is lately tinged with a sense of guilt because he now can conjure Agnes, Lachlan and Gail more vividly than he can his own family. He has discovered that to those who remain behind, death is not a state but a gradation. The dead become deader. The images of Lachlan and Gail are colourful, while his family is gradually sinking into historical sepia, fading to some indiscriminate eternal radiance.

As Franz lies down to his three blankets and his medical textbook, Lucy lies down to her fatal curettage. But he is in no danger. His bed is on the south side of the river, as far from Clydebank as city boundaries permit. He sleeps the healthy sleep of his years and awakes, momentarily disoriented by the unfamiliar wallpaper. The family breakfast is interrupted by the shrill ring of the hall telephone. And so it is that news of obliteration on the other side of the city comes to them from Rassaig. And despite his assurances and remonstrances Franz is prematurely summoned back that day. And on the other end of the line, Lachlan, having employed sterner tones than the boy's recall demanded, returns the receiver to its cradle and leans, suddenly weary, on the hall table.

'He's safe.'

'Thank God. My prayers are remembered.'

'What about the prayers of the people of Clydebank?'

'I'll get a cloth for your waistcoat.'

Having assured Lachlan that the city is safe, Franz's visit to the centre, to catch the train north, gives him the lie. There is the movement of the displaced, hordes of people appearing both tragic and confused, carrying bundles, ridiculous miscellanies picked at random from warm rubble. And overall, in the faces of those around, he senses an air of determined embattlement. His train is delayed. He has no way of getting in touch. When, in darkness, the train draws into the rural station Murdo met him at a lifetime ago, he sees two figures, petrified with cold, levitating in smoke, anxiously scanning the carriages. For the first time he abandons his Gladstone bag to chance, drops it on the platform and runs towards the old couple.

Lachlan's caution proves well advised. The night of Franz's return, 14 March 1941, the bombers return to Clydebank. The night after that, Lachlan, sadly vindicated, paraphrases aloud from the late edition, expurgating as he sees fit.

'They used Dorniers and Junkers . . . Dropped landmines the first time. Landmines! On civilians. How do they sleep?'

'Is it a quiz?'

'Don't be absurd, woman. It says here there was still a distillery burning the second night to guide them back . . . Dropped incendiaries the second night and burned what remained . . . You'd think with all that fire they might have been more accurate. Didn't get a single shipyard, or the Singer factory.'

'Were they looking to blow up sewing machines then?'

'Apparently it has been converted to make sten guns.'

'Who makes the sewing machines then?'

He momentarily folds down the top half of his paper to stare at her in exasperation.

'What has that got to do with incendiary bombs dropped on Clydebank?'

'Folk need things sewed. Even if there is a war on. Especially if there is a war on, all those uniforms and badges.'

'We managed well enough before sewing machines were invented. We'll do so again.'

'We?'

He flicks the paper vertical and resumes.

'One theory for their inaccuracy is that the German navigators saw Great Western Road in the moonlight and mistook it for the Clyde. Personally I don't see it. I can see a moonlit road being mistaken for a canal, but not a river. If they can afford all that ordnance to drop on innocent people you'd think they could afford decent maps and a compass. And they can't even get it right when the place is lit up like a roman candle. So much for the Luftwaffe.'

'Their airforce isn't much good either.'

'For once, Agnes, we find ourselves in agreement.'

'Has Lucy come back?' says Franz.

44

It is a question Gail and Harriet have been asking with increasing urgency for two days now. With his concern for the boy, Lachlan has forgotten all about Lucy. The girls haven't. Risking welcome interruption from her, Harriet looks through Lucy's things. Almost all her life is up for public scrutiny. She is not the kind of girl to keep a diary. Introspection is not in her nature. There is no address book. The only lead Harriet can find is a piece of scrap paper with a London telephone number written on it.

The McHargs don't have a telephone. The Campbells do. Both girls agree they don't want to make the call from the Drovers or the public telephone on the promontory. Gail makes the call, prepared for sarcasm or to be rebuffed – given the tenor of their last exchange. She anticipates a relative, not a London pub. It sounds as if she has interrupted some perpetual party, contrived to affront the Luftwaffe. There is ragged singing in the background. A man takes the call. No, he's not her father, he's the publican. No, he doesn't know her personally but some of the girls who work here might. Can she hold? Without waiting for a response he goes to fetch someone else. Gail reflects that everything about this is in keeping with Lucy: the capricious departure without letting anyone know, the contact being a pub. She will probably arrive back momentarily irate that they have gone through her things, and then offer good-naturedly to forgive them when it is she who should seek forgiveness. A girl comes on. There is a suppressed hilarity in everything she says. She sounds like Lucy. Yes, she knows her. They both worked here till she decided to go to some Godforsaken place to pitchfork shit. Oh, that's where the call's from. No, no one's seen her since Christmas. Yes, she'll ask. Lucy's brother comes in here. And Gail's number?

She returns from school the following day to Eileen Campbell's news that a young man called and would call back at eight o'clock. This is said with the rising intonation of a question. Hamish makes sure she has the hall to herself when the call comes through. It comes from the same pub. The perpetual beano is still in full swing. The caller is Lucy's younger brother. Either he is drunk or has been given a garbled interpretation of her last call. He expects to speak to Lucy and is under the impression she lives there. No, he hasn't seen her, has she? No? Why did she call? Gail gives a patient reiteration of her last telephone conversation. He interrupts to add his order to the list being circulated. She finishes to a vacant silence.

'Well?' she is finally obliged to ask.

'Well what?'

'Do you think there are any grounds for concern?'

'Well, I'm not concerned.'

But the mother is. She calls at some unconscionable hour from a public box. She gets out the news that no one down here has seen either hide or hair of her before a siren goes off in the background.

'How did she seem before she left?'

'I . . . I didn't see her just before she left.'

'She's a good girl. There's no harm in her.'

'Shouldn't you take shelter?'

'Suppose. She hasn't done this before. Get her to telephone me. If I hear, I'll telephone you.'

'I will. Please go.'

Something of the older woman's panic has communicated itself. She looks out the window towards the sleeping village and feels guilt in her seclusion, imagining people huddled in Anderson shelters and on tube platforms. The following day Douglas Leckie sheepishly gives Harriet the same name he gave to Lucy, someone who knows someone who can help. Gail again makes the call. She speaks to a woman in Inverness.

'I'm only looking for my friend. I don't want to resort to threats.'

A snort of laughter at the other end of the line. 'Take my advice, dear, don't try. You don't have the accent.' And without further prompting, 'Ellinger Terrace. There's no point in looking. It's not there any more.'

'Why.'

'It's in Clydebank. You know where that used to be?'

45

A telegram has arrived in Rassaig. No one recalls this having occurred before, which would make the event portentous enough. But a war and a telegram draw the inevitable conclusion. The messenger has collected a retinue of schoolchildren, who run following his bicycle. Opening the door, Liz McKinnon almost faints at the sight and rallies against the cool of the doorjamb when he explains he is only looking for directions. She looks at the address and points in the direction of the other poor bastard. The children have only been able to keep up as he hesitated from street to street. Confident of his way, he stands on the pedals to accelerate and leaves the breathless group hovering on the edge of the village.

Following the discovery of Lucy's destination, Gail and Harriet have spent the night at the Campbells'. This was done at Eileen's insistence. Lucy's silence has grown eloquent. Both women draw the same conclusion. Harriet offers to call the number Lucy left them with. Difficult as the news is to pass on, it is going to be more difficult still to take. Gail reasons that scant as her association with Lucy's mother is, it would be better if she heard this from her and not yet another stranger.

The tiresome singing has abated to a hubbub. She leaves a message for Lucy's mother to call back and two hours later walks to the ringing hall telephone with a sense of dread. She can't explain why they think Lucy was in Clydebank without revealing the reason. Rather than have this teased out in instalments, she has prepared a mental script which she recites.

She gets to the end of this without faltering, her purpose deterring interruption, and is confronted with a dreadful silence followed by sobbing. This is cut short by the line going dead.

Numbly she walks back to her room. There is only one mental topic. She imagines Lucy, sitting in a tawdry waiting room, or worse, recuperating alone, frightened and in pain, perhaps half-way down a stairwell when everything is reduced to constituent atoms. In a way the sight of Angus is preferable to this. To have nothing to dispose of leaves a hole the same shape as the person missed. And the way they parted leaves the gap ragged.

There is a pile of corrections in the corner. She can concentrate on nothing. There is a gentle tap on the door. Harriet, yet a shade paler than sleeplessness has left them both, noiselessly crosses the room.

'There's a telegram . . .'

46

Eileen telephones Agnes. For once she is not motivated by the compulsion to circulate information she has the thrill of knowing first. There is no pleasure in this at all. She calls Agnes to ask her to send Lachlan across when he comes back.

Lachlan, weary, returns not to the anticipated aroma of dinner in the making but to news that Gail's fiancé is lying dead in Tobruk and that, according to Eileen, she is in 'a bit of a state'. He pulls back on the coat he had just shrugged to his elbows, picks up the bag and goes. He is prepared for the worst. Of all people Gail is the one he would least like to see discomposed. Eileen's vicarious description suggests melodrama. He suspects this has more to do with Eileen than Gail. Hamish Campbell meets him in the darkened yard.

'How is she?'

'She's a good one, her.'

The house is in silence as he is shown into the hall. Eileen hovers nervously outside the bedroom door. Lachlan nods as he passes. Eileen looks through the door as he enters, only to find it gently closed upon her. She doesn't know what she expected but finds she is holding the doctor's hat.

Gail is sitting in the only armchair. Harriet stands behind, stroking Gail's hair. Gail does not appear to be in a bit of a state. She is merely pensive, staring abstractedly at the floor. Lachlan sits wearily on the bed, older than him. The springs protest as much as his knees.

'Do you want me to go?' Harriet asks.

'No. How long has she been like this?'

'There's no need to talk about me in the third person.'

'Perhaps a cup of tea,' Lachlan concedes, wanting his dinner. Harriet goes.

'Who sent for you?'

'Eileen called Agnes. She said you were in a bit of a state. I doubted it. I think she thought you might be in the kind of state she would be in if she had had this much bad news one after the other.'

'I parted with both of them badly, you know.'

'I didn't know. A last parting will always be inadequate, unless you recognize it for what it is, and how many times does that happen? You can't go around making farewells assuming they will be the last.'

'There was a fair chance with Clive it was the last. I knew. I think he did too. He was frightened and I didn't have it in me to give him what might have helped.' She begins to cry almost silently. He sighs, shifts his weight to the accompaniment of groaning springs, leans across to take her hand.

'Perhaps it wasn't in you to give.'

'And I fell out with Lucy. Perhaps I'm the common denominator.'

'That girl would try the patience of a saint. Underneath my best professional manner I fell out with Lucy. I think even she realized, which shows how professional my professional manner is.'

'Why are you here, Lachlan?'

'Because I want to help you any way I can. If you want, I can give you a sedative at least to help you sleep.'

'Why would I want a sedative? Why postpone things?' He does not say, but he knows from personal experience that delay can be a merciful safety net to allow the impetus of death to intrude gradually. 'I don't want medicine, I want an explanation.'

'I'm sorry, but that's the one thing I find myself uniquely unqualified to provide.'

47

Ewan McHarg is standing in front of a seated Lachlan. The patient is staring doggedly at the ceiling, the sight chart, the colourful cross-section of the respiratory system, at anything that will distract from the embarrassment of the moment. This contrived preoccupation is not working.

On his arrival Lachlan cordially invited him to sit. Ewan coughed in preparation for his memorized delivery. The doctor appeared not to notice his patient's paralysed embarrassment as he squinted in a rather peculiar manner at Ewan from the other side of his desk, and then again from another perspective as he swivelled his chair around to the side. Returning to his original position, Lachlan proceeded to pull a large book from the bottom drawer and scribble mysteriously for a few minutes before closing the tome with a satisfied thump and cheerfully asking, 'Well, what can I do for you?'

There follows a period of prolonged swallowing on Ewan's part before the apparatus, sufficiently lubricated, will recite the script he has prepared. Even if the symptoms are harmless, which Ewan doubts, the nidus is a sign from God, a mark of His disapproval of his recalcitrance. Why would it appear there unless it was a sign of his transgression?

It seems that description alone is not sufficient. He had hoped to conclude his recital and be given something, a powder, a pill, a balm, but it seems not. He reflects, bitterly, how easy it is for others: the Catholics would get a prescription from the doctor, three Hail Marys and an Act of Contrition from the priest, and that would be that. But then, they're all damned anyway. And so, following instruction, Ewan stands, excruciated, trousers and underpants down, his stingy penis exposed to the curious gaze of this godless old man whose understanding of the situation stops at pathology.

As a matter of fact, Lachlan, thoroughly enjoying himself, is fully appreciative of both the physical and metaphysical aspects of Ewan's condition. He may not share the theology but he understands both what he is looking at and what it signifies to Ewan. To Lachlan it is a hard, insensitive lesion that is the first manifestation of syphilis. To Ewan it is the first infinitesimal indication of the limitless and eternal torment that awaits those who come by these symptoms.

'That, Mr McHarg, is what we in medical circles refer to as a chancre . . .'

48

Gail's next appearance at the Drovers is two weeks after she has received her telegram. In the interim she has given herself over entirely to work, devoting more time to this than the task merits. Her social circle at this time has shrunk to Harriet, events drawing the two girls closer, the Campbells and the occupants of Lachlan's house. Her after-hour lessons with Franz are now invariably talks across her desk on topics which seldom wander near the arbitrary curriculum. With him she never mentions Lucy or Clive or her sense of loss. He has lost far more than she has. She feels admiration tinged with shame because she thinks he has coped better than her. In the very inconsequence of their talks she is aware of a reversal: she is taking instruction. Nothing is demanded of her at the Campbells'. She can sit in companionable silence. When she wants to talk she visits Lachlan.

It is Lachlan who tells her to go to the Drovers. He tells her he enjoys her company, but that at her age she shouldn't limit her exchanges to the narrow rote of school, the Campbells and his house. He knows it is inevitable she'll run into Murdo, but in his mind the risk this presents is less than the consequence of entrenching herself into a routine whose comfort becomes a trap. He tells her he admires the way she has immersed herself in work.

'What else am I to do?'

'Others wallow.'

'If I don't occupy myself I'll go insane.'

There is an element of truth in this statement. She is not

being melodramatic. She feels that if she gives herself time for introspection she will go under. Apart from correcting school work she does not read. She avoids the news. Her insistence on being constantly occupied even involves volunteering to Hamish what help she can give after hours.

'There's not much you can do after dark. Go to the Drovers like Doctor McCready says.'

She feels this is some kind of public prescription. She tells herself she will prepare for this first drink, imagining the embarrassment of being confronted with a deferential silence. She thinks the village's opinion classifies her as some kind of emotional invalid.

The following night she has arranged to go to Lachlan's for dinner. He awaits her in the hall, coat already on.

'I've told Agnes we'll eat in the Drovers.'

'I'm – I'm . . . not sure.'

Ignoring this, he takes her arm. 'The food's inferior but at least we don't have to sit through grace.'

'I heard that.'

Putting his hand in the small of her back, he propels Gail back out the door she just came in by. He takes her arm, talking cheerfully as they walk down the hill. She stiffens as they approach the lights. Sensing the tension, he momentarily stops and turns to face her.

'Indulge an old man.'

And so she comes back. Harriet is there. There is no dampening of noise at her entrance. The only comments that come her way wouldn't have been out of place a month ago. If anything, she is diplomatically ignored. She feels the whole thing has been stage-managed by Lachlan. She watches him order at the bar. There is respect in the space automatically made for him. When she first saw him and how he was treated she did not understand the reason for deference. It was more than just age and a rural doctor's status. She understands now. Turning, he finds her watching and speaks across the gap.

'Stovies?'

'Stovies,' she agrees, with an upwelling of feeling towards him. She knows he knows. Perhaps he has seen the symptoms before. To give her time he consults with Harriet who has been waiting for them to arrive before she eats. The plates arrive at the table a moment after he has seated them with drinks. For a reason she cannot explain Gail blurts a laugh and takes her face in her hands. Looking out between splayed fingers, like a child, she sees Lachlan waiting to say something.

'Was I right?' His manner is almost mischievous.

'Yes, Lachlan. You were right. The food's inferior.'

And so she comes back.

She views the letters sent to Clive since New Year as a rambling apology that was never properly made and now cannot be. When he was alive she felt guilty at not loving him enough. Now the obligation has been removed she cannot work out whether it is him she misses or, perversely, the burden of failing to requite. If nothing else, a sense of guilt gave her emotional ballast. It held her down. It held her back. Angus is dead, and Lucy, and Clive, and Franz's family, and thousands upon thousands of others she will never know. The world is on fire. Perhaps Lucy had the right idea. What's wrong with fun? Lucy ignored the consequences, ran up a tariff and paid the compound debt in one fatal instalment. Not everyone does. Some live at a pace that outstrips consequences their whole life. Some never pay anything. And who's to say that everything we enjoy carries with it a debt? Continue thinking that way and she might as well throw in her lot with Gavin Bone. Some end up the same way Lucy did without having had any enjoyment. There is no equity. Who knows how much time is left? Perhaps it's time to stop counting costs.

She always thought of Lucy as childlike in the assumption that she deserved to have something simply because she wanted it. All Gail's better instincts, what she had learned at home and seen brutally corroborated here, tell her that if there is a purpose to anything, it's not just getting what you want. Happiness is ancillary. It is earned. It occurs, it is not invoked, and not at someone else's expense. At any other time she would pay attention to the dictates of conscience. To find him now is to do violence to her nature, to consent to be the beneficiary of someone else's misery. But the cumulative effect of all the deaths she has apprehended, either indirectly through Franz or directly in the sudden removal of Angus and Lucy and Clive, has left her morally concussed. Distinctions normally clear to her seem less so. She feels that her loss gives her some kind of dispensation. And in this blunted state she is prepared to grasp happiness, or if not happiness, anything that might temporarily pass for it, any way she can.

She begins to revisit the harbour after school hours. Blustery March turns to blustery April, scudding clouds and bloody sunsets. Green walls of water shudder the promontory in repeated explosions of foam. Observing this behaviour, Franz contrives to detain her, but she will not be deterred. It has become necessary to her, this lustral exposure. The more severe the weather, the greater her enjoyment and sense of being cleansed. She knows the interpretation Murdo will put upon this. She tells herself she cannot help what he thinks, but she knows she can, and she knows her exposure is not only for the sensation of feeling clean.

He does not approach her while she is out there. As before, her willed isolation deters. As before, he stands at the doorway and watches her pass on the way back. As before, she sees him watching.

From his eyrie at the top of the house Franz sees her

standing alone at the crossroads. She is waiting. There can be no mistake. She waits till he comes. From his window Franz sees the figures meet and begin walking together till the roofs intervene. In agitation he jumps off the table. She has cut short their after-hours lesson to go there and meet him on the way back. There is nothing accidental in this. She has chosen, perhaps without realizing what he is. But she has chosen. He does not know what to do.

While she stood waiting for Murdo her mind ran through the possible alternatives of what he or she might say. Who would speak first? There is no reason for her to be there besides the obvious one. She feels cheap, but the feeling does not deter her. As he turns the corner she feels her heart grow hot at his approach. All her speculations about what might be said are wrong.

'Where?' he says simply. His assurance is arrogant.

'I . . . I don't know.' She did not expect it to be reduced to this brutal simplicity, but she does not disagree either.

'My boat.'

'No.'

'Are you frightened of water or are you thinking of your friend and Douglas Leckie?'

'I didn't know it was common knowledge.'

''Course you did. He was so worked up he couldn't scull without trembling.'

She imagines Murdo's boat: some masculine space, tackle, no adornments, no concessions to comfort he probably considers effeminate.

'I don't want to become public knowledge the way she was.'

'At least you're honest. Where then? We can't go to mine. What about your room?'

'No. They go to bed early but not that early. And there are

dogs.' She does not want him in her room. She does not want the Campbells' hospitality abused. She wants him immediately, piercing her, and she wants him kept at arm's length.

'The schoolroom,' he says by process of elimination, and taking her hand begins walking.

Nothing in Rassaig is ever locked. He crosses the brief hallway racked at her waist height with pegs for children's coats. There is only one classroom. An intermittent street-light just beyond the short playground casts a sodium glare, throwing rhomboids of light on the opposite wall. By now he is pulling her. This place, the hanging drawings and pressed leaves, the clumsy mounted projects, a place for children, somehow it is wrong.

'No,' she says. But, like Lucy, she feels she has set in motion a train of actions she cannot now stop, only guide. She points towards the shelved store cupboard at the back of the class, still stacked with old slates and the detritus of itinerant teachers and successive years. He drags her in, kicking the door behind them so hard it ricochets open again. By this time he does not care. He pushes her against the unshelved wall, pulls open her blouse, takes her left breast in his huge hand and squeezes so hard the nipple bursts though the gap of encircling forefinger and thumb. Bending down, he takes this in his mouth. She can feel the rasp of a day's growth on the areola. She grasps his hair, pulls his mouth from the bursting nipple, tilts his head and bites his lip. Released, he takes two steps back and pulls at his clothes. She makes no move to undress but watches. In the aquarial gloom his body is a section of overlapping angular planes. Looking up, he sees her watching and momentarily stops. She marvels at the prominence of his collarbones, ribs, corrugated stomach, the density of his thighs and his penis, heavy with blood but still pendulous. He is breathing like the Minator, the sound immense in the close space. Without stepping forward he reaches across for her, pulling her so hard that both her feet leave the floor. She struggles to undress lest he tear her clothes.

'Put your arms round my neck.' It is not a request. Bending, he takes the crook of a knee in each hand. She is lifted and splayed, held in a moment of exposure that brings with it an intensity of anticipation she feels cannot be appeased till he pushes into her with an explosion of force that triggers her ferocious release. He continues to gore her, snorting. She spasms again and feels him arch till finally he leans against her, shoulders heaving, shuffling forward till she is sandwiched against the wall, her breasts pressed, her back indented against the exposed masonry.

'Poor Clive,' she thinks. Like Franz she has just made the discovery that the dead become deader.

49

It seems to Lachlan that beyond Rassaig the world continues to tear itself to pieces at a furious pace. Tobruk, a place no one had ever heard of, continues to dominate the headlines as others die, to line up statistically with Clive and generate posthumous telegrams. His reading of the evening newspaper is as thorough as ever, he understands the words in front of him, but somehow the outside has lately come to be less real to him. Since the arrival of Franz, the completion of his own world has relegated what lies beyond this domestic sphere. His greatest concern is not for the outside world but for its intrusion on this one. He is not thinking of himself.

He begins to tally the passing of the weeks not by the ebb and flow of hostilities, the campaigns he monitored so diligently and still abstractly follows, but by his weekly visit to the cinema in Oban with Franz that has become a staple of their routine. They drive there for Saturday matinee showings. Agnes goes with them only once. Make-believe of any kind entails for her an anticlimax. Why drive all that distance to see people dress up, walk about and say a lot of memorized words? Lachlan, with conscious irony, tells her she has no soul. But there is another reason she doesn't go. She knows Lachlan treasures time alone with Franz and she thinks the boy also enjoys it more if she stays behind. The cinema has given them a shared appreciation of something that eludes her and she is happy to leave them to it.

To Franz's embarrassment and the irritation of those in surrounding darkness, Lachlan keeps up a whispered commentary over the Pathé News reports, translating the euphemisms of war reportage. But when the main feature comes on he sits in rapt attention. Franz has never seen him transported. They take turns at choosing the films, by unspoken mutual consent avoiding anything with a contemporary war theme. The exception is *Waterloo Bridge*, Lachlan's choice, at which he weeps unashamedly. Robert Taylor's pained recollection, pacing the bridge, straining through the mist of amnesia to recall poignant instalments of his past love affair with Vivien Leigh, has Lachlan honking like a migratory goose into his handkerchief. Dramatic effect is deflated when the lights come up and he pragmatically states, 'I don't think that was an accurate portrayal of remission from amnesia.'

Franz thinks the tears were an anomaly till Lachlan's next choice. *That Hamilton Woman*, with Vivien Leigh as Lady Hamilton being again rendered inconsolable, this time by the death of Laurence Olivier as Nelson, leaves Lachlan equally tearful. In return for confidences, Lachlan has told Franz something of his own history, leaving out mention of his wife. The boy marvels that a man who has served in a theatre of war, who is confronted with disease as part of his everyday business, who has the constitution to return from a deathbed to his dinner, is reduced to tears by the situations counterfeited on the screen. His own preference is for action. He chooses *The Sea Hawk* and *Zorro*. The trip home involves Lachlan pontificating on the relative merits of what they have seen till the boy inevitably falls asleep. Tyrone Power as Zorro is a 'fop', only marginally better than 'that ham Fairbanks who did it before. Best thing about sound was that it got rid of him.' The only saving grace is Basil Rathbone. Errol Flynn as the swashbuckling privateer in *The Sea Hawk* is a 'posturing hormonal lout'. The only saving grace is Claude Rains. Lachlan chooses *Pride and Prejudice* to glimpse his screen sweetheart, confiding to his sleeping passenger that 'parts of me long dormant are quickened by Greer Garson. She is a fine, fine woman.'

Making another exception to their unspoken rule, they see *The Great Dictator*. Franz is enthralled, Lachlan only enjoying it because of the boy's delight. They see *His Girl Friday*, both enjoying the rapid-fire dialogue; *The Philadelphia Story* – 'That Cary Grant can teach the Americans something about diction'; *Rebecca* – 'Never trust a man with a moustache', 'But the bad man was clean-shaven', 'Don't trust them either'; *The Little Foxes* – 'You know, there are patients I've wanted to deny medicine to the way Bette Davis did today.'

They eat fish and chips out of paper in the car before the drive back and Franz falls asleep to Lachlan's running commentary and the pervasive smell of malt vinegar. Like exhaust fumes recalling his departure from Prague, it is one of the smells that will evoke for him exact reminiscences for the rest of his life.

Gail meets Murdo twice more on the way back from the harbour. They adjourn to the cupboard. Periods between meetings are sufficiently long to mark the occasions with the same urgency. In an attempt to convince herself that this is something more than a mercenary exchange she persuades him to stay with her one Saturday night in a hotel. Oban is too small, too local. Braving the possibility of more bombs, they choose Glasgow and travel separately. On the train she tries unsuccessfully to read. She sits in the room awaiting his arrival. He has been drinking by the time he arrives. They fuck without preamble. Getting up for a bath afterwards she catches sight of herself in the mirror. There is a bite mark on her shoulder and a dull bruise on one buttock where his hand cradled her. He lies sprawled on the bed behind, sleeping off the beer, his long muscular frame compressed by the perspective. She has not prepared herself for this scrutiny and in her face catches a look of complete misery. She wakes him while she dresses. He does not care where they eat, it is all fuel to him, as long as there is beer.

Over dinner she makes several attempts to get the conversation going, employing the prompts she has mentally rehearsed during the journey down when her book defeated her. She is trying to introduce an element of normality into the situation, to have the kind of exchange normal couples do, even though she knows normal couples don't rehearse inconsequential conversation in advance. She is desperately trying to help herself temporarily forget that she is having an affair with a married man since the thought of the wife she has only ever seen at a distance now insinuates itself between them, even during the act. It does not work. He is civil enough in his responses but each attempt is a cul-de-sac. He no longer employs the caustic humour of their first meetings because he has no need to: he has achieved his object and will continue to do so when she is near and the impulse is upon him. She realizes he is more interested in the beer and in the thought of resuming their activities.

As soon as the food is finished he pays quickly. On the way out he takes her arm and holds this at a height that leaves her heel on his side barely touching the ground. He walks too quickly back to the hotel. She is about to say something when she realizes she has no ground for complaint: it was this kind of handling she waited for at the crossroads. Despite having done this three hours before he again treats her with the same urgency he has shown in the schoolroom cupboard. He falls into a light doze afterwards. She can hear him swallowing loudly in his sleep. She begins to calculate how long it will be till she can remove her cap. She knows he will wake and want to do this again so it will all depend on that. Perhaps he will want to do this again before they have to check out. It did not seem to occur to him to provide condoms. The timing of the whole night has really been dictated by what he wants. What, she wonders, does she want, really want?

He duly wakes an hour later, roused by the proximity of a warm woman in his bed. As he moves across he notices the pillow is wet. This one has been crying, he surmises, as he turns her on to her face and kneels up.

Catriona Bone, wife of Gavin, is staring doggedly at Lachlan's sight chart, framed between her parted thighs, as was the molten globe Lucy witnessed emerge from the abortionist's floor before it expanded to render her visit redundant. From Catriona's supine perspective the arbitrary letters descend from knees to pubis in dwindling legibility, the bottom row being lost in the grey smudge of Lachlan's hair.

Her contrived preoccupation does not work either. Lachlan straightens, turning away as he does so to conceal the smile that he knows has formed itself on his face. He turns back when he has schooled his features.

'That, Mrs Bone, is what we in medical circles refer to as a chancre . . .'

Abandoning the idea of walking to the harbour, Gail turns from the schoolroom in the direction of the Campbells' farm. Although still drawing down early the evenings have lengthened. When not staying late at school she can get back in daylight, watch bright cold sunsets over a cup of tea from the kitchen window. Late-afternoon gusts hum in the fence wires, flattening her dress against her legs.

All concessions to discretion have been hers. When she returned, alone, from Glasgow, she found that Murdo had accepted a lift there and back from someone in the village. She has already concluded that he has made little attempt to conceal their meetings. She reasons that if she becomes common currency, as Lucy was, she has only herself to blame. She thinks of her exchanges with Lucy and considers herself a hypocrite. She once thought Lucy's moral development was as retarded as Angus's literacy. She lacks this excuse for her behaviour. Eileen Campbell has been more reserved of late. Perhaps she knows. If she does, it's a matter of time before everyone does. Eileen's opinion is of little consequence to her but Lachlan's isn't. Nor is the opinion of at least another dozen people she likes up here. Lucy could afford to be blasé. She didn't teach. Gail wonders how tenable her position will be. Behaviour like this has corroborated Gavin Bone's opinion. The night she spent with Murdo didn't dispel the qualms she felt on the way there, if anything it increased them. She had gambled that the pleasure of sexual release was sufficient antidote to the guilt of fucking another woman's husband, and she was wrong. She is struck by her own selfishness.

These thoughts are running through her mind when she hears her name being called, propelled by the wind behind her. She turns. Isabel Dougan is coming into sight round the bend. With one hand she is pushing a large creaking pram. The other holds the hand of a small boy, who must be no more than three, trotting beside her, trying to keep pace. With the wind at her back Isabel is having difficulty balancing the ensemble. They are on the stretch of road that runs out of the village. There are no diversions until the entrance to the Campbells' farm. There is no pavement. Continuous farm traffic has left the surface uneven. Isabel is struggling with the pram through the ruts. Hating herself, Gail turns away and starts to accelerate, her loose scarf a whirling plume before her. Her name is called again, high and plaintively. Worst of all, it is her Christian name. Refusing to turn she walks doggedly on, wondering what to do if this pursuit continues all the way to the farm. Perhaps she should continue walking past the entrance.

'Gail! Gail! Please don't make me run.' This is cut short by the sound of the boy crying. Gail turns. The child has fallen. Having suddenly stopped while still holding his hand, Isabel is trying to prevent the skewing pram veering into the ditch. Despite the gap Gail can see her crying. She runs back against the wind to where they are and stoops to the boy. His knee is bleeding. Her obvious thought is why is he wearing shorts in this weather? Picking him up and turning to Isabel, the answer is obvious. The pram is battered, the covers good, but Isabel is very shabby. What money she has been given has obviously gone to them. And that night in Glasgow he disdained her offer of dividing the bill and paid it all as a point of principle, paid it prematurely in a hurry to get back to fuck her.

She despises herself.

'You wouldn't want him if you knew. I've got the marks and I still want him.'

'Look . . . I'm . . .'

'Please don't take him. Please.'

Gail turns her attention to the knee, unable to look at the other woman's face. She takes her handkerchief and wipes the blood away. The scrape almost immediately turns bloody again. She wipes it again, and asking him to stand ties the handkerchief round in a loose bandage. The mother watches this, waiting for Gail to look at her.

'I don't know if he can walk back.'

'Say you won't see him again.' The boy limps to her and wrapping his arms round her legs buries his face in her thigh.

'I'll carry him.'

'I can see to the boy. Don't pretend to make this about the boy. Say you won't see him again.'

'I already decided . . .' This sounds limp. How insulting would it seem that she has already given up someone this woman is prepared to abase herself to keep? Better to let her think her appeal has prevailed. 'I won't see him again.'

'Promise.'

'I promise.'

At this Isabel turns her attention to the boy. She hauls the pram round to face the village. Facing into the wind it seems more steady till she lifts the boy and balances him sitting across the pram, knees crooked over the side rim. The whole thing gives a precarious lurch. Holding the handrail, she busies herself with the unseen baby. Satisfied with the arrangement, she braces the handrail against her stomach while using both hands to tighten her headscarf. The whole thing is done with intense preoccupation. Having got what she came for Gail feels herself dismissed.

'It'll be hard, all the way back . . . I'll carry him.'

The other woman turns. The face is ravaged. 'All the way back? To my house? To meet him and explain? You might even meet my mother-in-law.'

Leaning at an acute angle she pushes the pram forward into the wind. Progress is laborious. Gail watches till they approach the bend. No amount of standing on an exposed sea wall will wipe this away. The pram stops, Isabel leaning forward. She turns, holding the handkerchief, and throws it limply in Gail's direction. The wind snatches it and carries it high towards the sea.

52

Gavin's ablutions are in vain. The lengthier, the colder, the more rigorous, the more petrifying, all have been to no avail. Perhaps it is a sign, a test, he a latter-day Job. There is some comfort in this. But if so, would he not be informed? He is chastising himself to make atonement for a sin he cannot place having committed, but is that not the scheme of things? Iniquity covers its own tracks and it cannot be for nothing that these things have appeared where they have. Morning and night he mortifies his penis with cold water only to watch it slowly revive with its marks of sin still intact.

He has been tested in his faith before now and found wanting. Some time ago, when these symptoms first presented themselves, he had gone to that heathen doctor. The cough had been a pretext, an introduction to allow him time to assess the doctor's competence. The consultation had degenerated when the subject of that other heathen, the one who tried to pollute the children of their congregation with the heresy of evolution, came up. The whole incident had been a sign that he had no business seeking help from pagans. True succour only comes from Him.

If only he knew Lachlan would be delighted to measure the skull again, the last reading botched by Gavin's restless aggression, and say: 'That, Mr Bone, is what we in medical circles refer to as a chancre . . .'

53

Her manner in the classroom is subdued. Morning and lunch-time break the rain continues to pour. Confined indoors, the children are restless. The windows are covered in condensation. Her head feels like a pressure cooker. By two o'clock the rain has abated. Released for the afternoon break, they pour frenziedly into the playground, a little compound of puddles. She takes the window pole and opens each window in turn. The smell of wet vegetation after rain blows through, lifting the condensation, easing her headache. She leaves the children longer than normal before going out to sound the bell and eases the short remainder of the afternoon by reading aloud to them.

Franz approaches when the rest have dispersed. She is cradling her forehead in her hand and recognizes his shoes on the other side of the desk. Without looking up she says, 'Not this afternoon, please,' more abruptly than she intended. She looks up apologetically but by this time he has turned and is walking away. She thinks: 'Yet another thing I have misjudged.'

He is not offended but concerned, as he lugs his Gladstone bag towards home. His destination is next right, up the hill. He sees Murdo walking towards him. If he does not make the turn before Murdo reaches it they will pass each other on the pavement. He stands indecisively wondering whether to go back in the direction he has just come from. Over any distance Murdo will catch up. Summoning himself, he runs towards the turn-off, towards Murdo, and makes the junction before he does. He pants up the hill and turns back to look down and see him pass.

If Murdo has even seen him he shows no recognition. His face is set as he walks purposefully towards the school. Franz has seen him often enough at the croft to know what that look presages. Confused, he looks down at the bag. If he goes for Lachlan it will slow him down. If he gets Lachlan what will he do? He is old. Murdo is strong. Lachlan will call someone before he leaves. All this will take time. In a fit of indecision he drops the bag, runs half a dozen paces up the hill, stops, returns. His breathing is accelerating. Agitated, he opens the bag and looks in to reassure himself.

Gail is making her rounds with the pole, closing the windows, when she hears the outer door open and close. He walks in with as little forewarning as Gavin did that day. She knew the meeting would be inevitable but wanted more time. She would have preferred some other venue, somewhere she could have walked away from. It doesn't yet occur to her to be afraid.

'You didn't come.' There is no rising intonation, no incredulity or sense of disappointment, just a flat statement of fact.

'No. I'm sorry. And if I had come it would only have been to say we can't meet again.'

'You're upset because of your friend.'

'He was my fiancé.'

'I was thinking about the girl. Whatever he was it didn't stop you.'

'No. You're right. It was all wrong. I was wrong.'

'You're out of sorts.'

This elicits a surprised ironical laugh. The conclusion she came to, the self-reproach for suspending her conscience, the humiliating encounter with Isabel, all reduced to an evaluation that just might adequately describe an overtired child. Looking at him, she realizes he is serious.

'I thought I had an excuse. I was wrong. Other people have lost more and don't behave as badly as I did.'

'I think you should think more about yourself.'

'You mean about you and me.'

'Aye. At least with me you weren't miserable.' She forbears to tell him that this isn't true.

'You make it sound as if you were doing me a favour.'

'Maybe. You'll forget more easily – with me.'

'Sex as a miracle cure. Doctor Dougan. You missed your calling, Murdo. And what were you trying to forget?'

As she says this she turns away, missing the frown that has descended on him. No one ever practises sarcasm on him, least of all a woman. Looking up, she sees the cast of his features and for the first time feels wary. Nor does she like the solitude they have so recently sought. She was going to mention his wife but doesn't. What was it the poor woman said? Something about bearing marks. At the time she thought this was said for effect, figuratively. Now she is not sure. Somehow she senses that if she does say something he will take it out on Isabel. She looks at him resignedly, leans against the desk and sighs. He takes this as a concession and nods in the direction of the cupboard.

'I can't. You're married.'

'What the fuck has that to do with anything?'

'If you don't understand I can't explain.'

'Well, you better try. And you better explain how me being married last week and the week before that didn't matter then but does now.'

She only realizes he is angry as his voice gets quieter and quieter. In the otherwise silent classroom she has to strain to catch the last words.

'I wasn't thinking about your wife and children then, only about myself.'

234

'Well, don't think about them. Leave me to think about them. They've got fuck all to do with you.'

She realizes there is no reasoning with him.

'Murdo, please go. I'm sorry. I really am. I had no right to let you think . . .'

'Get in the cupboard.'

'It's finished.'

He walks past her towards the cupboard. Instinctively she expects a blow and shrinks. But he does not touch her. His left hand reaches the handle and wrenches the door open. He stands for a moment, as if committing the interior to memory. Looking back briefly to her, his right hand reaches across the gap and grasps her hair. He looks back towards the cupboard and in one convulsive movement yanks her towards him and propels her in.

Her head collides with the shelf of redundant slates. Momentarily dazed, it takes her a moment to grasp what is happening. He walks in, slamming the door behind him.

54

As Lachlan returns from a late house call he finds Agnes in the drive, ill-dressed for the cold, gesturing to him. He has not seen a similar look on her face since she handed him the Clydebank headlines. She shouts something that is obscured by the crunch of gravel as he stops the car in a skewed diagonal and climbs out.

'Franz.' She waves towards the house. He snatches his bag and hurries, making for the stairs. 'The lounge,' she says. He walks in. Franz is sitting in Lachlan's chair staring rigidly before him, rocking slightly. The intermittent blinking reminds Lachlan of the first time he met the boy, but a bat would not hear the surf from here. He takes both his hands and looks as intently into the boy's face as he did that first night, illuminated by car headlights on the clifftop.

The lips are forming a word, again and again, which he fails to enunciate. Pressing his hands, Lachlan nods in time with the rocking, agreeing with what he has not heard, teasing out the sound.

'Gail. Gail. Gail. Go to Gail.'

'Where?'

'Go to Gail.'

'Where is Gail?'

'Gail.'

He goes into the hall to the telephone and asks the operator to connect him to the Campbells'. Agnes dons her coat while he waits for the connection.

'Where are you going?'

'The school. If you go to the farm pick me up as you pass.'

The number rings out. When asked if he wants to hang on he drops the receiver and makes for the car. He would not leave the boy alone but there is no help for it. He is barely out of the drive when he comes across Agnes. She climbs in. He drops her at the bottom of the hill, a minute from the school, and accelerates off towards the Campbells' farm. The suspension protests at the same surface that rattled Isabel's pram. He is jostled so violently his foot leaves the accelerator. He drives straight into the yard, leaves the engine running and walks through the front door. He shouts from the threshold. No one responds. He walks to Gail's room, looks in just long enough to assure himself she isn't there, and goes back towards the car, absently noticing the trail of slurry his hurried entrance has left.

He swerves out of the yard. It is dark now. He puts the headlights on, shading the ruts in the same cratered road back. He stops with a screech in the playground. The door is locked. He bangs, shouting.

55

Having looked in his bag and overcome his indecision, Franz
begins walking back down the hill towards the junction. Gravity helps. When he reaches the flat his resolve deserts him and
he has to gather himself, pick up the bag and again begin
walking. The outer door is closed. He pushes this open tenta-
tively. Rows of vacant pegs are visible in the deepening gloom,
each shadowed by light coming from the open door of the
classroom beyond. He pushes this door further open and walks
slowly inside. There is no one here. He had not known what
he would interrupt but did not expect to find the classroom
empty. He stands in the middle of the room and looks around.
There is an added apprehension at the novelty of being here,
alone, at this time.

He stops at the sound of a stifled concussion, tilts and slowly
rotates his head, trying to discern the source. At the repetition
he is utterly certain that it comes from the cupboard. He has
been there once. The fact that this noise comes from some
dark, unused alcove terrifies him. Walking slowly across, he
pauses at the door. He hears something like a sob. Very
gradually he turns the handle and lets the door swing inwards.
It takes him a minute to assemble the image in his mind to
realize what he is seeing. Murdo is standing with his back to
him. His free hand is tugging at the opening of his trousers.
His other hand is otherwise occupied, holding a dark coil
mostly obscured by the bulk of the small of his back. Only
when he sees the heels of the woman's shoes either side of
the heels of Murdo's boots does he realizes he is witnessing the

same spectacle he saw in the croft from another perspective. The man is standing between the woman's parted legs. The boy's next moves are very slow and deliberate. He puts the bag on the ground, opens its yawning mouth and reaches inside.

Straining bent across a broken trestle, Gail sees the light from the classroom on the far wall. Murdo doesn't. His eyes are closed. With the half-dozen or so women he has done this to he finds greatest arousal from the struggle. When they are subdued the remainder is automatic until the explosive conclusion. He has even found the need to galvanize himself through the passive interval until the urgency again takes over. His wife no longer offers the stimulation of resistance as she did on the first few occasions. The temporary suffocation that he improvised has turned out to be a happy experiment, the struggle for air simulating the same spasms he is about to enjoy again.

The first bang is so loud in the acoustics of the deserted classroom that it arrests even him. His first thought is that the roof has collapsed. Anyone coming in from outside could be forgiven for confusing cause and effect: the explosion of the display case, mounted on the classroom wall above the cupboard, coincides exactly with the detonation. Shattered glass rains down like ice, vivid fragments of butterfly wings spiralling through the smoke to come to settle on the littered floor. At the next roar the heel of Murdo's right boot blasts off to career against the opposite wall, taking with it an ellipse of bone and tissue from the base of Achilles tendon to rear instep. The force of this pivots him away from Gail to face in the direction of the light. He lets go of her hair and looks down. He thought there was something in the cupboard that had pushed him. He has automatically transferred the weight on his right foot to the ball to make allowance for the heel that is no longer there. In its place he sees a ragged bleeding concavity.

Looking up, he sees the smoke disperse to reveal that skinny little Jewish kid with eyes like saucers staring down the wavering barrel of the service revolver that he holds with erratic determination. The gun looks immense in his hands. Another report and the shelf to Murdo's immediate left fragments, driving splinters of wood into his shoulder and neck.

'You fucking little kike!' he screams. Only as an adult, when sufficient time has elapsed to allow him to look back at this emblazoned moment with some kind of impartial curiosity, does Franz wonder if Murdo was incensed at the loss of his heel, or the theft of his gun.

The next report detaches part of the doorjamb to Franz's immediate left. He is wavering violently. He could have just as easily hit Gail's heel. Now it looks as if he lacks the accuracy to hit anything within the frame of the door. Murdo attempts a step forward with his truncated foot and nearly falls when he transfers the weight to the other leg. The span of his huge arms is almost the breadth of the oblong cupboard. Spreading his arms to steady himself by touching alternate sides, he begins to slide towards the boy. Extending his damaged foot first and catching it up, he repeats this in jerking progress to the door.

He is now looming in the frame, completely obscuring Gail, presenting a larger target. He must be aware of the risk. He had wanted to fight. His idea of being under fire didn't encompass some fucking little yid making him a fucking cripple with his own fucking gun. He is screaming now, a hoarse, continuous ululation, his immense reserves of anger boiling to a state rendering him incapable of speech. Concentrating on the gun without looking up, Franz discharges the two remaining rounds in quick succession and continues to pull the trigger. The cloud before him seems to him enormous; the noise temporarily deafens. He anticipates Murdo lurching out the smoke to grasp him. He is too frightened to move, the paralysis complete with the exception of his hands.

The fifth shot dislodges one of the splinters sticking out of Murdo's shoulder without touching the flesh. At the sixth a crimson flower instantaneously blooms in his throat. The bullet passes clean through the larynx, windpipe and carotid artery and embeds itself in the wall behind, above Gail's cowed head, with a spattering of blood and tissue. Had she stood up more quickly it would have continued its trajectory through the back of her skull. Stopped dead by its puncturing momentum, Murdo clasps his throat. Blood spouts frivolously from the severed artery out the ragged hole in the back of his neck. His shattered foot, unable to take the sudden weight transferred to it, retracts. He slumps against the wall of the cupboard and slowly sits, the leg with the damaged foot folding unnaturally beneath him. The screaming stops abruptly with the disappearance of his vocal cords. The pierced whistle that escapes him descends in register to a gurgle. From his sitting position he leans forward, one hand to his neck, the second on the ground, as if intent on continuing towards the boy. The gurgling, after some moments, concludes in bloody frothing. He collapses, the impact of his forehead with the parquet twisting his head, forcing him to look back and upwards into the cupboard.

Gail stands slowly, trembling with shock. She pulls down the skirt he had forced over her hips and turns to see Murdo lying on the floor looking senselessly at the ceiling. A black puddle is radiating from the back of his head. Above this, framed in the doorway, Franz is disclosed through the dissipating smoke, holding some kind of monstrous gun. In the ensuing silence the only sound is the remorseless click of the hammer descending on empty chambers that slows to a stop as the boy's fingers cramp.

56

At his repeated banging Agnes opens the door and pulls him inside.

'For God's sake keep the noise down!'

'Is she here?'

'In there. Where's your bag?'

'In the car.'

'What use is it there?'

'Does she need help?'

'None that you can give without your bag. Go and get it.'

In the past she has inveigled money out of him for whatever cause she thinks he should subscribe to, she has cajoled him into providing assistance for this or that, she has implored, entreated, importuned, petitioned and persuaded, but she has never ordered him to do anything. Until now. If the case was not so desperate he would have a word with her about her tone. But instead he goes to the car. As far as he is concerned it is the work of a moment to retrieve the bag and return. Infuriatingly, she has locked the door again. Again he bangs.

'I said we had to keep the noise down.'

'Where is she?' This time he will not be deflected. He precedes her into the classroom. Gail is sitting behind her desk. From this distance there is an ominous semblance of normality, aside from the smell that reminds him of recently discharged fireworks. As he gets closer he notices her colour. She is paler than Franz.

'What happened?'

Agnes indicates a point on the floor. From his perspective this is obscured by the surface of a desk.

'Whatever you do, lock the door behind me.'

'Where are you going this time?' Despite the gravity of the situation he cannot keep the asperity from his voice. But she has already gone, and both infuriated and anxious he dumps his bag, goes back to obey her instructions and locks the door. As he approaches Gail again he is aware of crunching underfoot. Looking down, he sees glass fragments and some kind of coloured scraps he is walking through. Looking up, he notices some kind of stain radiating out beneath the closed cupboard door that Agnes had obviously been pointing to. Doing his best not to stand in this, he opens the door.

Very few things shock Lachlan. He says nothing, and forgoing his punctiliousness walks into the cupboard and lifts a wrist to take the expected reading. The blood has radiated out from the wound to the point of coagulation on the cold floor. Lachlan drops the wrist and steps back over the body blocking the doorway. He now adds congealed blood to the slurry on his shoes. His feet make sticking noises as he approaches Gail, still silent.

Looking up at him she whispers, 'He's dead.'

'Yes,' he says, not knowing if she is looking for confirmation, not knowing he also is whispering, and adds, 'Any death is a tragedy but I can't find it in myself to say I'm sorry.'

'He was shot while trying to rape me. I don't think it was the first time he's tried to rape anyone. Those poor women didn't have anyone to intervene. Where's Franz?'

'At home.'

'How is he?'

'His sole concern appeared to be you.'

The door sounds again. The sound seems very loud. They

exchange a startled look. Both begin to speak at once. Politely he defers.

'He saved me. That bastard would have raped me and then done God knows what. He's been through enough. He's not taking responsibility for this.'

'I couldn't agree more.' He stands stiffly and walks towards the door. Michael is alone. For the first time in his life Lachlan is frightened of a uniform.

'Agnes told me to come here. You look as if you were expecting someone else, Lachlan.'

'You'd better come in.'

Curiously, Michael locks the door at his back. He takes the same route as Lachlan's last entrance, crunching through the same glass, pulverizing the same friable wings. Attracted by the same stain, he opens the same door and stands in the same attitude of contemplation Lachlan did before checking for the pulse he knew he would not find. Deciding not to repeat the examination, he simply looks at Lachlan and says, 'Dead?'

The question is so ridiculous that in other circumstances Lachlan would laugh. But he cannot laugh. He merely nods assent. At the thought of due process taking its course he is, again for the first time in his professional career, crestfallen. Who knows what the law would decide would be appropriate punishment? The best they could hope for would be some kind of exoneration, mitigating circumstances, testimony of character witnesses . . . But any kind of investigation is likely to bring the boy's credentials to light. The only paperwork he has is a dead woman's impassioned plea in three languages. His being here cannot be legal, whatever that abstraction might mean in a world where each half of its population is intent on destroying the other. It is difficult enough to divine meaning in normal circumstances. From the colossal turmoil of the world beyond Rassaig Lachlan can only tease out one thread of sense and he cannot give rational account of it: for whatever reason the boy arrived and Lachlan was here to receive him. This is the only thing that matters. An enquiry will separate them. He has no doubt of it. Realizing his despondence is not helping the boy, he rallies.

'I know there has been a crime and therefore there is the question of accountability—'

'It was me,' Gail interrupts simply. Having said this she seems to think she has said sufficient to settle the issue. Michael is again looking into the cupboard. Holding the doorjamb, he leans forward without stepping into the stain. The question seems to come out of the cupboard.

'And how was this accomplished, miss?'

'He pushed me into the cupboard and bent me over . . . something. He was behind, trying to rape me when the weapon was . . . discharged . . .'

'I'm assuming he was shot in the heel first because the other wound looks like it finished him. It's interesting that you managed to shoot him in the heel when he was standing behind you.'

'She's overwrought. I'm prepared to take responsibility.'

'I've no doubt you are, Lachlan.' He straightens and turns, evidently satisfied with his scrutiny. His voice no longer comes from the cupboard. There is another bang at the door. 'This isn't just another thing you can shoulder or fix simply because you're the village doctor.' He begins to walk towards the entrance. Lachlan feels that unless they reach some kind of accommodation before the door opens, the boy's fate is sealed.

'Michael!' It is a shout. 'As long as it stops here, with me, I'll sign anything. If you agree I'll even write a statement at your dictation.'

'Everyone knows no one can read your writing, Lachlan.'

He has reached the door and unlocks it. Agnes comes in

with Fraser Laing, the harbour master, one of Lachlan's frequent chess opponents. Agnes locks the door at her back and gestures the two younger men towards her. They are both so much taller they have to bend as she talks in an intense undertone. Michael nods and turns to the classroom.

'Lachlan says he's prepared to take responsibility.'

Agnes says, 'Don't be so silly, man. It's not your responsibility to take.'

'And Gail over there shot a man who was standing behind her.'

Agnes continues, 'If we bring them in on it do you not think they'll put two and two together? Where's the gun either of you are happy to admit having used? Between here and the surgery or more likely in the Gladstone bag it came out of.'

'For God's sake!' He is speaking to them all. His tone is an entreaty. 'That boy's endured as much as it's humanly possible to take, more than could reasonably be expected of anyone three times his age. To institutionalize him now . . .' He falters, again a first, publicly at a loss. There is a brief silence. Agnes leaves Michael's side, walks across to him and touches his cheek.

'Lachlan dear, you're a bright man but sometimes you haven't got the common sense God gave you. No one's going to destroy that lovely boy's life. Certainly not for a fornicating wastrel like that. Much as I would have liked to settle this among ourselves I know we can't. Realistically there's a minimum number we need. We have to let some know to stop everyone knowing. What you'd call irony. That's why I brought my cousin.'

'I didn't know Michael was your cousin.'

'That's because he's not. Fraser's my cousin.'

'Michael's my cousin,' Fraser says.

'But to get rid of him effectively he's going to have to go in a boat,' Michael says.

'His boat,' Agnes says, with conviction that carries the moment.

Lachlan reflects that impoverishment of the genetic pool aside, he always knew there was advantage to be found from living in a small community.

57

At the combined insistence of all the cousins Lachlan is persuaded to go home. 'This is heavy work,' Michael insists, nodding to the cupboard.

'You're no spring chicken, Lachlan,' Agnes says.

'Neither of us are, Agnes. And tell me, do you intend heaving a corpse around in the night? You think an old woman and a cadaver won't attract some attention?'

'You're wandering again, Lachlan. As long as you've known you've taken care of everything and everyone you come in contact with. You've done more than anyone could expect. It's time for the younger ones. Go home. Take Gail. For once let someone else cope.'

The sense is obvious. Once he agrees, a great weariness possesses him. He has trouble picking up his bag. Seeing this, Michael picks it up for him and goes with him to the car. Agnes brings Gail. All four return to the house in Lachlan's car. Agnes puts Gail to bed. Lachlan administers a sedative. Agnes calls the Campbells to say Gail has been taken poorly on a visit and will stay at least the night. Agnes puts Franz to bed. Lachlan kisses him goodnight and tells him everything is being taken care of, that he will not let anything happen to him. From the doorway Agnes watches the exchange. Lachlan returns to the lounge where Michael is waiting. Agnes appears with three large whiskies.

Michael delves into the abandoned Gladstone bag and pulls out the revolver.

'Fortunate he shot that bastard on Friday. If it had been a

school day tomorrow we might really have been in trouble.'

When Lachlan is at last persuaded to go to bed Agnes goes to her kitchen and returns with a bucket, bleach and various cloths. She directs Michael to the linen closet to take what he needs.

'Have you any rope? Tarpaulin? Anything we could use.'

'Try the garage and the shed. Take anything.'

They return to the school, the headlights out. Michael parks a distance away. Fraser lets them in. They lock the door. The two men take what Michael has brought and go into the cupboard. Fraser goes to fetch his van. The last Agnes ever sees of Murdo is his shrouded figure being heaved out the schoolroom door, which she locks at their backs.

As she sweeps the glass and butterfly wings into a dustpan a rowing boat sculls quietly out. As she kneels down with cloths and bleach to the congealed stain, two boats, all lights out, throttle quietly out the harbour into the dark expanse.

She has to make repeated trips to the toilet to wring out the cloths and refill her bucket. With the forethought Lachlan has taken for granted all these years, she has stolen his penknife to prise what bullets she can find from the woodwork and masonry. Michael returns in the early hours for her. He stands on a desk to dismantle what remains of the mounted case. He will arrange for someone he knows to come and replace the shattered doorjamb and shelf. He drives her back, leaves the car in the driveway and walks down the hill, whistling. She rinses the bucket, brings her dressing gown to the kitchen and undresses in front of the iron range. Raking up the fire, she throws her clothes into the flames one item at a time, followed by the wrung-out cloths that hiss on contact. She wraps herself in the gown and goes upstairs to run a bath. Finally, clean by her own standards, she dries herself, dresses for bed and makes a quick inventory, looking in on all three before going to her own room. The last thing she does before putting out the light is to locate her bedside rosary. In the darkness she begins a decade for the repose of Murdo's soul. Her mind's eye sees a bundle, nestling in silt, fifty freezing fathoms down. The tarpaulin exudes a wraith that rises through the blackness, breaking the surface without a whisper of turbulence to be drawn further up, like morning mist sucked towards the sun, ascending to its luminous reckoning. She prays for an easy quietus, her mouth forming the words in little susurrations, slowing as she tires, sleep concluding her whispered conversation with God.

58

During a bright May morning in 1942 Dr Lachlan McCready stands near the edge of the platform contemplating the rails. At some distance, because he has detached himself from the little group, stand Agnes, Gail and Franz. The Gladstone bag is no longer the boy's constant adjunct. It has become a dispensable accessory. It sits on top of Gail's bags. It is on this forlorn little pyramid that Lachlan now concentrates, looking anywhere other than at the people he has just walked away from. The only other people on the platform are an elderly couple, awaiting a relative, who sit in the doorless waiting room in chatty conclave with the postman. He is regaling them with some shaggy dog story to the old man's sniggering amusement. The wife is pretending to be scandalized and casts reproving looks around to advertise her disapproval, lifting her hand to her mouth from time to time to conceal her smirk. Lachlan bets what he is saying is really unfunny, some seaside postcard toilet humour. At any other time he would take keen interest in the size and shape of the three skulls and perhaps even eavesdrop, correlating shape to the banality of the exchange. But he is too preoccupied. The three chortling from the booth are in marked contrast to the dismal silence that has descended on the good doctor and his companions. Lachlan walks back to the group who all look at him expectantly. Agnes is in the middle, holding the other two by an arm each.

'Franz, I want you to look out for the train's arrival and tell me the instant it comes into sight.'

'All right.'

He wants as much notice of the train's arrival as possible because he has still not decided what it is he wants to say. He wants to give the boy something to take with him, some appropriate distillation of what he feels, that encapsulates what they have gone through, something uplifting that will help sustain him.

It was Agnes who came and told Lachlan the boy would have to go, at least for a while. In doing this she merely articulated something he already knew. She started by saying, 'There's no going back from a killing,' and he sat, wordless, listening to the cards fall into place and her inexorable reasoning towards the conclusion he had already reached.

Morag Dougan bore the news of her son's disappearance stoically. Perhaps she had had an inkling of his behaviour and recognized it merely as a matter of time before something happened. Isabel accepted the news differently. By this time Franz had told Lachlan more of what he knew and Lachlan, this time summoned to the clifftop house by the mother for the benefit of her daughter-in-law, was again confronted with the full force of human despair. Again the inevitable sedative made an appearance. It defeated Lachlan that a woman could look deranged with grief, faced with the loss of a man who habitually raped her. He left the croft both confused and disappointed at the vagaries of the human heart.

The village rallied. Isabel was entitled to a pension. Materially she would be better provided for but her grief was so public as to give force to Agnes's argument. Having discussed the events of that evening with Agnes, Lachlan has gone over them again and again in his mind, looking for loopholes, some weak spot that will allow news to haemorrhage. Two boats left the harbour and one came back. Fraser could only pilot one. Michael was not in the second. That's someone else in the know. Michael found some tradesman to put the doorjamb and shelf to rights and plaster the holes in the walls. That's someone else. All it takes is some drunken unintentional divulgence. Agnes is right: there's no going back from a killing.

Since the incident he has kept Franz with him as much as possible. Is it his imagination or has the boy attained a quiet notoriety in the interim? He has tried to view the reaction of others as impartially as possible, which for him is impossible. He is a creature of prejudices and knows enough of himself to recognize this. He also knows he has become overprotective towards the boy. His custodial manner could eventually rouse suspicion. Perhaps Franz also senses a change in public attitudes towards him. Since the events in the schoolroom his manner to the world at large has become more withdrawn. He has compensated for it by becoming more forthcoming with those he trusts.

Gail wanted to leave almost immediately. She was only prevailed upon to stay by the combined efforts of Lachlan and Agnes. Lachlan wanted her to delay leaving until Murdo's disappearance ceased to invite speculation, clinching the argument by telling her that this would be in the boy's best interests too. It might come as news to her but her affair with Murdo wasn't a secret. If Murdo's wife knew, does she seriously believe that everyone else who's interested, who is everyone else, didn't? Eileen Campbell knew. That meant everyone knew. An affair, a death, a sudden departure: imagine herself impartial, what would she conclude? For the sake of burying the news with the body she should stay till the gossip subsides.

Lachlan's patronage is not extensive but select. He has written to the headmaster of his old school, giving an indication of Franz's abilities. He has followed this letter with a telephone call, reciting invented antecedents. Lachlan is only good extempore. The other man extends the courtesy of pretending the halting performance sounds plausible. A place is obtained. The boy will receive something like an education appropriate to his gifts. Lachlan does not want the boy to become a boarder. He does not want him swallowed by another institution, no matter how intentionally benign. He wants him to come back each night to something approaching a home, to be with someone he recognizes as a friend.

To this end he has arranged three interviews for Gail at different Edinburgh schools. The same headmaster he has already discussed Franz's education with can vouch for the calibre of these places. He has also arranged accommodation. He would have done as much for Gail anyway, the only difference being he would have consulted with her first.

And having convinced her to stay, he let a reasonable interim elapse and raised with her the topic of the public attitude to Franz. Is he being overprotective? If he is, she concedes, he has reason to be. He begins to reiterate Agnes's argument. She pre-empts him.

'Lachlan . . . This is difficult. I have been thinking about it a lot and I – I think Franz has to go. You can't leave. That would turn too many heads. I was always going anyway, sooner or later. I think he should go. I think he should come with me.'

And letting her know she has reached the same conclusion he and Agnes independently arrived at, he begins to talk to her about Edinburgh. She is a teacher. The city is bursting with schools – good schools. Why go back to England? England is full of memories. England is being bombed. Why risk it? Scotland has had its quota of bombs and even if it hasn't the next ones will land beside the last ones, in Glasgow. Edinburgh is not a munitions factory. Edinburgh is the city of the Enlightenment, of Scott, of Adam's visionary architectural symmetry, of Burke and Hare, of . . . of Greyfriars Bobby, of . . . of . . . of three teaching vacancies for each of which she has an interview.

Behind the well-intended coercion there is a persuasive logic to what he says. And she feels she owes it to Lachlan to keep the boy within visiting distance. She has no intention of going back to Winchester. She sits three interviews in two days and has her choice of two positions. She calls Lachlan to let him know the news and says she may stay another day or so to try to locate reasonable accommodation for her and Franz. He plays his trump card, reads the address over the phone and tells her the rooms are ready for habitation.

'You're a scoundrel, Lachlan. You've had it all worked out all along.'

'I'll call the headmaster I talked to and ask him his opinion on which of the two schools is better.'

'I think I'm capable of making up my own mind on this one.'

'It never hurts to be well informed.'

'You've thought of everything.'

'One tries.' In self-congratulation he blows a fragrant blue cloud from his cigar into the hall cornices.

'Have you thought of how you'll tell Franz?'

The consultation Lachlan has that evening is the most halting of his career. The hundreds of occasions on which he has had to confront the bereaved have polished his delivery. He has learned to speak slowly, expound clearly and with sympathy. While inference from personal experience leads him to understand what his listeners are often going through, he has developed a sense of professional detachment. Bad news seldom disturbs his constitution.

All of the inarticulate pauses that evening are his. Franz hears out without interruption the halting catalogue of reasons, and at the end says simply, without hint of complaint, 'But I don't want to go. I want to stay here. With you.'

On the kitchen side of the hatch Agnes stops in her

preparations and looks determinedly at the scarred table. After a moment of consideration she decides to make a novena for the two of them. Consoled by this solution, she continues chopping.

'The train is coming.'

Gail refuses Lachlan's help with the bags. Franz looks merely comfortable carrying his. He no longer has that obsessed, proprietorial air. As the train gets closer Lachlan becomes more agitated. He helps them both on. Franz immediately pushes down the window and, leaning out, kisses Lachlan. The old man steps back. This is the time to say what he has been preparing. But like Franz's father, attempting to put pen to paper on the eve of another departure, Lachlan finds himself unequal to the task. He says nothing at all and listens to the last-minute inconsequential exchanges between the women, confirming arrangements that have already been made for the sake of saying something. He and Agnes are to visit the weekend after next. They are to telephone tonight to let them know they are settled. They have the address of the Edinburgh Rabbi it has been arranged for Franz to meet. Gail is to provide Lachlan with the boy's school booklist. The doctor plans a jaunt with Franz round the same bookshops he used to haunt when he was nearer the boy's age than his own.

A succession of doors slam. The boy is going. Lachlan takes these concussions personally. A whistle blows. The boy is going, waving. Behind the regret Lachlan can see something else in his face. A sense of excitement at change, anticipation of seeing the place Lachlan has praised to mitigate the shock of yet another dislocation. The boy is going, in smoke, like a conjuror's trick. This is the difference between them: he is travelling forward into the future that is opening before him, Lachlan is going back to what remains. The boy is gone.

He stands until the train has turned out of sight and makes

no show of moving. Agnes stands with the patience of a monument. Finally she takes his arm.

'You will be seeing him in less than a fortnight.'

'It was delight in small things . . . daily exchanges . . . I can't explain.'

'You already have. You know, it's all right to cry.'

'Don't be foolish, Agnes.'

But she has steered him round and he looks at the car that will take them back to the village, suddenly impoverished, and a house without the boy's coat on the hall peg. Through the thickness of his sleeve she senses the spasm of grief.

'Just concentrate on the weekend after next, Doctor McCready. Think of it as twelve dinnertimes away. Speaking of which, I have made your favourite this evening.'

'Really?' She recognizes in him the anticipation he saw in Franz's departing face. He reflects that she is right. He should look at this as an interval till they next meet, not a farewell. The boy will fare better there. There is not enough substance here for one of his gifts. He would have reached a state of inertia that would have been painful to watch. Their absence will better qualify him to chart the boy's development than he would have been able to had they been in constant contact. Lachlan is prepared to be pleasantly surprised. The school has a chess club he looks forward to hearing Franz has overwhelmed. Or perhaps he is being too complimentary to his own game. Since his encounter with Franz he is now reconciled to the fact that there is stiffer opposition than the petrified tactics of a country doctor. It would be good if the boy excels, but all that matters is that he gets a chance and is happy. And it should not matter that she has made his favourite for dinner, but somehow it does. And there is that claret he has been keeping. In one of those extraordinarily rare moments of self-doubt Lachlan wonders if he is superficial to be cheered by such mundane home comforts. But he dismisses this thought almost as it arrives: life is made up of the quotidian, it is the warp and weft; only fools, or those who read too much, fail to take consolation from the texture of the everyday.

The tension in his arm slackens. She begins to guide him towards the car.

'And another thing, Agnes, after all this you can't go back to formal terms.'

'We'll see, Doctor McCready.'

With thanks to Christopher and Mary, agent and editor respectively, for having the foresight and taking the trouble when no one else would.

An Interview with Michael Cannon

In *Lachlan's War* you render the isolation and beauty of the Scottish landscape brilliantly. Is it important for you to set your novels in Scotland?

Scotland fitted the bill for a number of reasons: although Rassaig is fictional I've visited and passed through so many of those communities that realizing it didn't demand the kind of imaginative leap that would have been required had I set the novel elsewhere. It provided the tension for the secular/Presbyterian confrontation that's essential for the novel's structure and the Highlands encompass many isolated rural communities that would allow the kind of activities that would attract attention in the larger world, to pass unnoticed. That said, there was an underlying reason more compelling than the obvious rational ones: the novel describes emotional extremes and some of the characters betray fanatical traits; in my mind's eye I found it easier to envisage such drama against the backdrop of all that austere beauty. The landscape both provides a context for and fashions the dramas enacted within it.

Your portrayal of the wartime bombing of Glasgow is very strong in your novel. Growing up in the city were you aware of this part of Glasgow's past?

I was only aware of it anecdotally, the way I was aware of the London blitz and the bombings of the other British cities. I'd a vague idea that anywhere with a shipyard was fair game for the Luftwaffe. As a child I'd heard the kind of stories that grow with the telling: someone who knew someone who missed the late bus and slept at a friend's, the most fortuitous accident they'll ever know, only to make their way home the next morning to find a smoking hole where their tenement once stood. When I decided to incorporate the bombing I began to read methodically. But to put it in some kind of perspective, Glasgow didn't suffer the way London did, and London didn't experience what Dresden was subjected to.

You have written three novels whilst working full-time. Do you find it difficult to find the time to write and do you think your day job hinders or helps your creativity?

I can't think there's anything I do in my day-to-day job that lends anything to my writing. Business correspondence doesn't afford much scope for flashes of lyric prose. Working does maintain the dozens of daily transactions with other people that I think full-time writing would preclude. Writing is a curious activity to engage in, when you come to think of it. For me it has involved coming home night after night and ransacking my imagination. Doing it full-time might be lonely. I don't know because I've never had the luxury. I have a fond image of being able to produce literary work in proportion to the time I can devote to it, but I suspect that's not the case. Maybe I'd spend all morning putting in a comma and all after-noon taking it out. Like lots of other people, I've been repeatedly asked where I get my ideas from. I usually reply that I don't know, because, if I did, I'd go back and get some more. I'm not being facetious when I say that. If I get a strong idea I'll devote all the spare time I can to realizing it. If I didn't have to work full-time I'd probably realize it quicker, but I don't know if the luxury of not having to work would lead to more ideas.

Scotland has a long literary tradition. Are there particular writers from Scotland you admire?

Muriel Spark. I think she's in a class of her own, and, going further back, Robert Louis Stevenson.

Which writers inspired you to become a novelist?

I'm more a fan of books than of writers. That said, a few writers are responsible for more than one favourite book. But I don't think they inspired me in any direct sense. I liked school reading books from a very early age, and they contained simplified extracts of various novels: *The Adventures of Tom Sawyer*, *The Coral Island*, *Kidnapped*, *Ivanhoe*, that sort of thing. I also pored over children's versions of Arthurian legend and invented and wrote stories about a virtuous knight called Sir Ibert, who went about kissing lepers, helping effete character-less women and killing bad knights whose motives for going off the tracks always eluded me but who gave themselves away by wearing black armour – even in bed (Sir Ibert's motives didn't require elucidation because virtue was its own reward). So I think the inclination to write, if not the discipline, was ingrained from an early age and I don't think it's attributable to any specific authors.

Do you see your books as character-driven, in the sense that characters assume a life and identity of their own?

I've met other writers who, when questioned, enthuse about how the characters they created do unexpected things, i.e. they assemble characters on the page and are surprised what each says and does. I've no idea whatsoever what that would be like. No doubt there are some exceptions, but it sounds too

265

much like Pinocchio with as much likelihood of producing great literature as automatic writing has. All my characters are chained to the oars. I'm the helmsman and the captain and the guy beating the drum. They do what they're told when I tell them to do it. Things that are too rigorously plotted might run a risk of eliminating scope for improvisation, but it's a slight risk in comparison to the potential menagerie of unplanned dialogue and action. *Lachlan's War* was written in a very episodic way. This was mainly due to the constraints of the circumstances of its writing. I wrote much of it longhand on the twenty-five-minute train journey home each evening from Glasgow Central to Clarkston. I planned each chapter in advance to the extent that I knew what each character would have to communicate to the others, in dialogue, gesture or action, but not exactly how it would be expressed. To that extent there was an opportunity for the characters to extemporize, but they'd better do it by the time we reached Clarkston because we were all getting off the train at the same time.